SPACE COWBOY

JUSTIN STANCHFIELD

For Shealan, Colter and especially Connie, with all my love.
You make everything possible.

Many thanks to Gisele LeBlanc, Sarah Stewart and
Megan Larkin for all their help and guidance.

First published in the UK in 2008 by Usborne Publishing Ltd., Usborne
House, 83–85 Saffron Hill, London EC1N 8RT, England. www.usborne.com

A CIP catalogue record for this book is available from the British Library.

FMAMJJASOND/08   ISBN 9780746087121   Printed in Great Britain.

CHAPTER ONE

Travis McClure turned his tired horse west, away from camp, away from cool water and soft sleeping bags, away from everything he so desperately wanted. He glanced at the sky, greenish gold, not blue like the skies back home on Earth, streaked with pale clouds that twisted and streamed in the unending wind. Two suns hung low, bloated red Beta and tiny Alpha, so white it hurt his eyes. Twin suns that burned and bleached and stole the spit from your mouth if you let them. Travis tugged his hat down, the brim floppy and torn, and nudged his horse in the ribs.

"Let's go, Deuce."

Deuce snorted his displeasure but broke into a laggardly trot, hoofs smacking the rust-red trail. The narrow path was packed tight by the scattered bands of cattle and wild sheep the terraformers had released decades ago, an attempt to jump-start millions of years of evolution and create a living planet in a galactic heartbeat. Someday, long after Travis and his family had gone home, colonists would arrive with their factories and schools, cities and farms. But for now, only the scattered camps of geologists and stockmen, too desperate or too stubborn to leave, covered the awakening world. Aletha Three was a harsh planet, desolate and arid. Someday, the Company claimed, it would be a paradise of green meadows and shadowed forests. Someday, but not today. And not tomorrow, and not for as long as Travis could imagine being stuck here.

"Just one more season," Dad would promise. "One more season, two at the most, and we'll have saved enough money to pay off the loans on the ranch. Then we'll go home." Travis sighed. He was starting to think his dad's promises were as empty as the wind. He'd been eleven when they landed. Now he was sixteen. Five years chasing cattle from pasture to pasture, five years wondering if he would ever see Earth again.

The trail grew steeper as it climbed into the foothills. Travis urged his tired horse forward as they slipped around boulders big as starship hangars. Scraggly patches of sagebrush and juniper poked out of the dry soil. The climatologists at base camp had been promising rain for weeks, but so far, not a drop had fallen. No surprise, Travis thought sourly. Like everything else on Aletha, nothing quite followed anyone's carefully laid out plans. Weather satellites failed, burned up by the harsh radiation that streamed around the planet. On the surface, radios became useless for days at a time after solar flares or during the sandstorms that swept in from the deserts to pummel the grasslands. Even simple machines like vid-games and clocks tended to die early in the harsh environment. He glanced at his wristwatch, not certain if it was keeping time correctly. His legs and stomach certainly felt like it was getting close to supper time.

As if he had read his mind, Deuce stopped, refusing to go forward, and stood flicking his ears back and forth. Travis frowned and glanced down at the trail in front of him. He had been following the stray cattle all afternoon, hoping every time he topped a rise or turned a corner he would run headlong into them. So far, though, he was always one jump behind. The tracks were fresh, a few hours old at most, long scuff marks trailing where their hoofs had dragged. The little herd had been moving fast. So had something else. An odd footprint covered the cow tracks, the impression perfect in the soft red dust.

"Whoa, Deuce." He swallowed, his mouth so dry his voice cracked. "This isn't right."

Travis stepped out of the saddle and crouched beside the strange tracks. Three toes, spread wide like a hawk on the grab. He'd seen tracks like these the year before and shuddered at the memory. Three yearlings ripped apart, shattered bones covering the blood-speckled ground. He had been riding alone when he had heard the scream, a keening wail of rage and animal triumph. No one had believed him then. They said it was a pack of coyotes or feral cats. But Travis knew better. He patted Deuce then fished his radio out of the saddlebag.

"Dad? Are you on the net?"

A burst of static preceded Jim McClure's reply. "Where're you at, Trav?"

"About five klicks west of Needle Point." Travis paused. He didn't want to say what he had to, especially over an open frequency. "Dad, do you remember those tracks I told you about last year? The ones around those dead heifers?"

"Yeah, I remember." Even across the distance it was clear his father still doubted the story.

"I think..." Travis took a deep breath. Far away, too distant to be clear, a scream echoed down the canyon walls. "I think whatever made them is back."

Night fell as Travis reached camp. True night, not the long twilight of twin sunsets, the darkness menacing and grim. Glad to be back, he unsaddled Deuce and turned him loose in the corral. The horse rolled gratefully in the dust. Fewer tents remained tonight, the camp preparing to move again, gypsies on an endless trek. The geologists and hydrologists had pulled stakes last week. Soon, they would do the same. The grass here was finished, the waterholes nearly dry. Time to drive the herds to greener pastures.

On Earth, animals like bison and wild horses had once covered the grasslands, their hoofs churning the barren soil like a million tiny ploughs, spreading seed as they moved. Here, the scattered herds of hardy, more manageable cattle served the same purpose. Eventually, so the terraformers insisted, the animals would number in the millions and establish natural migration patterns as integral to the environment as rain. They were as much a part of the plan to bring Aletha to life as the weather satellites and water collectors scattered around the planet.

Travis wondered what other creatures the plan included.

He saw his dad near the cook-tent and hurried towards him. Most of the other herders had long since returned. One of them, a dark-haired man in his early twenties loitering outside the repair trailer, saw him and broke away from the knot of people waiting for supper. Travis grimaced. Bart Caddy was definitely not someone he wanted to see right now.

"Hey, Trav. Heard you found them tracks again." Caddy's voice was loud and piercing, about as musical as an untuned thruster pack. "They looked like bird feet, you say?"

"Yeah." Travis chewed on his lower lip. News had obviously spread fast. Out the corner of his eye he saw Caddy's friends approach, ringing him like a pack of wild dogs. "They look like overgrown-bird tracks."

"Well, do you suppose whatever made 'em looked like this?" Howling at his own joke, Caddy raised a crude, hand-drawn picture of an enormous chicken, big as a jump shuttle, a struggling cow clutched in its beak. Travis blushed, but before he could reply, his father pushed through the little crowd. McClure cleared his throat, his voice dusty as his cracked leather chaps.

"Don't you all have chores to do, or should I find you some?"

"No, sir." Caddy stuffed the picture inside his tight-fitting jacket, and left, followed by his pack of friends.

Travis looked away, embarrassed that he needed to be rescued, but grateful for it all the same. He followed his father towards their tent, a squat blue dome glowing with warmth and the promise of sleep. Travis paused outside the door-flap.

"I really did see those tracks."

"I'm sure you saw something." His father pushed the flap up and ducked inside. The stiff fabric rustled behind him. Travis stood outside a moment and stared at the sky. He felt like a scolded child. Someone coughed. Startled, he spun around. A stocky man in an expensive parka waited behind him. Allen Tempke, the Company foreman, the man who signed the cheques. The man who hired and fired. The boss.

"You saw something today, Travis?"

"I..." Travis was sweating despite the chill wind. "I think so."

"If someone has introduced a rogue predator into this environment, the Company needs to know about it. I don't suppose you recovered any physical evidence? You know, hair or droppings? Something we could test for DNA."

"No, sir." Travis didn't mention the scream he had heard. "All I saw were the tracks."

"That's unfortunate." A faint smile creased Tempke's lips. "I'm sure the bonus for that sort of information would be substantial." He nodded a goodbye, then left.

Travis watched him go, too stunned to speak, and not at all happy with the extra attention. Around him the night wind moaned low. Still shaken by the strange turn the day had taken, he lifted the tent flap and slipped inside.

CHAPTER TWO

He was up before daybreak. Travis tiptoed past his snoring parents, scribbled a quick note for them and left it beside his homework. A sturdy digicam hung by the wrist strap from one of the tent poles. He took it down and stuffed it in his shirt pocket. Across the domed tent, on top of a plastic footlocker, rested a battered carbine. Travis stared at the rifle, so old it was almost a relic, and wished he could take it along, but as quickly abandoned the idea. Dad didn't lose his temper often, but when he did it was epic, and borrowing his gun without his permission was pushing his luck light years too far. Instead, he grabbed a handful of ration bars and his canteen and started towards the door. As an afterthought, he snatched his tracker off the table and clipped it beside his knife sheath, just in case they needed to find him. He was anxious to pick up the trail of the strange animal before the wind destroyed the tracks.

Thoughts of the weird animal – and the bonus – spun in his brain. He'd waited a year to prove he wasn't just some kid with a runaway imagination, and refused to let the chance slip this time. As quietly as he could, he zipped his jacket tighter and stepped outside.

The wind was strong and bristled with static electricity. A storm was gathering, a change already in the chill air. Travis shivered as he hurried to the corral. No one else in camp had stirred out yet, nothing moving except for the little sentry bot crawling its rounds on the outskirts of the encampment, and the anemometer cups whirling above the meteorologists' station. He took a short cut through the uneven collection of tents and balloon-tyred trailers where the single herders and terraformers set up their bunks. Everyone called it "Bachelors' Row", despite the fact that more than half of the scientists and technicians were women. Life on Aletha Three had its own rhythm. They travelled like high-tech nomads, never in one place long enough to call it home, always on the lookout for the next move. But hell or high water, wherever the camp stopped, the same tents would somehow always pop up next to each other. Travis clipped a tent rope with his right foot and stumbled.

"Ouch!" Angry at being so clumsy, he picked himself up and slipped past the main generator to the portable corral on the very edge of the encampment. The horses looked up, startled to see someone so early in the day. They ran around the wide pen, heads high, tails streaming in the breeze. They were restless. Travis stood outside the gate a moment, a frayed halter in hand, and studied the animals. Over the years he had learned to read their moods, their behaviour as good a weather prediction as anything that came in from Base Camp five hundred kilometres to the south. The horses pranced, shoulders stiff as if they were stepping on broken glass instead of dirt and dry manure. No doubt about it, a storm was on its way.

The tall metal gate creaked on its hinges as Travis stepped inside the corral. Deuce saw him and spun away. Travis hazed him towards the long feed bunk. He stuck out his arm and pointed his finger at the horse's face.

"Whoa there, fella." The horse stopped, caught between Travis and the fence, nowhere left to run. He flinched a little as Travis looped the lead rope around his long neck, but stood patiently while he buckled the halter. "How come you're so nervous today?"

Still moving quietly, Travis saddled the horse, then slung aboard. The fenders creaked as he settled in, the slick leather seat as familiar as the taste of dust on a windy day. Deuce whickered over his shoulder at the other horses as Travis turned him away from camp.

"Come on, fella. You and me have a long ride ahead of us." He reached up and patted the horse's neck, then nudged him into a slow trot.

Red fire poured across the horizon as they headed west. Beta rose sluggishly into the dawn sky, a dull red hump half hidden by the jagged skyline. Deuce whinnied and tossed his head, protesting the early start. Travis kicked him up faster, concentrating on the trail ahead and not the dark fear gnawing in his stomach. The higher they climbed, the more he began to doubt what he was doing. Memory of that scream rang in his mind, and the idea that he might be up against something he couldn't handle left him cold inside. A few klicks out of camp he stopped in the lee of a narrow ridge to let Deuce rest. He leaned out of the saddle and studied the ground.

Sharp rocks littered the path. A century and a half ago, Aletha had been dormant, a dead planet with a thin, unbreathable atmosphere. The seeder ships had changed that. Millions of tons of microbes and genetically modified plants had been released from space, followed by drop-pods filled with the furnaces and refineries the terraformers needed to bring the rocky world to life. Now, Aletha had air, and if there wasn't a lot of water, there was enough for more complex organisms to gain a foothold. Organisms like rabbits and crows, cattle, horses and human beings.

And who knew what else.

"Come on, Deuce, let's go."

Higher into the foothills they climbed. Jagged spires towered above them, the stone painted in garish shades of red and orange. Hundreds of metres above, tall black cliffs rimmed the narrow valley. Travis searched for familiar marks, hoping to find the spot where the tracks had been yesterday. But the further he climbed, the less certain he was that he was even in the same canyon where he had seen the strange markings.

The trail dipped into a ravine so narrow Deuce leaped across from one side to the other, loose rocks rolling in his wake. Travis clung tight to the saddle as the horse scrabbled up the other side, then turned him west again. They followed the ridge line to the top of a high, rock-strewn bench. Finally, something familiar popped into view: a small mound of horse manure, less than a day old.

"Never thought I'd be happy to see a pile of horse apples," Travis muttered as he swung Deuce towards the little mound. The horse stuck his nose down and snorted, and broke into a slow trot as he tracked his own scent across the dry, open plateau.

Ahead, a jagged spine of lava poked upwards, dark against the red cliffs behind it. A vein of bright green crystals lay embedded in the porous black stone. They glinted as if on fire as Alpha, the smaller, hotter sun, joined Beta in the pale sky. Travis remembered the outcrop, and turned towards it. Tracks wound from one patch of grass to the next, broad teardrop-shaped imprints stamped in the dirt, the same hoof prints he had followed the day before. He backtracked along them, anxious to find the three-toed tracks.

"They've got to be around here someplace." Travis reined Deuce in a little and forced him back to a walk so he could study the ground. The horse tossed his head as they meandered towards yet another steep-sided hill. He was nervous, and had Travis let him, would have turned and run for camp without so much as a nudge in the shoulder. Travis reached down and patted the animal's neck. "It's okay, fella. We've been up here before. Nothing out there but rocks."

Travis wondered if the horse knew he was being lied to. Something was definitely out there, somewhere.

The twin suns climbed higher, and soon the air grew hot. Travis reined Deuce in and stepped out of the saddle. It felt good to stretch his legs as he peeled off his jacket and tied it tightly behind the cantle. The tie straps snapped as he pulled them tight and double-checked the knots. Mom would kill him if he lost another jacket. He checked that the digicam was still in his shirt pocket, then pulled his canteen out of the saddlebag. The water was lukewarm and tasted like plastic, but he swallowed it gratefully. Sunlight burned against his neck as he checked the cinch, then climbed back on. Deuce tried to turn around, but Travis swung him once more westward.

Time seemed to speed up as they crossed from ridge to ridge, the scattered tracks a confused path that criss-crossed back and forth at random. One minute he

17

would find a clear trail, the next it would be gone, the ground too rocky to hold a print. Sweat poured down from under his hatband as the suns neared the zenith, noon less than an hour away. Travis chewed on one of the ration bars he had brought along, his mouth so dry he could barely swallow the sticky-sweet granola. He took another swig from his canteen, and looked around, desperate to locate the strange tracks.

Everything looked familiar. He swore he had been past each boulder, ridden over every narrow, rocky ridge. It had seemed so simple when he left at daybreak: find the tracks, get some hard evidence, then collect the bonus Tempke had hinted at last night. Now, in the hard light of day, the task suddenly felt impossible. Frustrated, Travis pulled the reluctant horse around and started off once more.

They rounded a squat, rust-red boulder. Fresh tracks crept out from behind it. Travis's hope jumped, then sank again. The sharp prints were solid and half-moon shaped, with a tight band along the edge. Horse tracks.

"Great. Now we're following ourselves."

Dust whipped past, a gritty veil erasing any tracks that might have remained from the day before. Travis leaned on the saddle horn, head tucked down. It was hopeless. The chance had come and gone and he'd missed it. Part of him was relieved, the thought of those long-dead yearlings he had found last year all too fresh. "All right, Deuce. You win. Let's go home." Slowly, he gathered up the reins.

Behind them, just over the ridge, something screamed.

Buzz saws cutting through bone. Demons howling in the night. The sound sent chills down Travis's neck. He hobbled the nervous horse, then climbed to the top of the steep hill, using his hands to pull himself over the crest. Nothing could have prepared him for what waited on the other side.

A young bull lay in a shallow, rocky bowl, its throat ripped open. Pieces of flesh littered the ground. Travis stood on the ridge, swaying in the wind, stunned. His legs felt weak, the hair on the back of his neck standing high. It was just like before. Hand shaking, he snapped a quick picture. The photo on the little screen was disappointing, the details washed out and flat. He flicked the setting to flash to compensate and took a second shot, the camera flash lightning bright. Satisfied the camera was working, he stumbled down the slope. The warm, wet smell of ammonia and sulphur and a thousand other scents rode the wind, strong enough to gag him. Travis searched the ground, taking pictures, cautiously looking around for more signs.

Something small and gleaming white caught his eye, a thumb-sized sickle buried in the bull's flank. He prised the broken tooth loose. It was sharp and smooth and wickedly curved. He stuffed it in his pocket, then searched the ground around the carcass. A set of three-toed tracks ran past his left boot.

They led behind him.

Travis bolted for the ridge. The killer hadn't left. It had circled him. He had to get back to Deuce, get mounted before it was too late, and get home. No time to be brave, only time to run. Out of breath, he broke over the top of the hill and looked down.

A nightmare greeted him on the other side.

CHAPTER THREE

The thing was long and grey, a snake's head on a raptor's body, with a whipcord tail that thrashed the air behind it. A narrow strip of feathery scales ran down its lean back and rippled as it moved. It crouched low, stalking the helpless horse, hissing and clicking its teeth. Blood stained its muzzle, a grim reminder of the dead bull on the other side of the steep hillside. Travis gaped at it, shocked at its size. From snout to tail it was every bit as long as the terrified horse, and probably weighed nearly as much. Deuce reared, his front feet bound by the hobbles, unable to run. Circling upwind, the creature advanced.

"No!"

It whirled away from the horse and stared at Travis. Without thinking, Travis snapped a shot with the camera, the flash strobe still set to full. Startled by the light, the creature howled in rage. Travis fired another shot then darted to the left, buying time. A hurried plan formed in his mind. Eyes on the creature, he fumbled with the camera timer, then placed it beside a small boulder.

"This is crazy," he whispered as he inched towards Deuce, moving from boulder to boulder while the creature edged closer. It sniffed the air, flicking its long tongue in and out between razor-sharp teeth. Travis counted the seconds until the timer went off and tensed for a final dash to reach Deuce. Slowly, the animal advanced, head low, its powerful hind legs bunched to pounce. A bright flash caught it off guard. Faster than Travis could have imagined, it lunged at the camera. A brittle, sickening crunch snapped loud above the wind as the creature snatched the digicam off the boulder and shattered it in its jaws. Bits of plastic and glass sprayed around as it shook its head in defiance. Seeing his chance, Travis rushed towards Deuce.

The horse tried to bolt, but he grabbed the reins and held tight as he dropped to his knees and struggled to unfasten the hobbles.

"Please, Deuce, hold still!"

Precious seconds slipped away as Travis fumbled with the stiff buckle. Not twenty paces away, he heard the creature growl. He was so frightened he could barely breathe as he pulled the tongue out of the latch. The leather strap fell away just as the creature lunged towards them. Terrified, Deuce reared high, lashed out with his front feet and jerked away. Travis gasped in pain as the reins burned through his fist.

The horse slammed against him as he broke away and vanished down the slope. Off balance, Travis tumbled backwards, utterly exposed. The creature saw him and spun around, neck low to the ground. It hissed at him and took a step forward. With no way to outrun the creature on foot, Travis scrabbled backwards, desperate to find cover. A pair of large boulders lay to his left, a narrow cleft between them just wide enough to crawl inside. He rolled between the boulders and pressed his body tight against the hard stone. Wishing the gap was deeper, he drew his knife and waited for the attack.

Rocks shifted outside as the creature advanced. Travis tensed and forced himself to breathe. Without warning, a long, grey snout shot into the cleft. Travis swept the knife at it, hampered by the tight space. The blade drove hard into the dirt, the creature quicker than he expected. He pulled his hand back just as the thing made another attack.

"Get out of here!" Travis screamed. The bloodstained muzzle poked towards his boot, and instinctively he jabbed at it again.

This time the bright utility blade struck home. Travis

stabbed the knife into the bony snout and pulled back. A long, thin cut sliced across its slitted nostrils. The creature howled in rage. Its foul breath filled the tiny cleft with ammonia and the stench of rotting meat. Before Travis could pull his arm away, the creature lunged deeper inside the gap, thrashing and twisting, a wild blur of motion. The creature's snout struck Travis on the wrist and knocked the knife out of his hand. The blade hit the rock above him, then fell to the ground, out of reach. Unarmed, Travis scooted further against the boulders, trapped inside the cleft. Suddenly, his shelter had become a cage.

A loud crack cut past him.

Outside, a splatter of rocks and gravel kicked up beside the creature. The thing hissed as a second rifle shot pelted the ridge. A final scream and it leaped away, whipping its tail. Through the narrow gap, Travis watched it vanish over the ridge. Suddenly, he felt sick, too much adrenaline pouring through his blood. Shaking, he crawled out from between the boulders as his dad rode up, carbine in hand.

"Are you all right?"

Travis nodded and staggered to his feet. He swallowed, his mouth impossibly dry. "How did you find me?"

"You hadn't checked in for way too long, and I got worried. I followed your tracker out here. Looks like it's a good thing I did."

Travis had completely forgotten he was wearing the

little transmitter. He reached down and patted the compact device clipped to his belt. His hand brushed past the empty sheath, and he remembered his knife. He fell back to hands and knees and reached inside the gap to retrieve the blade. Knife in hand, Travis slumped against the boulder and tried not to be sick.

His dad jumped off his tall, grey mare. "What was that thing?"

"I don't know." Travis took a long, deep breath and began to feel stronger. "Not sure I want to know."

"Did you know it was out here?"

Travis nodded.

"That was stupid, riding off alone looking for that thing."

"I know. I'm sorry."

"You should be." His dad's face softened. "I should have listened to you, earlier. But why in the name of hell did you come up here like this?"

"The bonus." His dad stared at him, a puzzled look on his craggy face. Travis hurried through an explanation. "Mr. Tempke told me last night that if I could get him hard proof that thing is out here, he'd pay a bonus."

"So you risked your life because Tempke promised to pay you?" Jim McClure shook his head, his disapproval plain. "You should know by now you can't trust that man. He doesn't care about anything but his own career. Besides, what do you need the money for?"

"I was going to give it to you." Travis looked away,

unable to meet his father's eye. "You're always saying how we need just a little more to pay off the loans on the ranch. I thought if Tempke paid enough, maybe we could go back to Earth sooner."

"You did this for us?" McClure sank down beside his son and sat cross-legged, the carbine across his lap. He sighed. "I didn't know you hated it here so much. I'm sorry, Trav. Guess I haven't paid much attention to you and your mom lately."

"It's okay." Travis shrugged. "Besides, I had to prove to myself that this thing really exists." He glanced at the shattered camera. His heart sank. "Wish I could prove it to everyone else."

Suddenly he remembered the tooth he had found and smiled. He fished it out of his pocket, turning it slowly in his hand. It glowed crimson in the light of the double suns. His dad took the tooth and ran a finger over its point. His eyebrows arched in amazement as he studied the deadly little sickle. He gave the tooth back and stood up, then helped Travis to his feet.

"Come on. Let's catch your horse before he makes it back to camp. Don't know about you, but I want to be a long way from here before that thing comes back."

Travis followed him down the slope. The wind moaned around them while crimson clouds streamed like pennants across the green-gold sky. He stopped and listened. For one long, endless moment, far behind them, he swore he heard the creature howl.

* * *

They found Deuce a kilometre down the trail, standing on his left rein, unable to run further. The right-hand rein hung broken, dangling under his chin. He saw Jim's mare and whickered loudly. Travis approached the frightened animal slowly, arm extended, careful not to startle him.

"You okay, fella?" He wrapped the good rein around his hand in case the horse tried to bolt, and stroked his long, sweat-damp neck. He let his hand slide down Deuce's flank and under his belly, then down his front legs, searching for injuries.

"Is he all right?" his dad asked.

"I think so."

Travis tied the good rein to the broken one and made a single loop that hung over the top of the horse's neck. Deuce flinched and drew in his stomach as Travis tightened the cinch before swinging up into the saddle. Anxious to put more distance between himself and the creature – whatever the thing was – he pulled Deuce around and followed his dad down a narrow wash that wound gradually back towards camp.

They rode in silence. Travis was glad for the interval, a chance to sort out his thoughts. Part of him felt like a giant for proving at last that the thing he had discovered a year earlier was real and not a figment of his imagination. But he also felt guilty, ashamed that he had risked so much and put his, Deuce's, and his father's lives in danger for a bonus that might not even exist. They rode on, and at last broke out onto the wide valley floor, the ragged collection of tents and trailers shimmering through heat waves in the distance.

Travis raised his hat brim and wiped the sweat and dust off his forehead. Beta hung straight overhead, the arid landscape shifting from the warm reds of morning to a harsh, silvery glare, so bright his eyes ached. He wished he had remembered his sunglasses. Shielding his eyes with his hand, he glanced upward.

An orange teardrop danced in the pale green sky. A long cloud trail streamed behind it. Travis watched it grow larger as it curved downward. He spurred Deuce ahead until he rode side by side with the grey mare.

"Dad, is there a supply drop scheduled today?"

His father's gaze followed where Travis pointed. His eyebrows bunched together as he watched the ship begin its landing run. "If there is, nobody told me. I didn't think we had a ship due for another month." He pulled his transmitter off his belt and flicked it on. "McClure to Camp Seven, come in?"

Nothing but static rolled out the little speaker. He tried again, then stuffed the transceiver back on his belt. "Come on, Trav. Let's get home and see what's up."

They broke into a fast trot. The horses in the corral ran to the fence and stood with their necks outstretched, whickering as they passed. Deuce tried to stop, but Travis urged him ahead and followed his dad through the drowsy camp. A gaunt woman with spiky black hair stepped out of the meteorology trailer and waved as they approached.

"Hey, Alice." Jim McClure pulled his mare to a stop in front of her. "Whose ship is that landing out there?"

"Wish I knew." Alice Prevoroski shrugged her thin shoulders. Although she was officially a meteorologist, she did double duty as the local air traffic control whenever the rare ship happened to land. "I can tell you this much, it's not Company traffic. They weren't even on the right frequency for this area." She paused. "Don't suppose you could ride out and have a look? From their radar track, I don't think they have a clue where the landing field is."

"Sure. Let me water my horse, then I'll have a look." Travis's dad turned his mare around as a hard gust blew through camp, a rolling wall of grit that rattled the tents and tugged at their guy lines. "Is there a storm coming?"

Alice shrugged again. "I'd love to tell you, but I can't. Beta burped last night and knocked out the sat-net again."

Travis groaned inwardly at the news. Solar flares were notorious for knocking out the fragile chain of weather and communication satellites in orbit around Aletha. He had a ton of homework he had been putting aside for days, and without access to Base Camp's online library five hundred kilometres to the south, he was going to pay hell to get it done. He glanced at their tent. To his dismay, he saw three riders hurrying past it, heads tucked against the rising wind. Travis's heart sank. The last thing he wanted to see was Bart Caddy and his obnoxious friends. He twisted around in the saddle and looked at his dad.

"Mind if I go with you?"

"Sure you're up to it?" McClure asked, surprised. "You've already had quite a morning."

Travis watched the three riders as they pulled up on the far side of the corral. "Yeah. I'm sure."

"All right," his father said doubtfully. "Give your horse a drink, then let's get on our way. I'll go tell your mom you're coming with me."

CHAPTER FOUR

Wind poured across foothills, the air hot and filled with grit. Travis tucked his chin against his chest as he rode, glad for the goggles he remembered to grab. Already, Beta slipped towards sunset, the landscape softening as the colour shifted from silver to russet. Deuce tried to turn around at the next fork in the trail, but Travis pulled the reins tight and swung him north, following his dad and the tall grey mare.

"How much further?" he shouted above the wind.

"Not sure." Jim McClure pulled the mare to a stop, and sat hunched forward in the saddle studying the tracker in his hand. He panned the little device back and forth and scowled. "Can't get a decent fix on their locator beacon. The static is too heavy. We must be in for a blow."

Travis took a deep breath and nodded. The storm-taste was unmistakable. He had been caught out in sandstorms before, and had no desire to be again. He had already pressed his luck far enough for one day. Moving faster to beat the sunset, they pushed further up the twisting trail.

The trail opened onto a wide, boulder-strewn bench. Something fast and grey shot out from behind a patch of juniper bush to Travis's left. Startled, he jerked Deuce around faster than he should have, and the horse stumbled. The coyote paused, glanced over his shoulder, then slunk off into the scrub. Travis shook his head, disgusted with himself for being so jumpy. Heart still pounding, he bumped his heels against Deuce's ribs to catch up with the grey mare. His dad twisted around and waited for him.

"Trav, do you have your radio? I can't get a signal on mine."

"Sure." Glad his dad hadn't noticed his encounter with the coyote, he pulled his compact transmitter off his belt and clicked it on. Static blasted out the speaker. "Camp Seven, Travis McClure, come in?" He waited for a reply, but none came. He leaned out of the saddle and passed the radio to his dad. "Maybe you'll have better luck."

A wave of sand rushed towards them. The horses

turned their tails to the wind and stood heads low until the gust passed. Travis pressed his hand against his hat to keep it from blowing away. His dad gave him back his radio, then once more took out his tracker and sat shaking his head as he read it.

"Nothing."

"Maybe," Travis said, "they landed then took off again."

"Doubt it. More likely they missed the field and had to make an emergency landing. They could be anywhere around here. If we don't find them pretty soon, I'm going to call it quits until morning." Jim McClure stared northwards, towards another low mesa. He shook his head in disgust. "What kind of damn fool shoots a landing in weather like this?"

They pushed on. Travis said nothing as they crossed the empty flat. He knew his father's moods all too well, and this was no time for pointless chatter. By the time they reached the little mesa, the wind had shifted further north, bringing the flinty taste of sand. Deuce flared his nostrils at the smell and stopped, his long ears flicking back and forth. Something in the wind had caught his attention. Travis sniffed the air. He could smell it too. A faint chemical stench drifted down the sides of the flat-topped mountain.

"Dad, do you smell that?"

"Yep. Smells like rocket fuel." He pointed the grey mare up the steep hill. "Come on."

The horses lunged up the mesa, loose rocks trickling

behind them as they fought for each foothold. Nearly to the crest, the slope became steeper. A barricade of dark lava, worn smooth by millions of years of wind and weather, rimmed the plateau. A single, narrow gap lay in front of them. Just when Travis thought Deuce would tip over backwards if he took another step, they broke out on top. He let the tired, sweating horse catch his breath and looked around. An unmistakable shape stood against the horizon on the far side of the tabletop.

"There it is." Travis pointed at the starship. He had seen enough ships in his lifetime to tell something was wrong with this one. It sat crookedly, one of its three stubby legs shorter than the rest. A red beacon flashed at the tip of the elegantly rounded nose, the only sign of activity. As they rode closer, Travis noticed a thin vapour trail hissing out beneath the blackened thruster cones. The escaping fuel was so cold it froze in the air and fluttered around the ship like snow on a winter morning.

"Let's hobble the horses upwind," Jim McClure said. Travis nodded. They left the horses sheltered next to a tall, rust-red boulder, then started on foot towards the ship. "I hope to hell the airlock is open."

"I think it is." From where he stood, Travis could make out a dark rectangle near the base of the cone-shaped craft, the entrance bay caught in shadow. A narrow, recessed ladder led up the side of the ship into the airlock. The metal hull was still so hot from landing it burned through the tips of his gloves as he climbed up to the small, box-like entrance. The stench of escaping fuel was so strong he pulled his dusty bandana over his nose and mouth to block the fumes. To his relief, a green light glowed above the control panel.

"Let's see if anybody's home." His dad pressed his palm against the wide, triangular switch beneath the light and the inner hatch slid neatly aside. A blast of cool, fuel-laden air rushed out, the pressure inside the ship stronger than the pressure outside. A narrow corridor waited beyond, lit red by a series of emergency lights. He stuck his head inside the open hatchway and shouted, "Hello?"

"Hear anything?" Travis asked.

His father shook his head, no. Hesitantly, they entered the starship. The wind against the hull made the ship moan as if it was drawing breath, a slumbering dragon stranded on the high, empty mesa. The corridor curved upwards, a steep spiral that led, Travis hoped, to where the passengers and crew waited. The fuel smell was so intense it left him dizzy and light-headed, and by the time they reached the flight deck, he thought he was going to throw up.

It was dim inside the low chamber, nothing but emergency lights and the glow from the instrument panels to light the way. A switch lay beside the entrance into the cockpit. Travis brushed his hand against it, then shielded his eyes as the main lights came up. He almost wished he had left them off.

Two bodies were strapped to the twin pilot's chairs, their heads lolling forward, as still as death itself. Both wore thin green environmental suits and lightweight helmets. Long coils of flexi-tube patched between their face masks and the control panel, their air supply tied directly into the ship's system.

"Are they..." Travis's voice broke off. Growing up around animals, he had seen his share of death, but finding two human beings slumped in the high-backed seats, held upright only by the restraint harnesses, struck harder than he expected. "Are they dead?"

"I don't know." Jim McClure crowded into the tight cockpit and leaned around the padded chairs. An iridescent holo-patch on the pilot's chest showed his name as "Adrian Lebrie". Above the name hung a planet with enormous white wings sprouting from the equator, the letters FPS glowing above it. Something about the patch made the older McClure scowl. "Their visors are fogged, so they must be breathing. I'd guess the air supply is contaminated."

He reached down and popped the pilot's supply hose off the panel. A whiff of fuel and hot coolant blew out, so strong it made Travis's eyes burn. "Whew. That stuff's nasty."

"Let's just hope there aren't any sparks before we get them out of here. There's enough fuel vapour in the air to crack this ship like an egg if it blows." Without hesitation, Jim McClure swung the restraint up on the left seat. He grabbed the unconscious pilot before he struck the instrument panel, then pulled him out of the cockpit. Travis did the same with the body in the co-pilot's seat. It was heavier than he expected, and by the time he reached the airlock he was covered in sweat. He leaned against the hatchway, fighting down his rising nausea. The bad air inside the damaged ship was getting to him, too.

"Come on, Trav," his dad shouted from the base of the ladder. "Get out of there."

"Okay." A sharp gust blasted against the hull, so full of dust it seemed brown in the fading sunlight. Travis slung the co-pilot over his shoulder and stepped onto the ladder. His foot slipped, and he fell the last metre to the scorched ground. The co-pilot landed on top of him, and he grunted in pain. To his relief, he felt the co-pilot move as he pulled himself to his feet and hoisted the body once more over his shoulder. Stumbling under the uneven weight, he jogged away from the ship. The fuel leak had worsened, the ruptured tank venting geyser-like out of a jagged tear in the underbelly, a fine mist of volatile gas mixing with the grit-choked air.

Out of breath, he staggered behind the boulder where the horses stood, and gently as he could, laid the co-pilot on the ground. His father already had the helmet off the pilot. The man inside had a narrow face with a long, aquiline nose and thinning brown hair that came to a sharp point above his forehead. His skin had a sickly, greenish pallor, long red lines cutting across like scars where the helmet seal had pressed against

37

his flesh. He moaned softly, his eyelids twitching as he began to rouse. Jim McClure nodded at the co-pilot.

"Better get his visor off so he can breathe."

"Right." Travis fumbled with the neck-seal. It had been years since he had worn an e-suit, not since he was eleven during the long flight out from Earth, and it took him a moment to remember how to unfasten the stubborn headgear. After a few false starts, he pressed down and twisted on top of the helmet, and it broke free. Trying not to injure the prone crewman, he tugged the helmet off and set it on the ground. To his surprise, the face inside belonged to a woman. Her eyes shot open.

"Where'm I?" She struggled to sit up, but Travis stopped her.

"You're safe." Travis eased her back down to the ground. She was younger than he had at first thought, barely older than himself. "Your air supply was contaminated."

"My father?" The girl turned her head to the side and saw the pilot an arm's length away. A look of relief slid across her face. "S'all right?"

Her speech was slurred, and Travis leaned closer to hear her.

"The pilot? That's your dad?"

She nodded.

"He's going to be okay. You both just need some air." Travis smiled for her benefit, and hoped he wasn't lying. He took a closer look at her. She was pretty, or would be once the sweat and helmet lines left her face. Her skin was the colour of coffee with lots of cream, with brown hair matted above eyes so dark they seemed black. Her nose was long and narrow like the pilot's. She began to cough. Travis rushed over to Deuce and retrieved his canteen, then helped her sit up while he held the plastic container to her lips. She took a sip, and finished, nodded thanks. "You two are lucky to be alive," he told her.

"I don't feel lucky." She managed a weak grin, then sat up on her own. A slight accent filled her voice, the vowels lengthened until every word seemed to rhyme. "My head feels like it's going to burst."

On hands and knees, she crawled to the still unconscious pilot. She peeled off her gloves, and stroked his forehead. "Papa? Can you hear me?"

The man stirred. Finally, his eyes opened and he looked up at her. "Riane? Are you all right? Where's the ship?"

"I'll explain everything later, Mr. Lebrie." Jim McClure helped him sit up. "We need to get moving. There's a sandstorm blowing in, and I don't want to be caught out in the open."

Travis peered around the edge of the boulder. His dad was right. The wind was constant now, so strong it stole his breath. Dust snakes wove across the ground. It wouldn't be long until the true storm hit. A last burst of crimson spread across the sky as Beta vanished below the horizon. The swirling dust turned from pink to silver with only Alpha's light left to shine through it. Soon, Travis realized, even that would be gone. He checked his wristwatch. Less than an hour of daylight remained. Anxious to start home, he untied Deuce and led the nervous horse closer.

"Is anybody else aboard your ship?" Jim McClure asked the pilot as he pulled him to his feet.

"No," the man answered. He had the same strange inflection as his daughter. "Only Riane and I."

"Good." McClure took the hobbles off the grey mare. A wall of hard, biting sand rushed past, and for a few seconds, visibility fell to zero. "Let's go."

"Shouldn't we stay here? We can take shelter aboard my ship."

"Only if you want to die from asphyxiation. Mount up, it's time to go."

"I..." Lebrie stared at the horses, a blank, frightened expression on his face. "I've never ridden before."

"Don't worry. All you have to do is hang on. We'll lead them. Okay?" Travis's dad handed him his helmet and waited until he settled it over his head, then helped the still woozy Lebrie into the saddle. The man climbed clumsily aboard, and sat with both hands death-gripped around the saddle horn. Travis started to help Riane onto Deuce's back, but she brushed his arm away.

"I can do this myself." She retrieved her helmet off the ground, twisted it on and slid the visor open. Staggering from the effects of the gas and the wind, she put her foot in the stirrup and jumped up. Her leg buckled and she nearly fell. Before Travis could help her, she jumped again and somehow managed to crawl into the battered saddle. Deuce snorted with impatience as Travis gathered the reins in his fist, and following behind the grey mare, started towards the edge of the mesa, the sky around them thick with driven dust.

CHAPTER FIVE

Once, when Travis was nine and still living on his parents' ranch in northern Montana, he had gone outside to play and was caught in an unexpected ground blizzard. Unable to see, he had wandered around in the swirling snow, one direction the same as another, until he had at last stumbled headlong into the side of the barn. Blinded by the storm, he had felt his way along the rickety fence that framed the outbuildings until he reached the house and practically fell inside, half-frozen and disoriented from the moving flood of unceasing whiteness. Sometimes, he still had nightmares about it.

This was worse.

He leaned into the wind, one hand on his hat to keep it from flying away, the other wrapped tight around Deuce's reins as he fought to keep up with his dad a few paces ahead. Fine grit leaked past the seal of his goggles into his eyes, while bits of sand whipped under the bandana tied around his face and filled his mouth every time he took a breath. It ground against his teeth and coated his tongue in a rusty film. Tucking his head down, Travis glanced back at the girl sitting on Deuce's long back. She might as well have been a statue, the only movement the slick green cloth of her e-suit as it rippled in the wind. Travis sighed and wished he had a suit like hers to protect his sand-blasted skin. He turned around again, too late to avoid smacking his right foot against a sharp rock half buried in the trail.

"Ouch!" He danced on one foot as the pain exploded in his big toe. Before he could slip out of the way, Deuce bumped him from behind and knocked him face down on the hard-packed ground. He rolled aside before the horse stepped on him.

"You okay back there?"

"Never better," Travis muttered. He could barely hear his father over the wind. Toe aching, he crawled to his feet. It was so dark he could barely make out his father's silhouette against the undulating clouds of dust. For all he knew, Alpha had already set, the sand so thick the sky looked no different to the ground.

"How do you know where we are going?" Lebrie,

huddled tight against the mare's withers, shouted, his voice muffled by his visor. "I can't see a thing."

"Neither can I." Jim McClure took the mare's reins and tied them securely around the saddle horn. Lebrie followed his movement. Even with a helmet and visor hiding his face, Travis could see the man thought his father had lost his mind.

"What are you doing?"

"I don't know which way camp is." McClure took the reins from Travis's hands and tied them around Deuce's neck also. "We'll have to let the horses smell their way home."

"Can they do that?" Riane asked.

"I sure hope so," McClure said. Travis was glad to see a ragged grin on his dad's face. He put a hand on Travis's shoulder. "Grab onto your horse's tail and don't let go. Okay?"

"Okay." Travis took a hold of Deuce's long tail and wrapped it around his hand. The tough strands felt like they would slice through his skin if he pulled too hard. His dad wandered up behind the grey mare, took a hold of her tail, then slapped her on the rump. Now leading the way unguided, the horses set off again, noses pressed to the ground. Riane twisted around until she faced Travis, the worry clear in her voice.

"What should I do?"

"Don't fall off." Travis grinned. "And if you do, try not to land on me."

* * *

One foot in front of the other.

They plodded on, the pair from the downed ship silent atop the horses while Travis and his dad followed, holding the animals' long tails to keep from being left behind. Darkness fell, what little colour remaining in the sand-drenched world banished. Now and then they would pause and try the radios, still hoping a signal might punch through to camp. A broad, rounded outcrop appeared out of the dust, and they pulled the horses against it for a moment to let them catch their breath. They hunkered down behind the enormous boulder, the wind, if not broken, at least blocked a little. Travis leaned against the warm rock, glad for the rest, Deuce's tail still wrapped around his aching fingers.

"How much further?" Lebrie shouted to be heard.

"It can't be too far to camp." Jim McClure shrugged. He pulled his tracker off his belt and swung the little device in a wide, slow arc. He scowled. "Worthless junk."

Travis thought for a moment his father might fling the expensive tracker away in pure disgust. He understood the feeling. The Company loved sending them new toys to test, then complained when they were broken or lost. The trackers had been one of the more successful experiments, though the units still failed more often than they worked. He wouldn't have blamed his dad one bit if he had thrown the malfunctioning device as hard as he could into the sandstorm.

"Can you get any signal?" he asked.

"Nothing." Jim McClure jammed the tracker back in its holster. "It worked fine this morning when I found you. Now the damn thing just flashes 'no lock'. What a piece of junk."

"Yeah," Travis said, suddenly unnerved. In the rush to find the downed starship and get back to camp he had forgotten about the encounter with the unknown predator. Now, he could think of nothing else. Every shadow became a nightmare crouching in wait, every gust of wind a scream in the night. He couldn't shake the sensation that something was following them, waiting for the perfect moment to attack.

They pushed on, the horses still leading the way, the animals following scents the humans could not. Travis struggled to keep up. Suddenly, Deuce snorted and picked up the pace, as if he had discovered something hidden in the night.

"Slow down," Travis gasped. Thoughts of razor-sharp teeth and bloodstained talons swept through his mind. Desperate not to be left behind, he broke into a stumbling jog, Deuce's tail cutting grooves in his fingers.

Something grabbed his ankle.

"No!" Travis fell hard. The tail whipped out of his hand and left him stranded and alone. Panicked, he rolled to a crouch to meet his attacker head on.

Nothing came at him.

Still fearing the worst, Travis groped around behind him. His hand brushed a strong, taut line. Unbelieving, he closed his fingers around the thin rope, and followed the slanting line upward. A flapping noise met him, the scratchy touch of canvas against his face more welcome than rain as he collided with the tent wall.

"Travis?" Jim McClure's voice cut through the wind. "Where are you?"

"Over here. I found one of the supply tents!"

"I know." His father appeared beside him, bent forward against the wind. "The horses took us right to the corral. Come on. Let's get them unsaddled, then get ourselves inside."

Travis couldn't have agreed more.

CHAPTER SIX

Faces stared as they ducked under the flap and stepped inside the long, crowded mess tent. Sand swirled through the open door behind them until the heavy flap dropped once more in place. It was hot inside; the scent of canvas and strong coffee and too many people crowded together hit Travis hard as he pulled his bandana down. No one spoke. The only sound was the wind outside and the drumbeat crack of the canvas walls as they whipped against the tent poles. A short, muscular woman, her pale blonde hair bleached nearly white by the relentless suns, stepped out from behind a tall cupboard and stood hands on hips in the middle of the tent.

"What in the name of hell were you two thinking of?"

For a moment, Travis thought his mother was going to hit him. Instead, she threw her arms around his shoulders and nearly crushed him as she hugged him tight to her. "Mom," he gasped. "I'm fine. I promise."

"I know, I know." An enormous grin spread across her face, her eyes squeezed shut as if she couldn't make up her mind whether to laugh or cry. She pulled Travis's head forward and kissed him, then spun around and launched herself at his father. "Jim McClure, I ought to kill you. That was stupid wandering off like that with a storm on the horizon." She threw herself against him so hard he nearly toppled backwards.

"Now, Angie..."

"Don't you 'now Angie' me!" She stood on tiptoes and kissed him hard on the lips. Around them, the little crowd came alive, laughing and slapping them on the backs, everyone talking at once, a thousand questions and no time to answer. Travis let himself be led to the nearest table. Someone set a steaming cup of hot, sweet coffee in front of him. He took a grateful swallow. Suddenly, he felt so tired he thought he was going to melt into the table. From the back of the noisy crowd, Bart Caddy pointed at Lebrie and Riane, who were taking off their helmets.

"Who are they?"

"That's the pilot of the ship," Jim McClure said. "His name's Lebrie."

"Adrian Lebrie, actually." Lebrie smiled hesitantly.

"This is my daughter and co-pilot, Riane." He set his helmet down on the nearest table and stepped deeper into the tent, then held his hand out towards Travis's dad. "I believe we owe our lives to you and your hired man, Mr. Tempke. Thank you."

"You're welcome." McClure shook his hand. "But you've got the wrong man pegged. I'm Jim McClure, the stock foreman for Camp Seven."

"Yeah." Caddy nodded at the table where Travis sat. "And that ain't no hired man. That's just a Travis." The crowd laughed. Even Travis had to grin a little at the mild taunting, too happy to care.

"Ah, my mistake. I was told a Mr. Tempke would meet us on landing." Lebrie bowed slightly, the movement so easy it seemed he was used to the attention of large groups of people. He straightened, then looked at McClure and Travis. "But, you still have my thanks. Both of you." He smiled gratefully, then moved towards the back of the tent.

Alice Prevoroski bustled out of the walled-off kitchen, a plate heaped high with fresh cookies in her hand. In the harsh electric lights that swung from the tent poles, her spiked hair looked even blacker than usual. She passed them around until everyone had taken one, then set the rest of the platter down in front of Travis. She squeezed in across the table from him and leaned forward. "I tried to call you guys back as soon as I found out about the sandstorm, but we couldn't raise you."

"I know." Travis picked up a cookie and took a bite. It was still warm, the wonderful flavour of melted chocolate enough to make him forget about all the sand he had swallowed during the trek back to camp. "All we could pick up was static. The trackers were dead, too."

Around them, the crowd began to relax as people sat down or drifted off towards the tall coffee pots beside the kitchen door. Bart Caddy reached over Alice's shoulder to snatch another cookie, but she playfully slapped his hand away. He dodged, but managed to snag another with his left hand. Around a mouthful of crumbs, he stared at Lebrie.

"What are you all doing here on Aletha?" he called. "You must have made somebody in the Company awfully mad to get sent here." Everyone laughed softly. Lebrie smiled.

"Actually, we are not with Advanced Terraforming." Lebrie put his hand on Riane's shoulder. "We are from the Free Planet Society."

The room fell quiet, nothing but the sound of flapping canvas to break the uncomfortable silence. Lebrie stood, for once appearing self-conscious, the corner of his smile twitching. Beside him, Riane stood straight, her dark eyes defiant. Confused, Travis leaned across the table towards Alice and whispered. "Did I miss something?"

"I'll explain it to you later, kiddo."

The silence stretched on until even the smile on Lebrie's lips vanished. Another gust blasted against the tent, the canvas straining inward from the force of it. The lights swayed, casting odd shadows around the long room. Just when it seemed the cold silence might never end, Travis's mom stepped forward.

"Well, we're all glad you're safe." She took Riane's hand. "Come on and have something to eat. You must be starving."

The tension around the room slackened as everyone went back to talking. Travis watched uncomfortably as his mom chatted with Riane. "My name's Angelica McClure, but everyone just calls me Angie. And I think you know Travis?"

Riane smiled. "Yes indeed."

"It's nice to see someone his age around here for a change." Angie gave Travis's hand a squeeze. "Especially someone as pretty as you are. You just sit there, and I'll get you a cup of coffee." She left them and started towards the coffee pots.

Travis stared at his own cup, utterly embarrassed. He felt the blush spread across his face as he sat tongue-tied. Out at the ship, he had been utterly in charge of himself, working hard to bring the stranded pair to safety. Now, the situation had unexpectedly flip-flopped, leaving him a helpless, hopeless, gawky boy. Before he could fumble for anything that didn't sound stupid to say, he was spared by his father breaking into the silence. Jim McClure stood up and nodded at Alice Prevoroski. He looked angry. "Where's Tempke?"

"Base Camp, I think." She seemed surprised. "He flew off somewhere in the jump-bug. He's been gone since mid-morning. Problem?"

"Might be." McClure's gaze drifted to Lebrie. Travis had the distinct impression the newcomer was the cause of his father's bad mood. "I'll talk to you about it later."

He wandered off, casually working his way towards the back of the mess tent where Lebrie sat. Travis watched him, his sense of unease worsening. Riane took a cookie and bit into it, chewing slowly. "Your father seems like an interesting man," she said.

"Huh?" Travis turned around to face her. Of all the things he thought about his father, interesting was not necessarily one of them. "I guess he is."

"It must be exciting, living on an undeveloped planet like Aletha Three."

"Exciting?" Travis grinned, thoughts of the long day's events blurred in his tired mind. "Sometimes. Usually, it's pretty boring, though."

Riane nodded, then leaned forward and took another cookie. She smiled playfully when she caught him looking. Her dark eyes reflected the lamps hung overhead and seemed to glow. Travis couldn't remember ever seeing eyes shine quite like hers did. He fumbled for something – anything – to say. "So, what is it that you do?"

"Travel, it seems." She leaned back and surveyed the crowded tent. "Most of our time is spent between stars.

If I didn't have my lessons to keep me busy, I think I'd go crazy every time we broke ground."

"What grade are you in?" Alice Prevoroski asked.

"Oh, I finished my primary studies early." The girl said it as if everyone in her circle was long out of school. "I attended university on Procyon Station last year, but decided to take a year off to help my father. But, I like to keep up with my classes, so I audit them on disc. What about you?"

"Me?" Travis shrugged. Suddenly, he felt terribly young. "I, uh, get my assignments downloaded from Base Camp once a month. My mom helps me with them. She's like a teacher or something."

"His mom," Alice gave him a stern glance, "has a degree in astronautic engineering."

"Really?" Riane's neatly curved eyebrows arched higher. "I didn't realize there was any call for that on a project like this?"

"There ain't. I mean, isn't." The words tangled in his mouth. "She used to teach school here a couple times a week, but then the Garcias and the Hazadis left camp, so there was just me left. So, you know..." Travis was saved from further embarrassment by a commotion at the far end of the tent. He stood up, straining to see what was happening, but too many people blocked his view. His mother dashed out of the kitchen and pushed through the milling onlookers. Travis swallowed, his stomach suddenly twisted into a tight knot as he watched her drag his father away from the far table.

Lebrie stood, swaying slightly, his face pale in the electric glare. Travis didn't have to look any more to know Jim McClure and Adrian Lebrie had been arguing.

"Oh, no. What now?" He started towards the commotion, but stopped. Already, the argument seemed to have ended. His mother led his father into the kitchen. Neither said a word to him. Travis could barely force himself to look back at Riane. "I don't know what that was about."

"Probably the audit we are doing for the Free Planet Society." Her smile never wavered as she tossed off her reply like the empty cup in her hand. "We're here to put a halt to terraforming on Aletha."

CHAPTER SEVEN

The storm broke just after midnight, gone as quickly as it came. Everyone drifted out of the mess, back to their own tents to catch what sleep they could. Travis paused outside the glowing blue dome that had, for so long, been his home. A small crescent of sand had drifted around the tent, and glowed dull grey like crushed bone in the yard lights spread around camp. He took a deep breath. The air was cool, a faint trace of wind-driven grit still on the breeze. Aletha Three had no moons, nothing but the faint auroral glow that hung ghostlike above the northern horizon to mar the star-filled blackness. Strange stars, most of them not even visible from Earth, rippled and danced, the atmosphere unsettled. Travis felt unsettled too. He glanced back at the long mess tent where a pair of cots had been set up for Adrian Lebrie and his daughter.

"Why did you have to show up now?" Travis whispered. The wind seemed to have heard him, and rustled the tent wall behind him. For years he had dreamed of leaving Aletha's harsh surface and going home. But, to his surprise, the idea of having the project shut down didn't make him happy at all.

It made him angry.

Across camp, the horses stirred in the corral, biting and kicking at each other as they fought for position at the feed bunks, free at last from the biting sand. One of them squealed, no doubt a mare in heat, a high, piercing note that drove a cold spike through his spine. It reminded him of the other scream he had heard that morning. Travis looked away from the soft glow of tents and yard lights, past the safe, familiar ring of light at the dark wastelands beyond.

Somewhere out there, something unnatural stalked the night.

Cold and exhausted, Travis ducked under the tent flap and crawled off into his sleeping bag.

Morning broke, a brilliant scarlet haze that filled the eastern sky. Travis stepped out of the tent and rubbed his eyes. They stung from yesterday's sand and lack of sleep. Tired as he had been, sleep was long in coming. Too many things on his mind, too much happening in too short a time. The predator. The sandstorm. The unexpected arrival of the Lebries and their agenda to close down the project. Travis tugged his beat-up hat down lower and started across the encampment, unable to shake the feeling that his life had suddenly became more complicated than he had ever expected. Outside the corral, he heard his father's voice.

"All right, boys and girls, let's get a move on."

Travis shook his head and sighed. The last thing he wanted to do was chase cows all day. His entire body ached with a thousand scrapes and bruises that he hadn't even noticed until he squirmed reluctantly out of the soft, heavenly warmth of his sleeping bag into the chill red dawn. Moving slow, he headed towards the corral.

He ducked inside the battered tack trailer and started searching through the tangled pile of halters strewn across the metal floor. The narrow aluminium trailer was dim inside, and reeked of saddle soap and horse sweat. Travis kneeled on the floor and dug deeper into the mess of frayed rope and nylon, but couldn't find the green and white halter he always used on Deuce.

"I know I left it here last night." A vague recollection of tossing his tack and saddle inside the trailer after they unsaddled the horses and put them away the night before ran through his mind, but in the confusion he wasn't sure about anything. Frustrated, he plucked a ratty halter out of the pile and hoped it would fit. Already the day was off to a poor start. Mad at having misplaced his gear, he stepped back into the daylight in time to see Bart Caddy amble through the gate, a rangy dun gelding in tow. Travis stared at the horse and clenched his jaw so hard his teeth ached.

Around the gelding's muzzle was a green and white halter.

"Hey, that's mine!"

Bart turned and frowned. "What are you yammering about?"

"That halter." Travis pointed at the lead rope in Bart's hand. "That's the one I use."

"So? Looks like you found another one."

"Yeah," Travis said, his anger rising. "But that's the one I use."

"Then," Bart said, edging closer. "I guess you should hang it off your saddle instead of leaving it on the floor, huh?"

The tone in his voice left no doubt he had dropped a challenge. Travis reached out and tried to grab the lead rope, but Bart snatched his arm away. The dun, startled by the sudden movement, jerked back. Travis tried again to take the halter, but Bart pushed him on the shoulder, a rough shove that rocked him backwards. Too angry for caution, Travis grabbed the dangling end of the lead rope and yanked on it. The dun gelding threw his head high and pulled back. Bart and Travis stumbled as the rope burned through their hands. Off balance, Travis landed on the hard-packed ground.

A long shadow fell across him.

"What the hell is this about?"

Travis pushed his hat back and stared up at his father. He swallowed, certain he had gone too far. Bart started to say something, but Jim McClure cut him off.

"I don't know what it is between you two, but I've had a bellyful of it." McClure glared at both of them. Travis swore he could hear the teeth grind in his father's jaw. "I have enough problems to worry about without babysitting you two. Understand? Now, get saddled up. Those cattle are going to be scattered from hell to breakfast after last night."

Travis crawled to his feet and dusted himself off. He felt like an idiot for trying to pick a fight. He bent down and retrieved the other halter, then straightened. A dull, pulsing roar cut through the chill morning air. He craned his head skyward as the noise grew louder. Far in the distance but approaching fast, a dark speck glided above the desert. A thin vapour trail, tinged red by Beta's glow, spread out behind the jump-bug.

"Who in the hell is that?" Bart squinted at the little vehicle as it swung towards camp.

"Who else?" McClure snorted in disgust. "Looks like Tempke's back."

The jump-bug passed overhead, a wall of sound rumbling in its wake, so loud the horses shied as the machine zipped past. Travis watched the one-seat flyer swing towards the patch of bare dirt, spray-painted white with a wind sock planted beside it, that served as the camp's landing field. Dust billowed out from beneath the machine as it settled to the ground. The roar faded, replaced by the falling whine of the turbine as it spooled down. Beside him, Bart Caddy cleared his throat and spat.

"Don't you love it?" he muttered. "The Company complains if one of us loses a horseshoe, but it's fine for Tempke to burn more money flying back and forth to Base Camp than most of us could earn in a month."

"No one said life was fair." Jim McClure left without another word, and headed towards the landing field. Travis waited until his father vanished inside the cloud of dust around the jump-bug, then stepped up to the corral and opened the gate.

Horses scattered around him as he walked through the pen. Deuce saw him and spun away, not anxious to be caught. The old horse moved stiffly, favouring his right front leg, too lame to be ridden. "Looks like one of us gets a day off," Travis said, loud enough that Deuce flicked his ears at the sound. Travis looked around the pen at the horses left unsaddled. A roan mare with a short, bristly tail, hardly more than a colt, stood near the feed bunks. Hiding the halter behind his back, he started towards her.

"Easy, girl." Travis kept his movements slow and deliberate as he slid the lead rope around the mare's neck and buckled the tattered halter. He patted her on the neck. He had ridden her before, and while she was gentle, she was still a green-broke colt, and that meant doing things slow and easy. "Come on, Twitch. Guess it's your turn today."

The mare whickered as Travis led her out of the pen and tied her to the railing, nervous at leaving the other horses. He picked up a soft brush and began combing her back, using long even strokes as he worked around her front legs and under her belly to calm her down before he threw his saddle on.

Voices, sharp and filled with anger, drifted towards him.

"Oh no." Travis straightened up and looked over the mare's back towards the jump-bug. His dad and Tempke were arguing, both men speaking at once. He dropped the brush and hurried towards them, snatches of the heated conversation loud as he neared the landing field.

"Don't try to back out on this," Jim McClure said, his face red. "You damn near got my son killed yesterday."

"Me? I don't even know what you're talking about!" Tempke was mad too, his fists clenched at his side. Few people ever had the nerve to argue with him, especially in the open. "Don't you dare blame me because your kid can't stay out of trouble."

Travis winced as he realized the fight was about him. He stood self-consciously at the edge of the painted circle. His dad noticed him and pointed directly at where he stood.

"My kid got into trouble because you told him you'd pay a bonus if he found that damned monster." McClure stepped closer. "And if I hadn't found him when I did, that thing would have torn him to bits."

Tempke's face paled. He swung around and faced Travis, the argument suddenly forgotten. "You found the rogue?"

"I..." Travis tried to frame his thoughts. "I found something."

"What did it look like?" Tempke stepped towards him, speaking rapidly. "How large was it? Did you get any pictures?"

"Show him the tooth," Jim McClure said, still angry. Quickly, Travis fumbled in his pocket for the sickle-shaped tooth he had found yesterday. In all the confusion the night before, he had totally forgotten about the strange artefact. It felt slick between his fingers, knife-edged and deadly, jagged at the base where it had broken off at the root. Reluctantly, he held it out for Tempke to examine.

"What the...?" Tempke's voice dropped. His hand shook slightly as he took the tooth from Travis, as if he expected it to jump to life and bite him. Travis waited, unsure what to do next. Behind his shoulder, someone coughed.

"Mind if I have a look at that?"

Adrian Lebrie stepped closer, a hesitant smile on his thin face. Someone had found him a company-issued flight suit and a well-worn cap, the brim bent nearly in two. Without his e-suit, Travis thought, he didn't seem nearly as imposing as he had the day before. In fact, he could have passed for one of the techs wandering around between tents. "I hope I'm not intruding, but I couldn't help overhear something about a rogue. A rogue what?"

"Who are you?" Tempke cocked his head, a puzzled frown on his face. "I don't remember seeing you around here before."

"Forgive me." Lebrie extended his hand. "Adrian Lebrie. I believe we communicated briefly via flash-net several months ago. You are Allen Tempke, yes?"

Tempke stiffened, his eyes suddenly alert. Travis frowned, surprised at his reaction. For one brief moment, Tempke looked like a man who had forgotten something important and only now realized what it was. Still, he recovered quickly and nodded, a thin smile on his face. "Ah, right, I seem to recall something about that. Maybe you could fill me in on the details?"

"Of course," Lebrie said. "I'm with the Free Planet Society. My daughter and I are here to perform an environmental assessment on their behalf."

To his left, Travis felt more than saw another, smaller figure join them on the edge of the painted circle. Riane stepped up beside her father and bowed slightly at the waist. The too-large tunic and work pants she had borrowed couldn't hide how pretty she was. She glanced at Travis and smiled. He felt his face redden.

"This isn't really a good time," Jim McClure told Lebrie. "We're kind of in the middle of something."

"Actually," Tempke shook Lebrie's outstretched hand, "it might be a happy coincidence that Mr. Lebrie arrived when he did. Now I remember. You're the exo-biologist from the University of Procyon, right?"

Lebrie nodded. "I'm currently on sabbatical, but yes, I am on the university staff."

"Let's step into my office and discuss the situation." Tempke walked away, Riane and her father following, the tooth Travis had risked his life to bring back still in his hand. Travis looked at his father.

"What do we do now?"

"We get to work, that's what." Jim McClure spun on his heel and stomped off towards the corral. Travis stood a moment and watched Riane's retreating form until she vanished inside Tempke's trailer, then followed his dad back to the pen.

CHAPTER EIGHT

The day seemed endless.

The storm had scattered the herd across the foothills, away from the waterholes and scrubby meadows, cows and calves split apart from each other. Travis spent most of the morning chasing a stray calf that had wandered away from its mother and stubbornly refused to go back, up and down the sand-choked gullies. By the time he had finally returned the frightened animal to the herd, Twitch, the roan mare he was riding, was caked in dust and dried lather. He took off his hat and swiped his forehead with the back of his hand. A reddish-brown streak ran across his sleeve, the same colour as the dirt on the little mare.

"Bet we look good, huh, girl?" He leaned forward in the saddle and patted her neck, then turned towards camp. They topped the long, high ridge that arced like a crater wall south of camp. Already the twin suns had passed the zenith and begun the long fall towards sunset. Travis glanced at his wristwatch, but the little screen was blank, the watch dead again. "Don't know about you, girl," he told the mare, "but it feels like it's a long time after lunch."

Sparse clumps of yellowed grass waved in the wind. Travis stepped out of the saddle, hobbled Twitch, then sat down on a flat rock to eat the last of the ration bars he had grabbed before leaving. He chewed the sticky-sweet bar, all too aware his canteen had run dry hours ago. Behind him, the roan mare cropped the grass within reach, long stalks flipping back and forth in her mouth as she chewed the tough, sun-dried fodder. Far below and kilometres away, camp rose out of the arid plain like some strange weed. Dust streamed away from the little encampment, churned by every passing footfall and carried on the wind. It gave the illusion that the scruffy collection of tents was moving.

A smaller cloud inched towards it, other riders already returning. Travis pulled the radio off his belt and flipped it on.

"Here goes nothing." He held the little transmitter close to his mouth and pressed the transmit button. "Camp Seven, Travis McClure, come in."

To his relief, a scratchy, female voice responded. Alice Prevoroski sounded cheerful as usual. "Go ahead, Travis."

"Just checking in. I'm seven klicks south, on top of the Rim."

"Roger that." A burst of static broke out the speaker. "Travis, stand by."

He held the speaker close and waited. Without meaning to, his gaze drifted westward towards the jagged foothills. Somewhere out there, a monster roamed, and he was glad to be kilometres away from whatever the thing was. The radio crackled back to life.

"Travis, could you come on in? Seems our guests want to have a word with you."

"Roger that," he replied. Somehow, he had been expecting the order. "I'm on my way."

Feeling uncertain, he clipped the radio to his belt, then walked back to the mare, who was still trying to eat every bite of grass on the hilltop. "Let's go, girl. No telling what I've done wrong this time."

Tempke's office was, like everything at Camp Seven, crowded with the day-to-day clutter of living. The narrow trailer was crammed front to back with filing cabinets and storage boxes stacked one on the other right up to the low ceiling. A sturdy metal desk occupied the corner furthest from the door, a holo-projector glowing softly on its surface. Three familiar figures stood around it, studying the image that hovered above the grey projector plate. Travis stepped inside and stood a moment to let his eyes adjust to the change in light. The office smelled like hot electronics and coffee long gone cold. He cleared his throat.

"You wanted to see me, Mr. Tempke?"

"Come on in, Travis." Tempke motioned for him to come closer. "I'd like your input on this."

Riane stepped aside to make room for him beside the desk. Travis stepped closer, so near that their shoulders brushed. She smiled in greeting. Lebrie stood to his other side, whispering into a hand-corder. A translucent, three-dimensional view of the region covered the desk, blurred at the edges. Tempke pointed at the foothills west of camp.

"Can you show me where you encountered this thing you saw?"

"I think," Travis said, studying the map and trying to get his bearings, "it was somewhere around here."

He traced a circle in the picture. The image folded around his finger as if he had stirred the surface of a mud puddle. The holo, sharp as it was, left familiar landmarks oddly distorted, the aerial view unable to portray how steep the bluffs and arroyos really were. Tempke fiddled with the controls, and the map zoomed in around the area Travis circled.

"Can you narrow it down a little further?" Tempke prompted.

"Maybe." Travis leaned closer. On either side, Lebrie

and Riane leaned in with him, so close he could smell the scent of soap in her hair. It made it hard for him to concentrate on the map. Near the centre of the image he spotted a shallow bowl, the hill around it steep and covered with large boulders. He jabbed his finger at the small depression. "How old is this picture?"

"The satellite took it this morning," Tempke said. "Is there a problem?"

"No. I thought maybe I could spot the bull the thing killed, but I guess the sand's covered the carcass." Or, he added silently to himself, it had been completely eaten.

"Just how big is this animal?" Lebrie asked.

"I'm not sure. It was big. Almost as big as Deuce." Travis paused. "Deuce's my horse. I guess he'd weigh 500 kilos. Maybe a little less."

"This animal weighs as much as a horse?" Lebrie raised an eyebrow, his tone sceptical. "Very few predators reach that size. Especially on a planet like Aletha Three."

"Mr. Lebrie," Tempke said quietly. "We've been over this. There are no native life forms on Aletha. Every species here was introduced several decades ago after the oxygen atmosphere was stabilized."

"And yet," Lebrie waved his hand at Travis. "Here we are. Where could this rogue of yours have come from if not native to this world? Is Advanced Terraforming so lax with its record keeping that you forgot to inventory something larger than a Bengal tiger after you released it?"

"We didn't release this thing." Tempke's neck muscles tensed, his jaw set tight. He was angry. So was Lebrie.

"If you did not introduce this thing – whatever it is – who did?"

Riane glanced at Travis. "Can you describe what it looked like?"

"Yeah." Travis nodded. "It stood on its hind legs and used its front claws for reaching. It had a narrow snout, and a long tail that stuck out behind it." A shudder passed through him, the memory all too fresh. "And it stank. It smelled like cleaning fluid or ammonia or something."

"What colour was its fur?" Lebrie asked.

"No fur. It was slick, like leather. Kind of silver-grey with dark grey stripes. And it had a row of feathers down its back."

"Feathers?" Lebrie's eyes narrowed. "It almost sounds like a Pegasian bandit-rat, but they don't weigh more than ten or fifteen kilos at most. Are you certain you might not have exaggerated the size?"

"Yeah, I'm certain." Travis bristled. "You saw that tooth I found."

Lebrie pulled back, a surprised expression on his face. Apparently, Travis realized, the man wasn't used to having his authority questioned. The exo-biologist straightened and scratched his chin. "Very well. If this creature truly matches your description, we may be dealing with an undiscovered species." Lebrie turned back to Tempke. "And, if that is the case, I need to study it in its habitat. I'm sure your company will offer full assistance."

"And if we don't?" Tempke asked.

"Then, I will have little recourse but to file an injunction against this project on behalf of the Free Planet Society." A thin, arrogant smile curved Lebrie's lips, his eyes steady. "I'm sure you can see it's to our mutual benefit to gain a better understanding of this predator."

"I see." Tempke tapped his fingers against his desk. The image fluttered in time with the vibration. "What kind of cooperation are you talking about?"

"Supplies. Transportation and logistics." Lebrie paused, then looked at Travis. "And, I will need someone familiar with the region."

Tempke leaned across his desk. "What do you say, Travis? Are you interested in working as their guide?"

Travis stepped back from the holo-map, startled by the offer. Tempke continued. "We would, of course, be willing to pay you more for the extra work. What do you say?"

"He says no."

Travis spun around. He hadn't heard his father step inside the trailer. Jim McClure's spurs clicked against the bare floor as he approached the desk. He put his hand on Travis's shoulder and pulled him away from the desk. "My son risked his neck once to find this thing. He's not about to do it again."

"Dad, I..."

McClure's grip tightened around Travis's shoulder. "Trav, why don't you go feed the horses. I'd like a word with these people in private."

"But..." Travis started to protest. The hand on his shoulder tightened, a warning. "Fine. I'll leave." He felt everyone's eyes on his back as he left the trailer and stepped back into the glare outside. Feeling more like a child than he had in ages, he stomped towards the corral, thoughts of what he should have said spinning in his mind. More riders were returning, dust clouds streaming in. Travis stepped inside the tack room, found a sack of grain, and hoisted the heavy bag across his shoulders. Stumbling a little under the weight, he spread the coarse ground feed along the trough, then broke open one of the carefully hoarded bales of grass hay. They were nearly out of feed, the supply trucks long overdue. Sweating in the heat, Travis spread the hay thin enough that all the horses could get some of it, then wandered to the water tank and made sure it was full.

Deuce plodded across the pen. For a second, Travis thought the old horse was coming to see him, but the animal whisked his tail to chase off a cloud of gnats, then hurried to the feed bunk, desperate to eat his fill before another horse might crowd him out.

"Well, hello to you too," Travis said, disgusted that even his horse was ignoring him today. He shut off the water valve and turned around, shocked to see Riane leaning over the metal fence behind him.

"For what it's worth," she said. "They kicked me out, too."

A bright smile spread across her face. Twin suns poured through her dark hair and left it shining like a halo around her face. Travis had never seen an angel, but if he had, he decided, it would look like her. Unsure what to do, he said the first thing that popped into his mind.

"I'll bet your dad doesn't treat you like a snot-nosed pup."

"Sometimes he does." Riane opened the gate for him and waited until he stepped through. "Other times, he just assumes I agree with everything he says. I think it's a dad thing." She laughed softly, though her smile faded. "It was worse when he and my mother still lived together. Now, though, maybe he accepts me for who I am. At least some of the time."

"You're lucky. My old man treats me the same as he did when we came here, like I can't take care of myself. I mean, I'm sixteen years old, not eleven."

"Only sixteen? I would have thought you much older." Riane seemed surprised. Travis suddenly wished he had kept his mouth shut a little tighter. Her smile returned. "I hope your father lets you work with us."

"Yeah, like that's going to happen. Once his mind's set on something, that's it."

"You never know," she said. "My father can be quite persuasive, too. And I have a feeling Mr. Tempke will do anything right now to speed along our audit." She leaned closer and whispered playfully, "I'm not sure if you noticed, but I don't think we are particularly welcome here right now."

They both laughed. Riane squeezed his hand, then turned to go. "I'll see you tonight at supper, won't I?"

"Yeah. Sure," Travis said, flustered at the simple touch. "See you at mess." He waited until she was gone, then finished taking care of the stock. Done at last, he trudged past Bachelors' Row towards their tent. His mother was inside, typing away on a laptop. She looked up and smiled.

"You're back early."

Travis shrugged. "Tempke called me in to talk about that thing I found."

"Oh?" Angie McClure's face darkened. "What did he want to know?"

"Where I found it and stuff." Travis took off his hat and laid it on top of a nearby storage locker. "He asked me if I wanted to work as a guide for the Lebries."

"He wanted you to help with this damn fool audit?" His mother's tone left little room for doubt about which side of the fence she stood on. "I hope you said no."

"I didn't have to. Dad said it for me."

"Honey, he's just looking out for you."

"Is he?" Travis felt his anger rising again. "Seems like he's fine with me going off by myself as long as it's doing his work. But the minute I might try something he doesn't approve of, I'm just some stupid little kid again."

"Travis..."

"Mom, you know it's true. It's fine for you and me to work like dogs, just as long as we're doing it for him. Why is it any more dangerous for me to show the Lebries around than it is to chase cows all day by myself?"

"Honey." Angie McClure sighed as if she was suddenly exhausted. "There's more to it than that. Your dad trusts you. He relies on you. But these people, no matter how nice they seem, want to take everything away from us that we've worked so hard to achieve."

"Take what away, Mom? This?" Travis waved his arm in frustration around the tent. "We're not exactly living in luxury here."

"No one wants to go home more than I do, Travis." Angie paused. "Unless it's your father. But without this job, we can never pay off the debt on the ranch. If the Aletha project hadn't taken us on, we would have lost the place. It's that simple." She looked directly into his eyes. "He's doing it for you, honey."

"Yeah? Well, maybe he should have asked me first what I wanted."

She stared at him for a long time, then set the laptop aside and walked towards him. "What is it that you do want, Travis?"

"I...I don't know. I just want a say in my own life sometimes. Is that too much to ask for?"

"No," she said, her voice nearly lost under the wind's moan. "No, it's not." She pulled him close and hugged him. "It's hard for a parent to realize their babies do grow up, that's all. Why don't you get washed up and I'll start supper early."

"Oh..." Travis pulled away. "I kind of promised Riane I'd eat supper with her in the mess tent tonight."

"I see." A smile flickered across his mom's lips. "All right. But don't be out too late, okay? You still have assignments to finish."

"I won't, Mom. Promise." He turned towards the tent door, then paused, his hand on the flap. "Mom? Thanks."

"You're welcome." She sat down and retrieved her computer. "See you after supper."

CHAPTER NINE

By the time Travis had cleaned up and walked across the compound to the mess tent, a line had formed outside, hungry riders and technicians waiting with trays in hand for supper. Riane and her father were already seated at one of the long tables, flanked on either side by a survey crew up from Base Camp. Disappointed, Travis plopped down a few tables away and picked at his food. It might have been goulash, but he wasn't sure. Riane saw him and waved, then turned back to her own tray. Mad at his bad luck, and feeling totally out of place, Travis took a bite of the bland, overcooked food.

"Here, try this." Alice Prevoroski set a small bottle filled with green paste next to his tray. "Trust me, it helps."

"Thanks." Travis popped open the lid and sprinkled a generous dollop of the sauce across his supper. The strong bite of hot peppers rose off his plate.

"Hey, go easy." Alice sat down next to him. "That's strong stuff for a beginner."

Travis scooped his fork into the goulash and took a bite. A pleasant, hot-sour flavour masked the bland beans and corn. Without warning, fire erupted in his mouth as the hot sauce kicked in. He grabbed his water glass and drained it in a single pull.

"I told you it's a little on the hot side." Alice opened the bottle and upended it over her own plate, mixed the hot sauce in, then added a dash more for good measure. She took a bite, nodded in satisfaction, and capped the bottle. "So, how come you're eating here tonight? Guarantee if I had a choice between your mom's cooking and this place, you'd have to drag me out of your tent."

Travis grinned, sweat pooling on his forehead, and hesitantly took another bite. Despite the heat, the hot sauce did make the food better. "Guess I just wanted to see how the other half lives."

"Oh." Alice noticed Riane sitting at the far table and smiled knowingly. "I get you." She broke a hard biscuit in half and used it to sop up the gravy on her plate. Her eyes never left the table where the Lebries sat. "Must be hard to be sixteen in a place like this."

"It's not so bad." Travis stared at his tray.

"And you're a lousy liar, kiddo." Alice ran a hand through her spiked hair. "I'm not so old I can't remember what it's like to be your age." She lowered her voice. "Just be careful, okay? A pretty face can lead a person into a lot of trouble if they don't keep their eyes open."

Travis looked up but said nothing. Alice continued, her eyes deadly serious. "What I'm trying to say is, trust yourself. You're smart, Travis. Follow your own instincts, not somebody else's." She rose and picked up her empty tray. "You ready for seconds?"

"No thanks," Travis said. "I've had all I can handle for one night."

"Okay. See you tomorrow." Alice Prevoroski squeezed out behind him and started towards the kitchen, then turned around and set the bottle of hot sauce directly in front of Travis. "You keep this. I've got a whole case back in my tent. Just be sure to keep the lid on tight. The stuff might burn a hole in the floor if it gets out."

Sleep was a long time coming.

Travis lay in his sleeping bag, the air in the tent stale, the familiar scents and sounds of night in camp around him. He thought about Tempke's offer. The idea of helping Adrian Lebrie and his daughter hunt for the strange predator left him twisted in knots. Part of him wanted to go so badly he couldn't stand staying behind. He wanted to prove himself at something outside of chasing cattle or doing chores around camp. And, though he hated to admit it, he wanted to be around Riane. But, another part of him shrank away from the idea. Everything would change if he went. That much he knew.

And somewhere out there, prowling the shadows, was an animal so vicious it could bring down a bull and tear it to bits. He closed his eyes and the creature seemed to leap out at him, narrow jaws dripping blood. Travis sat up, unable to sleep, and wandered outside to the latrine.

The night wind was cool and the hair on his arms bristled, goosebumps on his skin. Travis hurried to the latrine, then, finished, started back to the tent. Halfway there, outside the feeble circle of yard lights, he paused and looked up. The sky was clear, so black it seemed to swallow every trace of light and warmth. Stars crossed overhead, relentless in their weary march. When they had first arrived on Aletha, Travis had spent night after night staring up at them, naming the strange constellations, conjuring stories about what they might be. A trio of bright red stars pointed westward, a silvery cluster behind it like foam behind a ship. He had named it the Pathfinder. It had always been his favourite constellation. Maybe, he had thought, he was meant to be a pathfinder too.

Travis smiled at the thought. He took a deep breath of the cool, flinty air, then went back to the tent, his decision made.

"No."

"But, Dad..."

"I said no." Jim McClure sat cross-legged on the tent floor and jabbed his spoon into the heaped bowl of oatmeal on his lap and took a bite. His frown deepened, as if the sticky paste had turned to sand in his mouth. "I don't want you working with those people."

"Why?" Travis set his own bowl aside. "I can handle myself. I do it every day. This would be a walk in the park compared to chasing cows."

"Honey..." His mother smiled and tried to ease the tension in the tent's main room. "It's not that we don't think you could do the job. But, the situation is a little more complicated than that."

"Complicated?" Jim McClure snorted in disgust. "The Free Planet Society wants to shut us down. What's so complicated about that? They're a bunch of rich, spoiled crusaders looking for a cause to chase."

"Then, wouldn't it be better if I was along to keep an eye on what they do?" Travis struggled to keep his voice calm. "And you've said it yourself, we could use the extra money."

He watched his parents, hoping for a sign that his argument had taken root. His father started to say something, but stopped. Slowly, he set his uneaten breakfast aside and sat stroking the corners of his unkempt moustache. After an eternity, he rose to his feet and stomped toward the tent flap. "You do whatever you think best."

Travis watched his father duck under the flap and vanish outside, his shadow a silhouette against the blue fabric. He turned to face his mom. "I'll be all right. I really can handle myself."

"I know you can, honey." Angie McClure sniffed back a tear. Her lips quivered, but she smiled anyhow. She helped Travis to his feet, then, before he could duck, threw her arms around him and squeezed tight. "Promise me you'll be careful?"

"I promise."

Travis turned away, embarrassed, and quickly started to pack what he would need for the trip. Extra socks and underwear, a change of shirt, his toothbrush and extra gloves. Everything else he would need was already on his saddle. He rubbed his face and thought about throwing in a razor, then laughed softly at the idea. He only shaved once a week at best, and besides, he decided, he might look older with a little shadow on his cheeks. As an afterthought, he tossed in the bottle of hot sauce Alice Prevoroski had given him the night before, then rolled everything up inside his sleeping bag and stepped outside.

Beta burned a hole in the sky, thin, high clouds the colour of dried blood twining overhead. It was going to be hot, no sign of rain. Travis slung his gear over his shoulder and walked to the corral. Tempke and Lebrie were already there, and he looked around for Riane. A lump formed in the bottom of his stomach when he saw her standing next to Bart Caddy. Already, he could hear Caddy, his voice twanging as he pointed at the various horses meandering around the dusty pen.

"Now, that bay gelding over there, I broke him myself. He might do you, but he's a little green. No telling how he might act. Maybe I ought to catch him and rough him out a bit before you step on."

"Forget it. She can ride Twitch," Travis said. He tossed his sleeping bag to the ground, and walked straight to where Caddy and Riane stood. "The last thing we need is one of your cast-offs, Bart."

"Who says you're going anywhere, Travy?" Caddy's mouth lifted in a crooked, ugly grin.

"I said he was." Tempke broke away from Lebrie and walked over. He ignored Caddy as he led Travis and Riane towards the gate. "You pick out whichever horses you want, then catch one of the mules. You know how to pack, right?"

"Yes, sir," Travis said.

"Good. You figure out everything you'll need, and I'll cut the requisition." Tempke held out his hand. Travis shook it, his grip strong. "Thanks for doing this." With that, he turned and strode off to his trailer. Travis grabbed a halter and stepped inside the pen.

Alpha was up, a fierce white dot, before they were

finally ready to go. Travis made certain the packs bulging on the tall, sorrel mule's back were secure, then double-checked Lebrie and Riane's saddles. He held Twitch while Riane climbed on, and handed her the reins. Behind him, Lebrie tried to put his foot in the stirrup, but the paint gelding Travis had picked for him backed away, swinging wide as the frustrated exobiologist danced on one foot, unable to swing aboard. Travis took the reins from him and pulled the baulky animal to a halt.

"You're supposed to get on from the left side," Travis said. Lebrie, his face flushed from exertion, walked around to the other side and tried again. The paint stood calmly and waited while the inexperienced rider struggled into the saddle. Travis looped the reins over the horse's neck, then sauntered towards the rail where Deuce stood patiently, swatting flies with his long tail. Travis had watched him carefully as he led him from the corral, looking for signs of lameness, but to his relief the horse seemed sound this morning. He swung up, the mule's lead rope coiled in his hand, and turned the horses away from camp.

He saw a familiar figure walk towards them, taking his time as he wandered past Bachelors' Row. Travis smiled, relieved, as his dad stepped up beside him. In his hand was his scuffed-up old carbine and a box of ammunition. Lebrie's jaw dropped open, his displeasure plain at the sight of the rifle.

"You're not letting your son take a firearm?"

"Don't see why not. He's a good shot." McClure passed the rifle up to Travis. The carbine felt heavy and reassuringly solid as Travis slung it over his shoulder. Standing at Deuce's side, out of earshot of Lebrie and Riane, McClure looked up at his son. "You be careful, okay?"

"I will." Travis felt a tear form in his eye, and he quickly blinked it away. Seated high on Deuce's back, twin suns burning down on them, Travis turned the old horse westward, and started off, the mule and the Lebries in tow, a lazy dust trail rising behind.

CHAPTER TEN

They rode for some time before swinging north towards the crippled starship, travelling far slower than Travis would have wished. Neither Adrian Lebrie nor Riane was comfortable on horseback, and the animals, sensing their riders' inexperience, took every advantage they could, baulking at shadows or stopping to crop at bunches of dry grass that stuck up through the hard-packed sand. The pair chatted endlessly, mostly to each other, leaving Travis isolated at the front of the string while he waited for them to catch up. Again and again, he found himself checking his watch, dismayed at how much of the day was already wasted.

A few klicks out of camp they topped a low rise and found a small group of cows and calves crowded around a muddy watering hole. The cattle looked up and noticed the riders, broke into a run and vanished into the scrub brush. Travis looked over his shoulder. Lebrie and Riane were pointing at the cattle and scowling. The exo-biologist took out his hand-corder and panned the area as he spoke into the tiny microphone. Travis felt a moment's guilt, knowing all too well what the off-worlders thought about cattle and the terraforming project in general. To the Lebries, anything that was done to change Aletha was "unnatural" and therefore wrong. In their opinion, cattle were just another symptom of the disease slowly strangling the once pristine planet. Travis sighed, unable to understand how anyone could prefer a lifeless ball of rock to a living, breathing world. He took a short drink from his canteen, then called back.

"We'd better hurry if you want to make Needle Point before dark."

Lebrie rode closer, grimacing as the paint gelding he rode broke into a languid trot. For a moment, Travis thought the man might bounce off the animal.

"Are you sure this is the way to my ship?" Lebrie squirmed in the saddle, unable to get comfortable. "I really need to gather my equipment."

"Yeah," Travis reassured him. "This is the way." He couldn't believe the pair were already disoriented. Riane rode closer. Though she sat with more confidence than her father, it was plain she was not comfortable aboard Twitch, either.

"Why is this Needle Point so important?" she asked.

"It's the nearest water. There's a little spring just south of it. Besides..." The knot in Travis's stomach tightened. "It's where I first picked up the predator's trail."

He spurred Deuce ahead, the mule straining on the lead rope as they moved out. The heat and glare worsened as the twin suns neared the zenith. Travis put on his goggles and ignored the sweat that pooled around the elastic band. Better to be uncomfortable than blind, he decided. More than once he had sun-flashed his eyes, and he had no intention of doing it again. Ahead, he caught the glint of sunlight off metal, the starship barely visible atop the steep-sided mesa.

"See." Travis pointed. "There's your ship. We're almost there."

Soon they broke out on top of the little bluff. The sandstorm had taken its toll on the starship, the hull scoured by the wind-driven grit. One of the sensor antennae hung tip down, torn from its socket, the cable beneath exposed. The disabled landing gear had settled further, leaving the ship tilted at a crazy angle against the skyline. At least, Travis thought, the fuel stench was gone, the tanks no doubt bled dry by now.

"I'll be a few minutes," Lebrie said as he crawled out of the saddle. The wiry man stumbled and nearly fell, his legs stiff from riding. Travis stepped easily to the ground and checked the mule. The hard climb had shifted the load, and he quickly readjusted the bulky pack while Lebrie and Riane disappeared inside the airlock. They returned a few minutes later, their arms piled so high with instruments and recording gear that they staggered as they walked.

"You can't bring all that," Travis said flatly.

"I most certainly can," Lebrie said. "I need this equipment for my audit."

Travis stared doubtfully at the mule. The animal was already loaded heavier than he would have liked. He turned back to Lebrie. "You'll have to leave some of it here. No way can I fit it all in."

"I thought you were experienced with pack animals," Lebrie said, his arrogance returned. "Perhaps I was wrong to think you could be our guide."

Travis gritted his teeth together. The insult stung, especially with Riane watching the entire exchange. Mad at himself for giving in, he started to loosen the heavy cinch straps on the mule to try and make room for the extra burden. Travis secured the bulky equipment as best he could, distributing it among the horses and the pack saddle, grumbling to himself the entire time. Lebrie stood and watched, fussing now and then over the more delicate items, until, at last, nearly an hour later, they were once again ready to move.

They started down the steep trail, moving slowly. At the base of the little mesa they stopped to let the animals rest, while the wind, rising once more in the afternoon's heat, made the juniper bushes and twisted stands of greasewood dance. Deuce shifted from foot to foot and tried to turn towards camp, but Travis swung him westward.

"Sorry, old horse." He reached up and patted Deuce's neck. "Home is the last place we'll be going today."

Dusk had settled by the time they reached Needle Point. The red stone pillar picked up the dying light until it seemed to glow, and Travis had the uneasy impression of an enormous, bloodied tooth sticking out of the boulder-studded ground. They let the horses drink from the sluggish spring, then found a sheltered spot to make camp. As quickly as he could, Travis set up a picket string and unsaddled the animals. He fed them and checked for cinch sores, then, satisfied they were all right, set off to gather firewood for the night. He dropped an armload of twisted juniper branches near their sleeping bags, then searched around for some rocks and built a ring, piling dry grass and twigs inside it and covering it with a few broken sticks.

"What are you doing?" Riane asked, curious.

"Building a fire." Travis pressed a lighter against the fodder and hit the trigger. Flames crackled in the dry material, and he hurriedly added more twigs. Smoke curled up, blue-white in the twilight. "Haven't you ever built a campfire, before?"

"No," Riane said.

"Fire," Lebrie said, his eyebrows furrowed as he glared at the little fire pit, "tends to scare away the animals we come to study."

"I know." Travis looked up at him, the memory of the predator riding close as darkness swept over them. Far in the distance, he thought he heard something scream. "That's exactly the reason I'm building it."

A thin sheen of dew covered the sleeping bags when Travis woke up. The fire was out, long cold, the horses sleeping on their feet, heads hung low. Riane lay in her bag, knees curled almost to her nose, while her father slept on the other side of the fire pit, snoring softly. Even the wind had stopped, the entire planet, it seemed, drowsing in the last moments before daybreak. Travis sat up, his sleeping bag bunched around his shoulders, and looked around. Something bothered him. Shivering in the chill pre-dawn air, he crawled out of the bag and pulled on his boots, then picked up his dad's carbine and walked as quietly as he could away from camp.

Cautiously, Travis made a circuit around the little clearing, climbing from boulder to boulder, crouching low. Strange shapes moved in the half-light, stunted trees and sharp-edged boulders taking on a monstrous aspect in his nervous imagination. A low sandstone outcrop lifted out of the ridge behind the spring, and Travis eased down in front of it to wait. He swung his head slowly from side to side, alert for movement in the brush.

Ten metres below, the horses suddenly woke. Deuce lifted his head and snorted while the mule and Twitch strained against the picket rope. Through the jumbled shadows, Travis saw a flash of yellow eyes just left of where Lebrie and Riane lay sleeping.

"Look out!" he shouted. Instinctively, he threw the carbine up to his shoulder and squeezed the trigger. Nothing happened. Shocked, he realized he had forgotten to chamber a round. Below, he saw the eyes again, glinting in the first blood-red streak of day. The creature, startled at the sound, spun around and vanished into the sagebrush, a bushy grey tail tucked between its crooked back legs.

"What is it?" Lebrie shouted, his voice thick with sleep and adrenaline. "What did you see?"

"Nothing," Travis said, laughing with relief. "Just a coyote."

"You nearly scared me to death," Lebrie said.

Riane crawled out of her bag and wrapped her arms around herself for warmth. Travis skip-walked down the steep hillside, rocks clattering under his boots. He made sure the rifle was unloaded, then set it down by his sleeping bag and turned to the cold fire and rekindled a small blaze. Still shaking from nerves, he huddled upwind of it, glad for the warmth. Riane slipped down beside him and held her hands out over the flames.

"Is this how you wake up every morning?" she asked, smiling.

"No, I'm usually much worse."

"How reassuring," Lebrie muttered behind them. He started away from the fire pit.

"Where are you going?" Travis asked, feeling chagrined.

"To the bathroom," Lebrie said sullenly. "Don't worry, I won't let any vicious coyotes attack." He disappeared into the scrub brush. Travis hung his head down and grinned.

"Sorry about that. Guess I overreacted."

"Don't worry." Riane tossed another branch on the fire. Sparks popped and shot into the air. "Father is always a little cranky when he wakes up."

"I heard that," Lebrie said as he returned. He sank down beside his daughter to sit cross-legged on the ground. He opened his mouth to speak, but before he could say anything, a shrill, high-pitched keen echoed down the canyon, far away, the sound of hell itself unleashed. Riane's eyes went wide, her voice low with sudden fear.

"What was that?"

"That," Travis said quietly, "is the thing we're looking for."

CHAPTER ELEVEN

For the first time in weeks, clouds bunched across the pale sky. Real clouds, dark-bellied monsters heavy with the promise of rain. The horses felt the change in weather. They were anxious, ready to run, starting at every shadow. Travis felt it too, an electric, primordial need simply to move. As noon approached, they climbed to the top of a wide, lava-strewn bench and let the horses rest a moment.

Behind them lay a broad canyon, the floor criss-crossed by dry stream beds. Mesas rose step-like from the floor, the rock banded in dazzling shades of red and purple sandstone. Patches of vegetation, more brown than green, were scattered about. It was perfect terrain for something to hide in, hundreds of square kilometres of sand and rock to search.

"What do you call this mountain?" Lebrie asked as he panned his hand-corder in a slow circle around them.

"I don't know," Travis said quietly. "I've never been here before. As far as I know, no one has."

The realization that they were travelling over uncharted ground struck harder than he had expected. Far to the east he could still make out Needle Point, a tiny black bump nearly lost among the dozens of other outcrops and broken cliffs. Somewhere beyond that lay Camp Seven, the pathetic collection of humanity beckoning to him like a siren to a lonely sailor. He had ridden off the marked trails dozens of times before as he chased stragglers or hunted for new waterholes. But this time, he knew, it was different.

This time, he wouldn't be returning to the safety of the camp at day's end.

Riane stepped beside him and opened her canteen. She took a sip and offered it to Travis, but he shook his head. As thirsty as he was, he had no idea how long it might be to the next watering spot.

"Better go easy on that," he told her. "Might be a while before we can fill up again."

"And just where are we going?" Lebrie put down his hand-corder and clipped it to his belt. "What makes you think this creature is down there?"

"You heard that scream this morning. It came out of this canyon. That makes it the place to start looking."

"Are you sure that was the creature we heard?"

Travis nodded. "Trust me."

He went back to Deuce and swung into the saddle. The old horse shifted impatiently while Lebrie and Riane struggled back aboard their own horses. At least, Travis thought, hiding his amusement, the pair were getting better at getting on and off. He coiled the mule's lead rope in his free hand, then turned Deuce once more towards the broad, desolate canyon.

"Tell me something," Riane asked as she pulled Twitch alongside. "Why aren't we riding down on the valley floor? If the creature is here, won't it be close to water, not exposed up here?" She swept her arm around the gently sloping lava field.

"Probably," Travis admitted. "But, do you see those clouds? Looks like we'll have thunderstorms this afternoon. We don't want to be caught in a flash flood."

"Is that really a concern?" Lebrie called from behind. "I think Riane is right. We need to find this thing's trail while we can. Especially if you expect storms. They would wash away any tracks it left before we can find them."

"I don't know..." Travis pushed his hat back and looked up at the sky. Strange mountains rose in the distance, jagged, sheer-sided peaks, their flanks cloaked by the rapidly growing thunderheads. A thin blue-white flicker of lightning shot between cloud and stone, so far away no thunder was heard. His gaze drifted down to the valley floor. It was rocky, criss-crossed by a disorienting network of ravines and washes. "This wouldn't be a good place to be trapped if a storm comes."

"No. But we'll have more than enough time to seek higher ground before it rains, yes?" Lebrie said, pushing his point. "I think we should concentrate on the valley, at least until a storm seems imminent."

"I..." Travis tried to find an argument against returning to the lower trails, but beyond a gut feeling he couldn't. Finally, he nodded. "All right. But, at the first hint of rain, we get higher. Okay?"

"Whatever you think is best," Lebrie said innocently. "You are the guide."

"Yeah," Travis muttered under his breath. "Sure seems like that so far." Angry at himself for giving in to the older, more forceful Lebrie, he spotted a narrow game trail that sloped down to the valley floor and started down it, the overloaded mule and the Lebries straggling behind.

Thick sand and gravel covered the bottom of the wash. The horse's hoofs crunched as they rode deeper into the twisted network of gullies and deep ravines. The afternoon seemed endless, a long, thirsty plod from one ridge to the next, the wind picking up as day wore on. The sagebrush and juniper thickened as they rounded a wide bend. The wind shifted for a moment, and the horses lifted their necks high and sniffed.

Travis let Deuce have his head and the horse picked up his pace as he felt the reins slacken, leading the way faster up the narrow trail. Ahead, less than a kilometre away rose a small stand of aspens, an oasis of green nestled against the garish, iron-stained rock. Travis grinned.

"What is it?" Riane asked. He pointed at the little glen.

"Water. Let's go get a drink."

A shallow creek led out of the trees, so narrow Travis could stand with one foot on either bank. It ran less than a hundred metres before it vanished once more into the porous soil, back to its subterranean passage. He stepped out of the saddle and let Deuce and the mule drink, long slurping swallows as they nosed the lazy ripples, then sank to his knees and cupped his hand in a deeper pool. The water was cool and sweet, and he drank his fill. Beside him, Riane sank down and took a hesitant sip.

"Perhaps," Lebrie said, staring doubtfully at the little stream, "we should filter that first before we drink?"

"Suit yourself." Travis took another drink, water streaming through his fingers. Riane caught his eye and laughed, then cupped her own hands and drank deeply. Their thirst slaked, they filled the canteens and water jugs while the horses grazed on the soft, green grass near the aspen copse. Leaves fluttered in the rising wind, and seemed to sparkle as they caught the double sunlight. Suddenly, the colours shifted, silver fading to brown as Alpha vanished behind a deep, black-throated cloud, leaving Beta to paint the land in darker shades of red.

"Looks like the storm is here." Travis stared up at the sky. "We'd better find shelter."

As if in answer, a low growl filled the air, the thunder so near it shook the ground. The horses stirred, flicking their ears, their tails swiping back and forth. Travis and the others mounted up and turned towards the higher ground behind the little spring. Deer trails wound between the tall greasewood, rising swiftly up the steepening banks. Travis nudged Deuce in the ribs, urging him faster as a second, louder peel of thunder cracked around them.

"Better hurry," he shouted back.

"Just a moment." Lebrie pulled the nervous paint to a stop, and crawled out of the saddle. The exo-biologist kneeled down and prodded the sandy ground. Travis rode back and looked down. A patch of disturbed soil stood out, flecks of bone and bristly clumps of grey-white hair littered across it.

"It's a deer kill," Travis said. "Lots of mule deer out here."

"Yes," Lebrie said. "But, look at the teeth marks on these bones." He held part of a shattered leg bone to the fading sunlight and turned the sharp-tipped flake in his hand. "Whatever ate this was large. Much larger than a coyote, I would suspect. Let's see if we can find some tracks."

"Over here," Riane shouted. Travis and Lebrie hurried towards her. She pointed at a vague scuff mark in the loose soil. As poor as the track was, the three-toed print was unmistakable. She glanced at Travis, her dark eyes filled with concern. "Is this what you saw before?"

"Yeah." Travis nodded. Suddenly, he could barely speak, his throat tight and dry. Nervously, his hand strayed to the rifle slung around his shoulder. "That's the print."

The sky unexpectedly brightened, the lightning strike so close the thunder crack followed immediately. The horses flinched at the noise and Travis rushed back and gathered up the reins before they could bolt. "Come on. It's about to get wet out here."

"But we'll lose the track," Lebrie protested.

"Then we'll find another one. Come on!"

A fat raindrop splatted against the sand and left a damp spot the size of Travis's thumb. More followed until, without warning, the storm broke in full. Already soaked, Travis fumbled to untie his slicker from the back of his saddle, and threw the long, stiff coat over his shoulders and shrugged his arms into it. Rain pelted him, a thousand tiny drumbeats against the waxed canvas. Lebrie and Riane struggled with their own rain-gear, their faces nearly hidden under yellow plastic hoods. Already, puddles formed on the ground, the soil so dry the water couldn't soak in. Tiny fingers of rainwater snaked between them and gathered together, dancing and jumping as the torrent fell faster. Squinting, the rain hard against his face, Travis spotted a shallow cave on the cliff face that framed the valley half a kilometre to the south.

"Get on your horses," he shouted. His stirrup was slick and his toe slipped, and he had to jump to get into the rain-wet saddle. He held Deuce tight, refusing to let the horse run until Riane and her father had mounted, then turned towards the high cliffs. Hunched forward, water pouring off his hat brim and down his neck, he picked a trail as best he could, holding Deuce back, afraid to let him run over the unfamiliar ground. As they climbed, the brush became thicker, the trail at times blocked by the prickly branches. Back and forth they rode, desperate now to find a path up to the narrow bench in front of the cliff face, the rain showing no sign of stopping.

The ground changed as they climbed, sand and gravel giving way once more to shelves of dark lava. A low rimrock blocked their passage, too steep to climb on horseback. Streams ran down the rock face and covered the ground in a single, wide puddle, deep enough that the horses kicked up spouts of water with each hurried step. Ahead, Travis spotted a shallow cleft leading upward. He kicked Deuce up and raced towards it. The ravine was narrow but short, and it looked as if they could reach the upper bench before the water grew deeper.

"Over here!"

He waved the Lebries towards him. They joined him in front of the narrow gap. Travis pointed up it. "You two go first. I'll bring up the rear."

"Why?" Riane asked, shouting to be heard over the storm.

Travis glanced back at the mule. "I'm not sure this is wide enough for him to fit through with the pack on." He jumped to the ground. Boots sloshing in the water, he handed Deuce's reins to Riane. "Just let the horses pick their way, all right? Once you get to the top, make a dash for that cave and wait for me."

"But..."

"Just go!" He swatted Twitch on the rump, and the little mare started up the narrow ravine. Travis watched them go, then grabbed the mule's lead rope and tried to drag him up the gap. The animal laid back his long ears and strained against the rope, refusing to follow. "Come on, you stupid idiot."

He tried again to force the stubborn animal into the ravine, but the mule baulked harder. Resigned, Travis pulled him around and started along the low rimrock, hoping he could find a better way to the top. He didn't have far to go before he spotted a second gully, wider than the first, but deeper, the rock walls sheer and unforgiving. Water gushed down it, ankle deep as it tumbled out of the narrow mouth and spilled into the thorny brush below. A deer trail cut along one side. Travis led the mule into the small canyon, keeping to the side trail. The overloaded pack brushed the wall as they climbed, the ground now so slick that both Travis and the mule fought to stay upright as the trail steepened. Nearly to the top, the ravine narrowed, barely wide enough to drag the frightened animal between the hard stone walls.

Another flash of lightning turned the black clouds overhead platinum white. Directly above them, Travis saw something move. He yelled in surprise as a long, narrow snout jabbed down and snapped, yellow eyes bright. Behind him, the mule pulled back, terrified as the predator struck again. Off-balance, Travis tumbled backwards. The rope burned through his hand as he landed hard on his back in the cold water pouring down the ravine. Thunder exploded around them as a second flash struck.

The predator had vanished.

Clutching the carbine, Travis hurried to where the mule stood. The animal flailed in panic, throwing its long head in mad lashes back and forth, unable to move. In its fear, it had become lodged between the opposite wall and a heavy boulder, trapped by the pack-saddle. Travis found the lead rope, wrapped it around his fist and pulled, ignoring the painful rope burn. It was no use. The mule couldn't break free. Unable to reach the cinch knot, Travis took out his knife and sawed through the thick rope that held the bulky packs fast. Free at last, the mule broke loose and charged up the ravine, the heavy packs breaking open as they clattered to the ground. Gear and supplies spilled out, the smaller pieces washed down with the run-off. Travis didn't care. All that mattered now was to get to the top of the rimrock and reach the cave before the predator came back. Carbine in hand, he scrabbled to the top of the cliff, and ran as fast as he could over the slippery rocks, feeling eyes on his back with every slogging step.

Behind him, shrill in the driving rain, he heard an all too familiar cry that faded like the thunder on the wind.

CHAPTER TWELVE

"**W**hat happened out there?"

Travis stumbled inside the shallow cave, out of breath and soaked to the skin. Riane hurried towards him and helped him sit down on a flat boulder. She asked him again. "What happened?"

"It came back."

"What came back?" Lebrie frowned from across the small opening, his face cloaked in shadow. The cave was little more than a narrow hole in the cliff face, stretching only five or six metres into the weathered stone. Rain ran off the ledge above, a shimmering curtain of icy water that splattered and danced as it struck the rocks below. It was deafening inside, the sound of wind and running water amplified by the stone around them. Outside, Deuce and the other horses huddled against the cliff, heads hung low, miserable in the downpour. The mule was with them, head high and nervous. Blood drizzled from a cut along his left shoulder, patches of hair missing where he had struggled to free himself from the rocky crevice.

Travis was bleeding too, blood seeping out of an angry gash on his right hand, another on his cheek just in front of his right ear. He had no idea how he had got the cuts. He began to shiver. Lebrie picked his way across the uneven floor and sat down beside Riane.

"You said it came back. What came back?"

"The predator." Travis stared at them as if they had lost their minds. "Didn't you hear it?"

"We couldn't hear anything," Riane said softly. "Are you sure you heard it again?"

"Heard it?" Travis laughed sourly. "It nearly tore my head off."

Lebrie and his daughter stared at each other, neither speaking. Beyond the wide entrance, the rain seemed to be slowing, the storm receding across the valley, a blood-red wall of precipitation in Beta's dull glow. Alpha poked out a moment from behind the dissipating clouds and silvered the valley below, shadows lengthening as sunset approached. Lebrie glanced at the horses, then turned back to Travis.

"Where are the supplies?"

"I had to cut the packs loose," Travis said. "The mule got wedged between rocks."

"You lost our gear?" Lebrie jumped to his feet. "Do you have any idea how much that equipment costs?" He stormed out of the little cave, ignoring the last of the rain.

"Don't go outside," Travis said, his fear rising once more. "That thing is still out there."

"I'll take my chances," Lebrie grumbled as he slipped down the rocky slope, following the mule's tracks. Riane looked at Travis and shrugged apologetically.

"I better go with him." She stood up. Travis grabbed her by the sleeve.

"You've got to believe me. I saw it again."

She nodded, but he could tell from the expression on her face that she doubted him. Without another word she left. Travis took a deep breath, forcing himself to calm down, then followed her out, his father's carbine clutched in his fist.

The suns were slipping below the horizon and a faint bluish glow rose out of the ravine he and the mule had struggled to climb only a few minutes before. Travis stepped to the lip of the narrow fissure and looked down. Lebrie was bent nearly double, a tiny blue thumblight in hand as he searched for the lost packs in the deep puddles left behind by the storm. Riane climbed down to meet him. She picked up a sack full of plastic-wrapped packages and held them out like a trophy.

"I've found some of the ration packs."

"Good," Travis shouted down to her. "Look, we can find the rest of the stuff tomorrow. It's getting too dark to search right now."

Grumbling in a language Travis didn't understand, the exo-biologist climbed up the ravine and stomped back to the cave, empty-handed. Travis helped Riane out of the ravine. Far below a new sound rose, a low, pulsing roar. Her eyes widened as she listened to the odd rumble.

"What is that?"

"Water," Travis said. "Right now, every gulch is flooded. We're lucky to be up here."

She didn't disagree. The valley seemed to flow, the water picking up the last light of day as darkness fell. Together, they hurried back to the little cave.

No fire. No cheery warmth to drive back the darkness. Travis hobbled the horses and pulled off the saddles. He found his first-aid kit in his saddlebag and tended to the cut on the mule's shoulder with an aerosol bandage. The animal tried to pull away as the cold spray hit the torn skin. Travis patted the nervous animal on his long, bristly neck.

"It's okay, fella. At least you believe me that that thing is still out there."

Satisfied he had done as much as he could, he dragged the saddles and blankets inside the cave and untied his bedroll. The sleeping bag was soaked through, water dripping out as he unrolled it and spread it over a boulder to dry. His toothbrush and personal kit fell out by his feet. He picked them up. Riane walked towards him, one of the ration packs in hand.

"Here." She held the package out to him. "It's a little bland, but it's better than nothing."

"Thanks." Travis ripped it open with his teeth and fished around inside, checking out the contents. Lebrie and Riane were already eating, using water from their canteens to mix the nearly tasteless food. Travis joined them, stirring the crunchy bits of dehydrated pasta in the wobbly plastic tray. He suddenly remembered the bottle of hot sauce Alice Prevoroski had given him, and dug it out of his kit. It helped, the hot peppers adding a touch of warmth to the cold, gloppy paste. He sprinkled a little more across the tray.

"What's that stuff?" Riane asked.

"Pepper sauce." Travis tossed the bottle to her. "Watch out though. It's kind of hot."

Riane added a small dash to her food and took a bite. She nodded, her eyebrows raising appreciatively as she chewed. Lebrie reached across her and took the bottle, then upended it across his own tray. Travis stared at him, shocked by how much he had used, but before he could warn him, Lebrie forked up a large bite and stuffed it in his mouth. His eyes shot open. Frantically, he searched for his canteen, slapping the rocks as he struggled to regain his breath.

"Like I said." Travis retrieved the bottle and quickly put it away. "It's got a little bite to it."

They finished supper in silence. The roar of the flash flood in the valley below subsided, the worst of the deluge over. Far away, a nighthawk trilled as it swooped out of the clear sky, chasing the insects that had risen now that the storm had passed. Travis sat, his slicker pulled tight around him, the carbine in his lap as he stared out the mouth of the cave. He forced his cold numbed fingers open, his grip around the stock so tight he could barely feel the heavy weapon. Riane, her own sodden sleeping bag around her shoulders, noticed him.

"You really did see something today, didn't you?"

"Yeah," Travis said softly. He was afraid to shut his eyes, afraid the thing might leap out of the darkness the moment he turned his back. "I saw something."

"This is what happens when you tamper with nature," Lebrie muttered from the back of the rock-strewn cave. "It's exactly the reason terraforming is a bad idea."

"Why?" As cold and frightened as he was, Travis felt his anger return. "Why is it a bad thing if a rock like Aletha becomes someplace people can live?"

"Because," Lebrie said, his tone condescending, "you cannot fully control the outcome. One mistake leads to another, and another, until at last you are buried in the avalanche it brings. What gives humankind the right to change the course of the universe?"

"I don't see it that way."

"And that," Lebrie said with a dismissive snort, "is because you don't know any better." The rustle of wet fabric fluttered around the cave as the disgruntled scientist curled up against a boulder and pretended to sleep. Travis sat stone still, too mad to speak, too ashamed at how badly the trip had turned out to argue. His first chance to really prove himself, and he had bungled it every step of the way. He felt like leaving, but couldn't face the thought of returning to camp a failure. Besides, even if he had really wanted to, he knew he couldn't leave the Lebries out here on their own. After a long while, Lebrie's snores drifted out from the rear of the cave. Something moved in the dark. Startled, Travis spun around as Riane eased down beside him.

"You have to forgive Father. Sometimes, he speaks without thinking." She paused. "But, he is right. Terraforming is wrong."

"Why?" Travis twisted around on the boulder. He could just make out her face in the darkness. "How can it be a bad thing to bring a planet to life? People need a place to live, and this gives it to them."

"Better that we stay home and fix the problems we have already created than to spread them from planet to planet." Riane's voice rose in pitch, her tone dogmatic as if she was reciting a grammar lesson to a stubborn child. "I suppose you think it is some kind of God-given right that humans colonize every corner of the galaxy."

"I don't know." Travis paused and thought about it. The idea that it was wrong to create a living, viable ecology on a barren planet had never occurred to him. For a moment, he began to doubt everything he had been taught, all of his and his parent's beliefs called into question. He tried to think of a counter-argument, but couldn't. "I don't know if there's a God-given right to anything," he said at last.

"Then how do you justify tampering with nature the way that you do?" Riane said, gloating a little.

"Wait a minute." Suddenly, Travis understood. "You and your Society don't believe in a God-given right to terraform, but then you turn around and talk about nature like its some kind of god, or goddess or whatever. You don't have any better leg to stand on than we do."

"That is circular logic," Riane said defensively.

"I don't care what you call it. It doesn't make you right. This outfit you work for doesn't have any more call to stop terraforming than the Company has doing it."

"That's what you believe?"

"Yep. That's what I believe."

"I should have expected that from someone with your limited education." She stood up and walked away, stumbling over the rocks as she joined her father near the back of the cave. Travis gritted his teeth and pulled his slicker tighter around himself, too mad to sleep, too conscientious to leave.

* * *

Sunlight woke him, Beta's glow bright in the rain-scrubbed air. Travis sat up, his body aching and cold, his clothes still damp from the storm. The boulder he had slumped against had proven a poor bed, and he rubbed his neck, then turned around to check on Riane and her father, but their sleeping bags were empty.

"Oh, wonderful." Travis stooped down and retrieved the carbine from his bedroll, then hurried outside. Deuce and the other animals whickered at him as he passed, begging to be set loose. "Hang on, fella," Travis said. "I'll be back in a minute...I hope."

Muddy footprints led into the ravine, long skids where the pair of off-worlders had slid in the fresh mud. Travis picked his way carefully down the deer trail he and the mule had climbed the night before. At the base of the low ridge mud and fine gravel had piled up, washed down by the heavy rain. Everywhere in it he saw fresh tracks, deer and coyotes, and the pair of humans. He breathed a sigh of relief when he didn't find any trace of the predator among them. Further down the valley, lost in the tangle of shoulder-high sagebrush and juniper, he heard Riane shouting, too far away to make out what she said.

"Now what?" Travis slogged through the ankle-deep mud and followed the boot tracks into the scrub. Before he had gone twenty metres, he lost the trail, the ground too rocky to hold a print. Branches slapped his face as he charged through the brush, tiny needles against his skin. Water dripped off the still-wet limbs and splashed over him until he was as drenched as he had been the night before. Lebrie's voice sounded somewhere to his left, muffled by the brush around him. Travis pushed another branch out of his way, but it snapped back and knocked his hat off. Bending down to pick it up, his foot slipped in the mud, and Travis thudded down, elbow first, on the stony ground at the base of a juniper tree. Pain shot up his arm.

"Ouch!"

Covered in mud, Travis picked himself up and struggled ahead, desperate to break out of the thicket. Again, he heard voices, Riane shouting frantically somewhere ahead of him. Ignoring the thorny branches, he charged out into the sunlight. Too late, he saw Lebrie in front of him and slammed headlong against the annoyed scientist. A small, black-bodied instrument mounted on a tall tripod tipped over and clattered to the ground.

"Would you watch what you're doing?" Lebrie scowled and bent down to pick up the fallen device. He dabbed a speck of mud off the lens, then tried to level it once more on the uneven ground. The ungainly instrument refused to stand straight, one leg of the tripod bent to the point of breaking. "Wonderful. Now this is broken, too. You certainly have a knack for destruction, don't you?"

"Sorry. I heard Riane shouting and thought she was in trouble."

"She was shouting," Lebrie said, his face bright red in Beta's glow, "because the radios we normally use when mapping out an area are full of water. They are full of water because someone cut the packs off the pack animal last night and let them fall into a flash flood."

"I said I was sorry."

Riane jogged towards them, a thin pole, striped red and white, in her left hand. She planted the survey marker at her feet and stood looking first at her father, then at Travis. "Is there a problem?"

"No. No problem," Lebrie said, the sarcasm thick. "The laser-transom is ruined too. Why should that be a problem?" He knocked the tripod over with an angry shove, then stormed away. Travis bent down and picked up the compact device and stood holding it awkwardly. Finally, he turned towards Riane.

"Look, I'm sorry all of your gear got wet. But what did you want me to do? Leave the mule trapped in the ravine? I had to cut the packs loose."

Riane shrugged. "Father thinks you panicked when you thought the predator could be nearby."

"Is that what you think, too?"

"I never said that."

"You didn't have to." Travis ground his teeth together, so angry he had trouble putting one word in front of the other. "I didn't panic. The danger was real. That thing was here last night – I saw it."

"Fine." Riane turned her back on him and walked briskly along the base of the rust-brown rimrock.

Travis followed, hampered by the rifle in one hand, the tripod in the other. She spoke without slowing. "You could have at least tried to save the gear, couldn't you?"

She stopped in front of a small pile of electronic survey equipment, took the transom and tripod from Travis's hand and dropped them with the rest of the ruined gear. Nearby, another pile waited, ration packs and spare clothing, much of it torn to shreds by pack rats and other rodents that had discovered the unexpected bounty in the night. Travis stared at the ground.

"I did the best I could." He glanced up at the girl. Though he was as tall as her, she made him feel small, like a scolded child. "So, what do you want me to do now?"

Riane stared at him, her dark eyes unforgiving. After a long, uncomfortable moment, she looked away and watched her father poking around in the fresh mud, still hunting for his lost equipment. "I think," she said quietly, "it would be best if you took us back to camp."

CHAPTER THIRTEEN

Daylight was nearly spent by the time they straggled back into Camp Seven, the horses tired, their legs caked with dried mud. Travis still rode in the lead, the mule still trailed behind, no different from when they had left. Beyond that, everything had changed.

"Hey, Trav." Alice Prevoroski poked her head out of the meteorology trailer as the little party rode past. "Didn't expect to see you guys back so soon." Her gaze drifted to the mule and the empty pack saddle.

"We ran into a little trouble," Travis said, his voice flat. He would rather have admitted to murder than confess how badly he had messed up. "My dad around?"

"No." Alice shook her head, spikes of black hair waving like grass on a windy day. "I think they headed south this morning, looking for pasture."

Behind him, still mounted on the tired paint gelding, Lebrie snorted. Travis heard him mutter something about terraformers, but ignored the comment. He was past caring. It had been a long, uncomfortable return, neither Lebrie nor Riane willing to forgive him for the trip's numerous failures. They had stopped at the crippled starship long enough for the exo-biologist to place the few samples he had gathered in storage, while Riane sent a flash message to the Free Planet Society. Travis could only imagine what the message said.

"Thanks, Alice." Travis turned Deuce towards the corral. The old horse found a new lease of life now that he was home and the feed bunk lay near, and he trotted happily towards the metal pen. Travis unsaddled the animals and brushed them down, working the clumps of hard red mud off their bellies and legs. Riane waited a moment, seeming torn between helping him and leaving, but finally followed her father towards Tempke's office. Travis bit down hard on his lower lip, as if the pain might drive the bitter taste from his mouth. More dejected than ever, he swung the gate open and turned the horses and the mule loose inside the corral. They hurried to the feeder, squabbling and nipping at each other to get the best spot for themselves. Travis sighed, locked the gate, and started back towards his family's tent on the outskirts of camp, his sleeping bag and his dad's carbine slung over his shoulder.

Far to the south a thin plume of dust rose, no doubt his father and the others returning. "Well," Travis said under his breath, "at least I won't have long to wait to hear how bad I screwed up."

Travis waited outside the tent, his hands stuffed in his pockets while he listened to the herders laughing and joking with each other. It was a familiar sound, the end of day ritual he had taken for granted so long he barely noticed it any more. Life in the camps might be harsh at times, but it wasn't without its reward. The smell of hot food. The taste of cold water or sweet lemonade after a long, thirsty drive. The welcoming softness of his sleeping bag. At the moment, Travis thought, none of it seemed to matter a tinker's damn. He glanced up and saw a lanky, dust-covered figure walking towards him, his steps slow and measured.

"Heard you had some trouble out there," McClure said.

"Yeah." Travis kicked a rock near his toe and sent it arcing into the trampled desert beyond the ring of tents. "News travels fast."

McClure grinned. "Always does." His smile faded, his wind-chapped lips set in a grim, straight line. "You guys got lucky. How close did that thing get to you?"

"Close enough." Travis shut his eyes, the memory of the predator striking down from the lip of the little ravine vivid. "I never had time to get a shot off at it."

"Just as well. No saying what that thing would have done if it was wounded. Especially with the mule trapped like he was. Yeah, I heard all about it. Lebrie was still ranting about the ruined gear when I checked in at Tempke's trailer." McClure stood a moment, then, to Travis's surprise, reached out and clapped him on the shoulder. "Don't let it get you down. You did the right thing. Sometimes, Trav, the best a man can do isn't enough. But as long as you tried, well, that's what counts."

McClure gave his son's shoulder a squeeze, then ducked under the flap into the blue dome. Near the door, a camp stove sat on the ground on four stubby legs, a pot on the burner, the lid dancing. Travis risked burning his fingers and lifted the lid, the wonderful aroma of thick brown stew leaping out in the steam. Feeling better than he had all day, he dropped the lid back over the pot, then ducked inside the tent, glad to be home.

He wanted to sleep on for hours, the air mattress beneath him soft and inviting, the warm blankets a gentle addiction. Travis prised his bleary eyes open. Sunlight washed over the tent. He bolted upright. It had been ages since he had slept through sunrise. He dressed quickly, the clean trousers and tunic stiff from being laundered, his boots still caked with mud and trail dust. He rushed outside and nearly tripped over his mother.

"And good morning to you too." Angie McClure smiled at him, then turned back to the little camp stove. Travis caught a whiff of hot iron as she turned up the burner. She wore a quilted vest against the morning chill, the pockets stuffed full of tools, her hair tied back with a thin leather strap that looked as if it had once been part of somebody's saddle. She reached inside a small plastic hard-box, pulled out a plate, then heaped a mound of scrambled eggs on it. "Here, have some breakfast."

"I don't have time, Mom." Travis squinted at the eastern horizon. Beta was fully up, a blood-red sphere dancing in the restless atmosphere. "Dad's going to skin me for being late."

"He's the one who said to let you sleep." Angie held out the plate until, at last, he took it from her hands. "Don't worry. Nobody's riding this morning. The storms filled the waterholes. Looks like we'll keep the herd here at least another week." She pointed at the ground. "Would you sit down or do I have to sit on you?"

"Fine." Travis plopped to the hard ground, dug a fork out of the same hard-box, and took a bite. The eggs were hot enough to burn his tongue, bits of crunchy bacon mixed in. He frowned. Something was missing, and he knew just what it was. He set the plate on the case, hurried inside the tent, then came back a few moments later with a small glass container. His mother laughed as he dosed the eggs with the potent green hot sauce.

"I see Alice Prevoroski has corrupted you, too." She smiled broadly. "I swear that woman would survive on nothing but coffee and tabasco if she had her choice."

Travis laughed, then dug back into the pile of eggs. He was hungrier than he realized, and quickly finished them. His mother tilted the frying pan over his plate and scraped the last of the steaming, dehydrated eggs onto it. He chewed more slowly, enjoying the unaccustomed luxury of a leisurely breakfast. Most days, it was eat fast then rush to the corral before somebody yelled at him.

His mom set the pan aside, then twisted around to close the gas valve on the stove. A multi-tool fell out of her vest pocket and she swept the sturdy pair of pliers back up with her free hand. Travis set his empty plate with the other dishes.

"What have they got you doing today?" he asked.

"I have to fix the motor on the comm-dish. Then, Alice asked me if I'd re-calibrate the ground antenna. Why?"

"Just curious." Travis swatted a fly away from his nose. "Mom, does it ever bother you, having to fix all the stuff around camp?"

"Why should it?" Angie McClure tilted her head,

startled by the question. "Things break, and somebody has to fix them. As long as the Company is willing to pay for it, it might as well be me." She dropped her voice and winked. "And just between you and me, your dad's one of the best stockmen in known space, but he's a lousy mechanic."

Travis laughed, then turned serious once more. "That's not what I meant. You have a college degree, right?"

"Two of them. Why?"

"I don't know. I just wondered if you ever think about doing something different?"

"Sometimes." A sad, dreamy expression softened the little lines around her eyes. "I'd be lying if I said I didn't miss home. But, if you mean would I rather be cooped up in some office making tons of money instead of living free, then the answer is 'not on your life'." She turned back to Travis and grinned. "That what you wanted to know?"

"Yeah. Thanks." He rose, his legs numb from sitting cross-legged too long. "I'd better find Dad and see what the plan is."

He didn't have far to walk. He met his father halfway through Bachelors' Row, heading towards the tent, his mouth set in a tight, hard line. From the look on his face, Travis knew trouble was brewing somewhere. "Your mom still at the tent?"

"Yeah, I'm here," Angie answered before Travis could. She stepped out to meet them. "Problems?"

"No." The way McClure said it made it sound like a yes. "That Lebrie wants to know if you're willing to go out to his starship for some extra work."

"He does?" Angie McClure leaned back and stared towards Tempke's office. Her eyes narrowed as she watched Tempke and the Lebries climb down the rickety steps. "Patching radios is one thing. Repairing a broken landing gear is another. Especially without cranes and a plasma cutter."

Jim McClure shook his head, the shadow from the brim of his hat sweeping back and forth over his weather-beaten features. "It's lab work. He said he needs a technician. He and Tempke have been arguing all morning, and they finally decided someone from our side should be there just to make certain he isn't cooking the results to get the answer he wants." He paused, obviously uncomfortable with the subject. "It would be double pay while you were there. I told Tempke I'd ask if you were interested."

Angie McClure took a deep breath, then nodded. "I suppose I could do it. Tell them I'll gather up my things and meet them at the corral in fifteen minutes."

"I'll go get your horse saddled, Mom." Travis started towards the corral. Behind him, his father cleared his throat.

"Don't bother, Trav. Bart Caddy is already down there."

A hard, cold lump landed in Travis's stomach. Something in his father's tone chilled him. Through the uneven gaps between tents, he could just make out the tack trailer. Two figures stood outside it. One was Caddy, leaning back against the metal wall, his hat tilted back at an easy, inviting angle. Riane was next to him. Travis gritted his teeth as he watched her slap Bart playfully on the arm, no doubt laughing at one of his idiotic jokes. She turned and saw him watching, then quickly looked away, the dismissal clear. McClure stepped up beside Travis.

"Sorry, Trav. Tempke asked Bart if he'd take over as guide when they go back out."

CHAPTER FOURTEEN

Empty. Hollow. Used up.

No one should feel like this at sixteen. But he did. Travis wandered away from camp, not caring where he went, one direction the same as another. Beta led Alpha across the pale sky, the mud from the storm long since dried, the noonday heat relentless. A lizard darted out from beneath a spindly clump of sagebrush and vanished under a tuft of crumbling lava. Travis barely noticed. Far ahead, something glinted on the sagebrush-covered bench. He squinted as he stared at it, the twin sunlight so bright it hurt his eyes. His dust-streaked goggles hung around his neck, and he knew he should put them on.

But right now, he didn't care about that either.

Sweat ran down his face by the time he reached the shiny object. Travis tossed a rock at the long discarded drop-pod. It hit the scorched hull and bounced off with a dull clang. Thousands of the pods littered Aletha Three, remnants of the early days of the project when seeds and machinery had fallen to ground like overripe apples from an untended tree. Travis laughed at the notion. He could barely remember the gnarled crab-apple tree behind the house back home on the ranch, how he would hide behind the yard fence with a handful of the hard, sour fruit to throw at his dad when he wandered in for supper.

He wondered if the tree was still there.

"What are we doing out here?"

His voice sounded small against the wind. Absently, he ran his hand over the scarred pod, the metal hot beneath his palm. A laser-etched label lay near the seam where the pod had broken open to release its cargo. A star and planet design, the company logo, filled the bottom of the label, the letters bright decades after it had burned through the thin atmosphere. Travis poked his head inside the pod. It was dark, the air rank with pack-rat urine and mould. The floor was covered with old sticks and dried grass, bits of bone and other litter that generations of rodents had carted inside and left. Travis sank to the ground on the shadowed side of the abandoned pod. Along the edge of the seam he saw another label, fainter than the first. He brushed the dust away until he could read "Assembled in Earth orbit".

"Looks like we're both a long ways from home." Travis sighed, tilted his hat over his face, and leaned back against the pod. Even in the shade, the metal was warm. Flies buzzed around him, a lazy drone. His eyelids fluttered, then closed.

A shrill beep startled him awake. He grabbed the radio off his belt and thumbed it on.

"Travis here, go ahead."

"Trav?" Even though he was only a few klicks away from camp, Alice Prevoroski's voice was broken by static. "Your mom called and wondered if you could come on in? Sounds like they need you out at the starship."

"Did she say why?"

"Not really." A crackle of static hissed out the speaker. "So, should I tell them you're on the way?"

Travis stood up and stretched, not anxious in the least to go back, especially where the Lebries were concerned. He put the little transceiver beside his mouth.

"Yeah. Tell them I'll be there in a while."

A bright green awning stretched out from the starship's airlock, the nylon billowing with every gust. A long tube tent had been erected beside it. Travis saw figures inside shadowed against the translucent walls. Reluctantly, he eased out of the saddle and led Deuce closer on foot. The old horse shied as the tent jumped and danced in the wind. Two other horses, his mom's bay mare and the paint gelding Lebrie used, stood in the lee of the starship, tails swinging a constant fight against the stubborn flies. He led Deuce beside them, and loosened the cinch, all the while looking around for more horses but seeing none. He wasn't sure if he was glad Bart and Riane were gone, or disappointed. Deuce's nostrils widened, his neck stiff as the odd scents around the crippled starship rolled over him.

"Easy, fella." Travis patted the horse's neck, then bent down and put the hobbles around his front legs. "I'll be back in a while."

It was hot inside the tent, the long passage filled with racks of computers and complicated equipment, a folding table at the far end. His mom turned and waved him closer. Lebrie stood beside her. He looked over his shoulder and muttered a half-hearted greeting. Travis walked down the narrow aisle, careful not to disturb anything.

"I have a few questions about this tooth you found." Lebrie held the gleaming sickle between his thumb and forefinger. "Are you certain it came from the creature that attacked you?"

"Yeah. I'm positive."

"It couldn't have been lying nearby, and you

mistakenly thought it belonged to the animal?"

"No." Travis glanced at his mother. She seemed doubtful, her green eyes full of concern. He turned back to the exo-biologist. "I prised it out of the bull that thing killed. It wasn't lying in the dirt. And I sure as hell didn't plant it there, if that's what you're thinking. I'm not a liar."

"Honey," Angie McClure said softly. "No one is accusing you. But this is important."

"You can ask Dad." Travis pointed at the tooth in Lebrie's hand. "Trust me, okay? That came from the predator."

Lebrie nodded, as if he had expected the answer. Carefully, he placed the tooth inside one of the scanners on the table. A fist-sized hologram flashed above it, the edges rippling around the edge of the field. A rainbow pattern swept over the image as a block of text appeared on a nearby screen. Travis studied the read-out, but the text was meaningless jargon to him.

"Do you know what DNA is?" Lebrie asked.

"Of course he does." Angie McClure glared at the thin scientist. "Just because he lives out here doesn't mean he's uneducated."

"No, of course not." If Lebrie was irritated by her outburst, he didn't let it show. Instead, he continued, pointing at the hologram as he spoke. The picture of the tooth vanished, replaced by a long, intricate chain of molecules wrapped around each other in an elegant spiral. "Well then, you will know that the DNA/RNA helix is unique to Earth. Life forms on other worlds have a similar mechanism to ensure reproduction, but this one..." Again, he pointed at the slowly turning hologram. "This could only have come from a terrestrial species. It's avian."

"Avian?" Travis searched his memory. "It's from a bird?"

"Originally, yes." Lebrie leaned towards him, his dark eyes piercing. "But this sample is unlike anything I've encountered before. And if it's what I think it is, someone needs to be called to account for it."

"I don't get it?"

"What he's trying to say," his mom said quietly, "is that thing you found is a product of genetic engineering. Someone created this animal, then turned it loose on Aletha."

"Why would anyone do that?" Travis asked, shocked at the idea.

"That," Lebrie said, "is exactly what I want to find out."

The mess tent was packed to capacity, every hand and technician in camp seated at the long tables or loitering near the walls, a constant rumble of voices and feet scuffling on the dirt floor. Scorched coffee and boot grease mingled with the fading scent of whatever lunch had been five or six hours ago. Travis wrinkled his nose at the wash of smell. Something else rode with it, the reek of nervous sweat and tension. This was a crowd ready to explode. Electric lights flickered on as sunset approached, the lamps casting crazy shadows against the gently fluttering walls.

A small figure with spiked hair appeared in the doorway. Alice Prevoroski hurried inside, saw Travis, and pushed through the crowd towards him.

"Did I miss anything?" she asked.

"Not yet," Travis said. "They're just getting set up."

Tempke sat at a table near the far end of the tent, Riane and Bart Caddy seated beside him. Adrian Lebrie moved behind the table, fussing with the large projection screen hung from the kitchen divider. Travis glared at them, and wished he could send waves of pain shooting at them like the characters in the worn-out vids he watched when he was a boy, but if they saw him at all, they didn't show it. His mom, Travis noticed with relief, sat at another table as far from the off-worlders as she could manage. Finished setting up the equipment, Lebrie leaned across the table and said something to Tempke, who nodded, then rose to his feet.

"Could I have your attention?" The crowd ignored Tempke, too many conversations happening at once. He tried again. "Everyone, could I have your attention, please?"

The door flap swept open. Jim McClure ducked through and marched down the centre aisle. "Listen up." His voice cut through the chaos easy as a sharp knife through rotten leather. "This is important. Let's hear what the man has to say."

Tempke glanced at McClure and nodded a brief thanks, then turned back to the crowd. "He's right. I want all of you to listen carefully to what Dr. Lebrie has to say."

Travis snorted at the way Tempke emphasized the word "doctor". He folded his arms over his chest and waited as the projector screen flashed on, the hologram blurred as Lebrie fiddled with the image. It resolved into a 3D view of the deer kill they had found near the little creek before the thunderstorm. A bland smile crossed Lebrie's narrow face, as if he had no idea the room was stacked against him.

"I want to thank all of you for coming this evening. I have some rather important findings to discuss that may affect you and your Company." Lebrie pointed at the hologram. "This is a picture of a deer kill I discovered in a canyon approximately thirty kilometres west of here."

"*I* discovered?" Travis muttered under his breath, his teeth grinding as the scientist claimed complete credit for what he had helped locate.

Alice Prevoroski poked him in the ribs with her elbow and warned him to silence. "Shhh. I want to hear this."

Sullenly, Travis waited for the scientist to continue. Lebrie poked his finger inside the display. The image expanded inside the field as the focus narrowed onto a single, three-toed footprint near the edge of the bloodstained sand.

"This track was left by the animal that made the kill."

"What is that?" someone near the front of the room asked. "Some kind of bird?"

"In a manner of speaking." Lebrie traced the outline of the print. "It has much in common with most terrestrial birds of prey, and well it should." The image shifted, this time to a pair of DNA strands slowly revolving in time with each other. "The genetic components are similar. In fact, most of this predator's genome is derived from various birds."

"What do you mean, derived?" Jim McClure asked.

"I mean, this creature, which apparently is loose in the area, is not a natural species." A hush fell over the crowd, the silence thick as the sand on the floor. "Someone went to a great deal of trouble to retro-engineer this creature."

"Dr. Lebrie," Angie McClure said, rising from her seat. "Why don't you explain what you're getting at in a little more detail?"

"Certainly." The exo-biologist pointed at the twisting helix on the left. "This strand of DNA is from a modern raptor, a North American bald eagle to be precise. The other strand comes from a saliva sample I recovered from one of the deer bones. They are very similar. You see, every cell, whether from this animal or from you or I, carries within it not only the information it needs to divide and multiply, it also carries a record of the entire genetic history of its evolution. Given enough time and experimentation – not to mention some extremely expensive laboratory equipment – you could activate enough dormant genes to recreate extinct versions of every species in the animal's background."

"And what kind of animal are we talking about?" asked the same man who had spoken earlier. Lebrie nodded thoughtfully, then once more changed the image. The tooth Travis had found flashed on, a dozen times its actual size.

"This tooth," Lebrie said, at last acknowledging Travis, "was discovered by one of your herders at another kill site, this time a bull cow." Snickers ran around the room at Lebrie's misuse of language, but he continued nonplussed. "It is nearly identical to one recovered in Mongolia several hundred years ago. However, the animal that particular tooth belonged to has been extinct for 60 million years."

Again, the hologram shifted. Travis stared at the new image. His chest tightened, and suddenly he found it hard to breathe. A long-necked creature with a narrow, vicious snout stood balanced on powerful hind legs, its stiff tail raised above the ground for balance. It wasn't the predator he had met, but it was close. Very close.

"This, ladies and gentleman," Lebrie said, obviously enjoying the moment, "is a computer rendering of a dinosaur called Dionychus, one of the most talented killers ever to have walked anywhere in the universe. And, I believe, something similar has been unleashed here on Aletha Three."

No one spoke. Travis waited, the hair on his neck bristling as if the hologram might come to life and spring at him. His arms ached, and he had to force his hands open, his fists clenched so tightly he had lost feeling in his fingers. Finally, his father stood up.

"So, how do we kill this thing?"

"We don't." Lebrie seemed startled by the idea of destroying the creature. "In fact, as of now, none of you are to do anything. I thought you all understood the legal implications here?" He fished a neatly folded piece of paper out of his pocket and gravely handed it to Tempke. "As of now, this project is under an injunction. Until further notice, no further terraforming work is allowed."

CHAPTER FIFTEEN

"They can't do that. Can they?" Lefty Eicks, a bearded man with an artificial eye asked as he stormed out of the mess tent, chasing Jim McClure. He bumped Travis in his haste, but didn't bother to apologize. He, like everyone around him, was angry and ready to lash out. "They don't have the authority to shut the project down, right?"

"That's what I'm trying to find out." McClure stared across the camp, his jaw clenched so tightly the muscles along his neck seemed ready to snap. Tempke and the Lebries had left the mess through the back door and, along with Bart Caddy, were hurrying towards the office. Travis followed his father, stepping fast just to keep up. Tempke tried to speed the scientist and his daughter along, but the McClures cut them off in front of the rickety metal steps. "We need to talk."

"Jim..." Tempke backed up a few steps. "This isn't the time to be rash."

"Rash? You don't know rash!" Lefty tried to squeeze past Tempke, his right fist tight against his ribs, ready to throw. McClure pulled him back.

"Lefty, back off!" He placed himself between Tempke and the angry herders behind him. "Let me do the talking, all right?"

"Just answer one question," Lefty said. His good eye narrowed. "Can they shut us down?"

"Yes," Tempke said, resigned. A tic beneath his left eye fluttered like a moth in a spiderweb. The man was obviously nervous. "He has a blanket order from the Federal Court on Betelgeuse Station to temporarily halt operations if any anomalies are found."

"Fine. So he has a temporary injunction." McClure stepped closer. Travis thought Tempke might tip over backwards in his haste to back up. "What do we have to do to appeal this thing and get back to work?"

"I...I'm not sure that we can. I need to contact Base Camp."

"Fine. Contact them. But tell them not to drag their feet, okay? We can't sit around for ever. Those cows are going to run out of feed and water, and every day we delay, the harder it's going to be to find new pasture."

"I'll do what I can. But, you have to remember, with that thing out there, it might be in your best interest that no one goes out until we have all the facts. It could be dangerous."

"I'm willing to risk it," McClure said.

"Well, I'm not." Tempke slipped around behind the others, using Riane and Lebrie as cover, and managed to step up into his trailer. He relaxed a little as he opened the door, his usual confidence returned. "Everyone, just stay calm while I try to work this out." He ducked inside and shut the door.

More herders had gathered behind McClure, joined by some of the technicians and survey crews. The little mob formed a ring around Lebrie and Riane. The exo-biologist, instead of being worried, drew himself taller, his face bright red in the fading sunlight. "What are you people so angry about, anyway? All I'm trying to do is make certain Advanced Terraforming complies with regulations."

"You worthless little piece of crud!" Lefty threw a clumsy punch at Lebrie, but Jim McClure knocked his hand down. Instinctively, Travis moved closer to his father to cover his back in case someone threw a punch at him. McClure held up his hand to quiet the people behind him, then spun towards Lebrie.

"Mister, I think it would be smart if you got the hell out of here before nightfall."

"Now, Jim..." Bart Caddy eased out from behind Riane, a crooked grin on his face. "I don't think you need to go ordering these people around—" He started to say something else, but McClure poked him in the chest with his index finger hard enough to rock him on his heels.

"Shut up, Bart. Go get their horses saddled and get them the hell back to their ship before real trouble starts."

"But—"

"I said, go."

Bart stared around him, his mouth hanging slack. He blushed, embarrassed and more than a little angry, but prudently turned and walked away towards the corral. As much as Travis disliked Bart Caddy, he couldn't help feeling a certain empathy for him. A day ago he would have been the one sent to saddle the horses for the off-worlders. Beside him, his father turned to face the growing crowd.

"Listen up, everybody," McClure said. "This isn't the time to go off half-cocked. The Company isn't going to let some piddly little injunction close us down. Go eat supper and let things cool off, all right?"

The crowd muttered, but broke up, men and women moving off in clumps, some towards the mess, some off to their own tents. Travis breathed a sigh of relief as the danger passed.

"Keep an eye on things, Trav." His dad nodded at him, then followed Lebrie inside Tempke's office. The trailer rocked slightly as the two men stepped inside and the door banged shut behind them. Only Travis and Riane remained outside the trailer. In the distance, a nighthawk trilled, welcoming the darkness. He stared at Riane and shook his head.

"I hope you're satisfied."

"What's that supposed to mean?" Riane's eyes narrowed, bright with anger. "We have every right to shut this project down. Advanced Terraforming has been careless. It's you who are breaking the law, not us."

"Nice." Travis laughed sourly. "So you shut us down on some stupid technicality. Did you ever wonder what that means to those cattle out there?"

"Cattle?" Riane drew back, a confused expression on her face. "I don't understand."

"I know you don't. If you did, you might not have been so quick to wave that injunction around. The feed around here is gone. And so is the water, or at least it will be in a couple of days. If we can't move the herd to the next pasture, guess what? They'll die."

"But, they're wild, yes? They were bred to survive." A note of uncertainty crept into her voice. "Won't they find water on their own?"

"Maybe. Maybe not. A few of them will probably get through, but the rest..." Travis let his voice trail off. "Cattle will stand at a dried-up waterhole until they drop dead, because they don't know where to go. They've never been to the next range. If we can't take them to it, chances are every one of them will die of thirst when the last of the water goes away."

"Oh." Riane stared down at her feet, her anger gone. Around them, the camp lights switched on, Alpha's fading glow replaced by the green-gold fluorescence. "I didn't know."

"Well," Travis said softly, "now you do." He turned and walked away, leaving her to sort things out on her own.

A pounding roar woke Travis before dawn. Wearing only his trousers, he rushed outside in time to see the jump-bug climb away from camp. A long streak of flame swept out behind it as the single-seat flyer arced steeply to the east. Cold wind blew across Travis's back and, chilled, he ducked back through the open tent flap and quickly sealed it behind him. A lantern flared to life.

"That Tempke taking off?" Jim McClure's voice was thick with sleep. Travis nodded. It looked as if his father hadn't slept more than a few minutes through the long night, the deep shadows beneath his eyes stark in the harsh light.

"Dad? He will get this straightened out, won't he?"

"I hope so." McClure ran his hand through his hair and left it sticking up at wild angles. "Who knows how long it's going to take, though? The Company never moves fast where legal issues are concerned."

"So, what about the cattle?" Travis shrugged into his shirt, then moved back into the main room. He stooped

143

low to keep from brushing the fabric ceiling, then sank down near his parents' air mattress. "We can't just leave them out there to die."

"I don't know what else we can do." McClure rubbed his eyes, his shoulders slumped in defeat. "Until this injunction gets lifted, nothing's going to move."

Angie McClure crawled out from the tangled sleeping bag, and smiled bravely. "Things are going to work out." She kissed her husband on the cheek. "I'll put some coffee on." She stepped outside. Jim McClure hardly seemed to notice.

The smell of propane drifted in through the tent door as the camp stove popped on, quickly replaced by the wondrous aroma of fresh coffee on the boil. Travis sat on the tent floor and chewed on his lower lip. Sleep had been a long time coming for him too, and it left him sluggish and sick to his stomach. Over and over the day's events had spun past him, refusing to let him rest. But, slowly, a plan had formed. He took a deep breath, then cleared his throat.

"I've been doing some thinking. That injunction is issued against the Company, right?"

"Right." Jim McClure nodded.

Travis continued. "So, that means they can't pay us to move the cattle to the next pasture?"

McClure frowned, his heavy eyebrows bunched above the bridge of his nose. "That's what it means. Why?"

"Well..." Travis hesitated a moment. "It doesn't say

anything about us moving the cattle on our own."

A smile lifted the corner of McClure's mouth and became a grin. He laughed out loud. Travis wasn't sure if his dad was pleased or if he thought he had lost his mind. His mom stepped back inside, the coffee pot steaming in her hand. She stared back and forth between them.

"Did I miss something?"

"Not much," McClure said, still laughing. "That son of yours just figured a way around the injunction. Now I remember why we keep him around." He ruffled Travis's hair, then pulled his boots on and headed for the door. "Hurry up and eat breakfast. We've got a long day ahead of us."

"Listen up!"

Jim McClure's voice echoed across the camp. The herders gathered around the corral. They were dressed for riding, their boots and chaps on, some with jackets or bedrolls slung across their shoulders. A few of the technicians stood with them, looking out of place but anxious to help. McClure waited until he had their attention.

"Here's the deal. I can't tell any of you to come with me today. Not officially. And I can guarantee none of you will get paid a dime if you do." He looked from face to face, then smiled. "But, if you want to tag along for the ride, I'd sure appreciate it."

A ripple of nervous laughter ran through the gathering. Travis laughed, too. For the first time in days he felt optimistic, the darkness that had chased him since their return to camp shredded at the prospect of doing something useful. He waited for his dad to line out the details of the coming ride.

"All right," McClure said. "We'll do this like always. Lefty?" He nodded at the man with the artificial eye. "You take a couple riders with you up Copper Creek. I'll swing east and gather the foothills. Trav?"

Travis looked up, startled to hear his name called.

His dad looked at him. "Did you see any sign up by Needle Point after the storm?"

"No," Travis replied. "Nothing fresh."

"Good. You know the waterhole behind Clay Banks? Why don't you take a couple of people with you and sweep that pasture." McClure pointed south. "We'll bunch the herd together at Mud Lake and let them water. I'd wanted to make this move nice and slow, but we won't get the chance now. It's fifty klicks to the next range, the last twenty through badlands. If there's any water there, we didn't spot it. Best we can do is keep the herd moving and get them to the West Amazon. Don't worry about stragglers. They'll have to catch up on their own. Just make sure the cows are with their calves, and bring what you can. Okay, any questions?"

As if on cue, a horse whickered. Travis stared, amazed to see Adrian Lebrie ride into camp, the spotted gelding he was on covered in dust-streaked lather. He bounced in the saddle so badly it seemed he might tumble to the ground at any moment, but he pulled up beside the corral gate and spoke in a loud, confident voice.

"What do you think you're doing?"

"Getting ready to move the herd to the next pasture," Jim McClure said. "You have a problem with that?"

"I most certainly do." Lebrie stepped to the ground. He pulled out the injunction and held it high enough for everyone to see. "In case you have forgotten, this project is under a cease and desist order."

"I haven't forgotten." A faint smile creased McClure's face. "Take a look at that paper. Who's the injunction sworn out against?"

"You know very well who it's against." Lebrie frowned. "It names the Advanced Terraforming Company."

"Well then, Mr. Lebrie, just so you know, all of us are currently laid off because of that injunction. We're not working for the Company today." McClure pushed through the crowd until he stood face-to-face with the flustered exo-biologist. "As far I can tell, that injunction doesn't apply to us any more."

"That is a blatant dodge." Lebrie's voice rose in pitch. "Your argument won't hold up in court."

"No?" McClure's eyes went cold. "Then I guess you better hustle off to the nearest judge and get their ruling. And you better hurry. There's a lot of light years between here and Betelgeuse Station." He brushed past Lebrie, leaving the scientist standing alone, the injunction fluttering in his hand. The other herders moved towards the corral, ignoring Lebrie as they passed. Travis stepped past him too, not bothering to hide the grin on his face. Lebrie sputtered something incoherently, then spun on his heel and climbed back aboard his horse.

"You haven't heard the end of this!" Angry, Lebrie kicked the paint gelding hard in the stomach. The animal snorted and jumped sideways. Off balance, Lebrie slipped sideways, then toppled to the ground. Laughter rang out around the corral as he struck with a thud.

Travis caught the startled paint and led him back to Lebrie. He held out the reins, his grin wider than before. Lebrie snatched them out of his hand, struggled back into the saddle and rode off without another word. Travis headed for the corral and caught Deuce. The old horse walked out behind him, head low to the ground as if he knew how long the next few days were going to be.

CHAPTER SIXTEEN

Travis let Deuce rest a minute as they climbed yet another narrow ridge. Morning was nearly over, Alpha a glaring white eye that scorched the air until it seemed to burn. He took off his hat and wiped the sweat from his forehead with his sleeve, then started once more uphill. The three riders with him, inexperienced technicians, straggled behind, uncomfortable with the steepness of the trail.

Rocks clattered behind them, knocked loose as they climbed. Travis leaned forward in the saddle, keeping his weight above the old horse's shoulders as they broke over the crest. A long embankment stretched out around them. The shallow, crumbling cliff formed an enormous horseshoe bend. Small patches of yellowed grass dotted the little plain below, half a dozen trampled, muddy ponds the only water for kilometres. Scattered groups of cattle wandered between the sumps, grazing as they moved along a madman's network of criss-crossing trails. Hot wind whirled around them as Travis turned around in the saddle.

"Here we go." He grinned for their benefit. The others, two geologists and a botanist stared doubtfully down the cliff face. "Don't worry. It's not as steep as it looks."

Before they could protest, he turned Deuce and followed the ridge to a low gap that led down to the dusty plain. The horses skidded and slid as they dropped, the trail so narrow it seemed at times they might fall off completely. A dozen pairs of long-horned cows and calves, their spotted hides caked with thick red dust, looked up, startled at their approach. Heads high, the animals bolted and ran, churning clouds behind them.

"Get on with you," Travis shouted. He flicked the reins and without further urging, Deuce tore after the fleeing cattle.

The riders spread out and gathered the scattered bands into a single, surging block of hoofs and horns bent on escape. Travis loped back and forth between the waterholes, keeping to the left of the herd, nudging the lead animals ever southward. The herd tried to break apart near the end of the long horseshoe cliff.

Travis slapped the reins against his chaps, loud as a whip crack. Deuce stretched out and ran headlong around the fleeing cattle before they could outrun the slower riders bringing up the drag.

Dust swirled higher, the ground lost in the gritty cloud. Through the murk Travis spotted a thin dark line directly ahead, the ravine narrow but deep. Before he could turn him, Deuce hit the edge of the ravine and leaped in a high arc across it. Travis clung with his legs, desperate not to lose the stirrups as they landed on the opposite side. Without breaking stride, Deuce ran faster. The cattle spun around and rejoined the herd, their escape thwarted by the gully. Panting, long tendrils of frothy spit spinning out their mouths, the animals strung out and turned south. Travis pulled back on the reins and forced Deuce to slow down before the old horse ran himself into the ground. Far in the distance, streaks of dust careened skyward, other bunches of cattle converging.

Travis called across the ravine to the other riders. "Fun, huh?"

One of the others shouted back. "If this is your idea of fun, remind me to skip your next party!"

Travis grinned, then trotted up once more towards the lead.

Beta slid below the horizon as the last of the riders straggled in, pushing the tired cattle towards the shallow, muddy lake where they would spend the night. The sound was deafening, two thousand head of cattle bellowing and bawling in the twilight. Cows searching for calves. Bulls eager to fight one another. Travis led Deuce towards one of the crawlers that had followed the drive, a long trailer hitched behind it. The low, tracked vehicle purred softly, the engines running as it pumped fresh, cool water from the tank on its back into a portable trough. The thirsty horse stuck his head in the trough and slurped greedily.

So did Travis.

The water tasted wonderful as it slid down his parched, dusty throat. He had whooped and yelled so much over the course of the day he had lost his voice, his tongue thick with the salty, alkaline grit churned up by the moving herd. Thirst slaked, Travis cupped his hands and splashed water over his face and scrubbed off what dirt he could, then led Deuce to the picket line and fed him. He let the weary horse eat as he pulled the saddle off his back. A perfect dark outline remained, drawn in trail dust, as if someone had painted it on his hide. Travis found a curry comb and dragged it in long, easy swipes over Deuce's back and flanks, while true darkness fell over the empty land. Weary to the bone, he trudged towards the circle of electric lights set up around the other crawler.

A line of people had formed in the lee of the vehicle, shuffling slowly ahead with trays in hand. Travis fell in step, dished up a bowl of something that looked vaguely like beans and bacon, then looked around the little camp for his father. He spotted him standing across the circle, his radio pressed to his ear. Travis wandered through the clumps of people seated on the ground eating, careful not to spill his own supper. His dad saw him and waved him closer.

"He just came in," Jim McClure said into the compact transceiver. "You can stop worrying now."

Travis laughed. Even from where he stood he could hear his mother's voice coming out of the little speaker. Legs stiff from the day's ride, he sank down to the hard ground and dug his spoon into the lukewarm beans. One bite convinced him something was lacking, and he fished inside his shirt pocket for the bottle of hot sauce. His dad sat down beside him.

"You know..." McClure nodded at the little glass container. "They distill that stuff out of rocket fuel."

"No wonder it's so good." Travis grinned as he added another dash to his food. "Want some?"

"No, thank you. I like my stomach without holes burned in it."

Travis laughed, then tore into his supper. There had been no time during the day to stop and eat, and he was starving. Finished, he set the empty bowl aside and leaned back on his elbow. A million stars wheeled overhead, brilliant points of light dimmed only by the fading crimson sunset. He turned towards his dad.

"How are things at camp?"

"Tense," McClure said, his voice full of worry. "I

don't want this getting around, but the Company is not happy with us."

"Should we turn back?" Travis asked, new doubts creeping into his mind.

"No." McClure shook his head slowly. "I don't care if we all lose our jobs over this one. We're doing the right thing." He stared out into the darkness, his face shadowed, so still that he might have been carved from stone. Slowly, his joints creaking, he stood up. "Better get some sleep. We're going to break up into shifts to ride night herd. I've got you down for the midnight watch."

Travis watched his father walk away, limping slightly on his right leg, the trail already taking its toll. He took his empty bowl back to the tender, found his sleeping bag and spread it out next to a jagged boulder, the rock scant protection from the wind. He squirmed into the bag, tucked his jacket under his head for a pillow, and fell asleep in a heartbeat.

The night was cool, and riding slow circuits around the edge of the tired herd, Travis felt every wild gust of wind as it blew down his neck. He pulled his jacket tighter, and turned Deuce a little to the right, hoping the horse could see better in the dark than he could.

"You need one of these."

Travis nearly fell out of the saddle at the strange voice behind him. Too startled to speak, he spun Deuce around. A dark shape, a short man on a tall horse, waited behind him. Travis must have ridden past without even seeing the other rider. Lefty rode closer and pointed at his artificial eye. A faint blue glow rose off the glassy surface as he swung it full on at Travis, laughing all the while.

"Yessir, kiddo. It ain't much to look at in the daytime, but the night-vision circuits sure come in handy for this."

"Yeah, I guess they would." The subject made Travis a little uneasy. "How far can you see with it?"

"Well…" Lefty scratched under his chin as he spoke. "Depends on the night. Right now I can see about two hundred metres. Course it gets a little fuzzy out towards the edges." Lefty swung his head around, surveying the cattle, then turned the glowing eye back on Travis. "What time do you have? My watch quit."

"Just a sec." Travis hit the light button on his own wristwatch, but nothing happened. He tried again, then gave up. "Mine quit too."

"I never seen a planet like this one for wrecking things." Lefty cleared his throat with a noisy gurgle then spat downwind. "Oh well, it's got to be close to the end of our watch. We'll make one more trip around, then wake those other fellers up. Sound good?"

"Sounds good to me," Travis said, relieved. He didn't want to admit it, but the darkness had him on edge. Too many shadows, too many sounds. Too many places for something to hide.

"I'll meet you back at the camp," Lefty said, but before he could move out, a shrill, bone-grinding scream slid in with the wind. The horses' heads shot up, their ears swivelling as the noise faded away. "What in the hell was that?"

"Lefty, no!" Travis tried to cut him off, but Lefty had already wheeled his horse and trotted into the darkness. Dreading what might lurk beyond the next rise, Travis pulled Deuce around and tried to catch up with Lefty. He found the other rider at the top of a low, grass-covered dune, staring out into the emptiness.

"Forty years of chasing cows, and I've never heard anything like that," Lefty muttered.

"I have." Travis shivered despite himself. "That's the thing that I saw out at Needle Point."

Slowly, Lefty turned his horse and faced him, his blue eye a faint glow. "Maybe you better wake up the others."

"Okay." Travis started downhill, then reined Deuce in. "What about you? Aren't you coming in?"

"One of us better sit out here and keep an eye on things." Even in the darkness, Travis could see the grin on Lefty's face. "And I've got just the eye for the job."

Despite being exhausted, cold and weary to the bone, Travis wasn't able to get much sleep once he finally returned to camp. He stopped off at the crawler long enough to tell the woman manning the radio that Lefty had stayed out with the herd, then took Deuce to the corral. After what seemed hours, he finally lay down, but spent so much time tossing and turning in his sleeping bag that by the time first light broke he felt more tired than he had before crawling in. Travis rolled up his sleeping bag and tied it behind his saddle, then gave Deuce a pan of oats. Feeling hollow inside, he wandered towards the rest of the herders and joined them outside the softly humming crawler. Part of him desperately wanted to know if anyone else had encountered anything strange on their watches, while another part simply wanted to pretend he had imagined the animal scream from the foothills.

The crowd around the vehicle thinned out as he poured himself a cup of coffee, then grabbed an enormous cinnamon roll off the still-hot tray. Breakfast in hand, he leaned against the back of the crawler and blew on his cup to cool it before he took a drink. Steam rolled off it, tinted red as Beta broke over the eastern horizon. Suddenly, he heard his own name mentioned from the other side of the vehicle.

"That McClure kid said he's heard it before. Damnedest noise I ever come across." Travis thought it was Lefty talking, but couldn't identify the others.

"What do you think it was?"

"Don't know. Could have been a bobcat, maybe."

"Yeah," someone else said. "Maybe you need an artificial ear, too, Lefty. Then you might be able to tell us just what you heard." There was weak laughter at the joke. The first man spoke again.

"So, what did the kid think it was?"

"Well," Lefty said, no way to know Travis could hear every word. "Between you and me, the kid's got himself a good dose of the nerves. Even if there is something weird out there, I can't hardly imagine it's tracking us here. I don't think there's nothing to get worried about."

Travis straightened, angry at Lefty for blaming the false alarm on him. It had been Lefty's idea in the first place. Not wanting to hear more, Travis stomped away from the crawler and ate what was left of his breakfast by himself, ashamed at what people thought of him. He was actually glad when the call went out to mount up.

If the day before had been a wild, headlong ride across the open grasslands, today was a trudge. The cattle were tired, too interested in grazing the sparse clumps of grass poking out of the sun-baked soil to move at more than a crawl. The heat was relentless, and long before noon a sullen mood had fallen over everyone, people and animals alike. Behind them, a dull haze choked the landscape, the distant mountains little more than shadows dancing in the heat waves. Ahead lay the badlands.

Travis sat bored in the saddle, shifting his weight from side to side or letting his legs dangle out of the stirrups to keep them from cramping. He was hot, and he was tired, and he had too much time to think about things he would rather forget. Thoughts of home crept in, far distant Earth, snowy days and friends around a Christmas tree. It had been a long time since he had thought about the long season of holidays, so long he realized he didn't even know what month it was back home.

Other thoughts struck at him too. Try as he might, he couldn't keep Riane out of his mind. The way she smiled, her dark eyes picking up the sun. The way she walked so gracefully around the boulders and scrub brush during that first long day of their ill-fated trip. But every time he thought of her, the memory was spoiled by the cold, unbreakable fact that now Bart Caddy, not him, was the one she smiled for while he was stuck in a dust cloud behind two thousand reluctant cattle.

And, over everything else, thoughts of the predator, whatever it was, banged around his head like an unhinged door in the wind. As sunset approached, the front of the herd finally reached the edge of the badlands. Travis came back to the present, no time to daydream as they worked to push the cattle into the arid breaks.

Towers of red rock, streaked with bands of black and dark green, lifted above narrow canyons carved by centuries of erosion. A narrow creek bed, the water long since dry, snaked down into the maze of washes and ravines. The herders forced the thirsty cattle down it, using the gravelly stream as a road, the walls rising on either side so high that the sky became little more than a silvery path above. Long shadows merged in the bottom.

No water, no feed, nowhere to hold the herd for the night that didn't offer a million hiding places for strange creatures with glowing yellow eyes and snapping jaws. Travis tried not to dwell on the idea as he put Deuce away for the night. So tired he could barely walk, he ate supper then fell asleep, desperate for a few hours' rest before midnight and his turn to ride herd rolled around again.

CHAPTER SEVENTEEN

A gentle boot-nudge against his shoulder woke Travis. "Time to roll out, kid."

He looked up, his eyes sleep-glued, and blinked. One of the other herders squatted down beside him, a steaming cup in either hand. He gave one to Travis. "Figured you'd want a cup before you headed out. That wind cuts right through a man."

"Thanks." Travis took a cautious sip, then looked up, startled at the taste. A strong, peppermint flavour swirled in the black coffee, an extra bit of fire that burned all the way to the bottom of his stomach. "What's in there?"

"Shhh..." The herder put his finger against his lips and grinned. "Lefty's got himself a bottle of schnapps. Figured we could all use a bracer on a night like this. But let's just keep it our little secret, okay?"

"'Kay," Travis muttered. Sleepy as he was, he knew the trouble they could get in if his dad learned someone had a bottle in camp. Still, the added warmth inside the cup did help drive the shivers away, and there couldn't be that much alcohol, not if Lefty was doling it out. The man had a cheap streak that was legend around camp. Travis took another, longer drink, then crawled out of the sleeping bag. "Thanks," he told the other man.

"No problem. Be careful out there. The cattle are pretty restless."

Travis nodded as he pulled on his boots and jacket. He finished his coffee, then hurried down to the picket line to saddle Deuce.

Walls of blackness rose around him, the cliffs without colour in the night. They had made camp inside what must once have been a shallow lake, the ground flat, covered with flaky alkaline deposits that gleamed pale as dried bone in the starlight. The cattle milled, feet crunching as they wandered, bellowing now and then, cow to calf, the sound trapped as it echoed off the steep walls. Travis rode slowly around the herd and did his best not to further upset the nervous animals.

"Hang on, Deuce." He patted the horse on the neck.

"Almost time to head back in." This was his fourth circuit, each circle taking at least half an hour to complete. The coffee was only a memory by now, the warmth long since worn off. He was cold, and wanted nothing more than to crawl into his sleeping bag. Far across the wide salt pan the lights of camp burned, the crawlers parked against the cliff to form a sort of barricade around the people and horses nesting there. He blew on his hands to warm them, and rode on. Not far ahead, he saw another horse and rider approach, a taller shadow above the moving carpet of cattle.

"How we doing, kid?" Lefty's artificial eye seemed to glow a little brighter than usual. "Cold one tonight, ain't it?"

"Yeah." Travis rode up a little closer. Lefty leaned on his saddle horn and sighed, his breath-cloud backlit by the lights mounted on the distant crawlers. Travis wrinkled his nose, the same peppermint scent he had found in his coffee strong around the other rider. Lefty had been hitting his bottle pretty hard, no doubt about it. Travis only hoped he had time to sleep it off before breakfast. "Reckon I'll head in after this pass."

"Right." Lefty mumbled something else, but Travis couldn't tell what it was. They broke apart, going in opposite directions, Travis letting Deuce walk a little faster than he should have, anxious to reach camp.

The wind picked up as he rode the last half-click, moaning down the hundred unseen canyons, mournful as the dead. The sound set the tiny hairs on Travis's neck upright. He had heard stories of the old days, the long drives back on Earth, where night riders sang to the cattle to keep them calm. The idea of him singing to the cows made Travis laugh. His singing voice rested somewhere between a lonesome coyote's howl and a worn-out compressor motor. Most likely the herd would pack up and leave if he broke into one of the few songs he knew.

A flood of relief poured through him as Travis reached the circle of light around camp. He led Deuce in and pulled his saddle off. The next two riders were already up, their horses shuffling impatiently near the water tank. Travis wandered towards them.

"Lefty make it in yet?"

"Nope. Not so far." Candy Ness, a heavy-set woman in a long quilted coat and Scotch cap shook her head. "He'll be along in a minute, I expect. Go ahead and turn in. We'll pass word you made it back when he comes in."

"Thanks, Candy," Travis said. Glad his watch was done, he stumbled to his sleeping bag and crawled in, knees curled against his chest for warmth, and quickly fell asleep.

Morning came all too soon. Bleary-eyed, Travis gathered up his sleeping bag and trudged towards the horses. Deuce looked as tired as he was, head hung low, resigned to another day of riding. Travis saddled and fed him, then jogged towards the crawler, anxious to get something to eat before they moved out.

Hot, fresh doughnuts, dripping with icing, covered a tray set above the big camp stove. Travis tore into one, washed it down with a swallow of coffee, then went back for another. One thing he had learned: doughnuts were scarce and it was every man for himself when they showed up. He snatched another off the top of the rapidly diminishing pile, then wandered around looking for his dad.

"Morning, Trav," Jim McClure said as Travis walked up to him. He had his radio out, a deep frown cut across his weather-beaten features. "Can't get a signal out. Canyon walls must be blocking them." Disgusted, he clipped the radio back on his belt. "How did everything go last night?"

"Fine," Travis said. He finished his doughnut and wiped his hands. He suddenly recalled that Lefty wasn't back when he came in, but didn't want to draw attention to the man if he was still half-drunk. Instead, he looked around the bustling camp, hoping to spot the one-eyed man in the crowd. Already daylight was filling the dry lake bed, the canyon walls garish in Beta's crimson fire. He started to say something, but stopped. His dad was staring out across the flat land, his eyes narrowed.

"Dad?"

"What's going on over there by that yellow boulder?" He pulled a compact pair of binoculars off his belt and focused them on the far canyon wall. Travis squinted in the same direction and tried to see what his father was worried about. The floor of the canyon was still in shadow, the cattle moving like ripples on a windy pond, the herd in motion. Jim McClure put down his binoculars, his face pale.

"Travis, go tell everybody to mount up. Looks like the herd is about to break."

They barely had time to mount up before the cattle hit them, a moving, surging wall of bodies bent on escape. The herders formed a line, everyone shouting at the top of their lungs to turn the herd. For a moment, the line held. Then a breach opened between two of the inexperienced technicians, and cattle poured through. The line fell back and re-formed, took the brunt of the motion and faltered again. With each break, the herd moved a little closer to the deep ravine that lead out of the badlands and back the way they had come.

"Hold that canyon!" Jim McClure shouted.

The riders pulled back again, fighting hard not to give up more ground. The noise was tremendous, a roar of frightened cattle and angry riders that bounced off the steep walls that ringed the dry lake floor. Again and again, they fell back, the mouth of the canyon so close Travis could see the tracks from yesterday leading up it. Sweat poured down his face despite the morning's chill, his throat raw from shouting. Deuce wheeled fast to the left as a pair of wickedly curved horns narrowly missed his front shoulder. Jim McClure galloped closer, and stabbed his arm towards the canyon mouth.

"Travis, block that hole!"

"Right!" Travis pulled Deuce around, already wondering how he could stop the frightened herd. An idea struck him as his eyes swept over the crawler. The canyon mouth was so narrow that the long-tracked vehicle might block the cattle's escape if he could reach it in time. Desperate to pull it off, Travis dug his heels into the horse's flanks, slapping the reins back and forth, urging him faster. They reached the nearest crawler and Travis leaped to the ground before the charging horse could stop. Too late to keep his feet under him, Travis struck the ground and stumbled, his ankle twisted, and fell face first against the hard ground.

"Ahhh." Travis gasped as the pain hit, but pulled himself to his feet and limped into the crawler's cab. The machine idled softly, the engine running to provide electricity for the stoves and lights. He slammed the door shut and added power. The tracks rumbled as Travis stuffed the transmission into forward and pushed the throttle. The heavy machine bolted ahead, stuttering, barely moving. Frantic now, Travis pushed the power to full, ignoring the red lights and alarms that screamed at him on the sloped dashboard. Something squealed beneath him, and he remembered the parking brake.

"Oh, brilliant, Travis," he muttered as he grabbed the release handle and pulled upward. Air canisters hissed as the brake released. The crawler jumped ahead as the treads churned the sand and rocks beneath it. Behind him, the long tables, covered with food and cooking gear, toppled over, their contents spilling onto the dry lake bed. Travis didn't care. He was too worried about driving the ungainly machine. He had driven trucks and tractors since he was barely able to look over the dashboard, but never sat behind the controls of something as big as the crawler.

The machine handled awkwardly, the steering a cumbersome combination of brakes and clutches. Travis managed to point the nose at the canyon and threw every bit of power he had into pure speed. Big as it was, the crawler charged ahead, rocking side to side with every boulder and rut it hit. Travis hung on, his head smacking the low ceiling with every jolt. To his left, he saw the herd break free once more, a dam unleashed, rivers of determined cattle flowing unchecked past the riders towards the canyon's mouth. He gritted his teeth and swung sharply towards it. Nothing mattered now but to reach the gap first.

Thirty metres became twenty, became ten. The front of the stampede was nearly upon him. Travis turned the long, bulky machine hard to the right, then straightened again just as he reached the narrow gap. The front of the machine slammed into the canyon wall, the crunch of metal against rock deafening inside the cab. Knocked out of the low, padded seat, Travis slammed into the dash as the engine killed. The cattle hit the machine, rocking the vehicle as they fought to get around it. With escape back in the direction they had come impossible, they turned at a run and followed the canyon wall, the dust so thick it hid everything from view as they surged away.

Bruised and battered, Travis shut off the electrical systems, the turbines winding down as he limped out of the cab. Camp lay a hundred paces behind him, a shambles, tables and food scattered across the bedrolls and loose gear. Deuce waited beside the other crawler, his head inside the feed bunk as he tried to steal a few bites of hay off the back of the machine. Travis grinned as he caught him.

"Leave it to you to eat your way through a stampede." He patted the horse on the neck, then gave him a once-over to make certain he hadn't been injured during the wild ride. Already, the herd was a kilometre away, a moving cloud pursued by riders as it spread out into the labyrinth of ravines to the south. A trio of riders approached from the other direction, his father in the lead.

"You okay, Trav?"

"Yeah. I'm fine." He left Deuce standing beside the feed bunk and walked towards the riders, trying to hide his injured ankle. The pair of herders who had relieved him after his watch last night sat on their horses, their faces grim. A cold, icy lump formed in Travis's stomach. "Want me to catch up with the herd?"

"No," McClure said. "Let the others handle it. You can come with us." He stepped to the ground and walked towards the crawler now blocking the little canyon. From the way he moved, Travis could tell he was upset.

"Where are we going?" Travis asked. Candy Ness looked down at him from the saddle, her broad face ruddy in the dust-streaked sunlight.

"We found out why the herd spooked. Something killed a yearling down by that yellow rock," she said.

"What do you mean, something?"

She tried to speak, but no words came out. Travis thought she was about to be sick. She cleared her throat and tried again. "Whatever it was, it tore the poor thing to shreds." She shifted her weight in the saddle. "Something you should know, Travis... Lefty never came in last night."

Travis felt the world drop out from under him, his own blood roaring in his ears. The ground seemed to tilt and he wasn't sure he could hang on. His father returned, a heavy pack in one hand, the carbine slung over his shoulder.

"Let's go."

Travis nodded, too frightened to do anything else. Deuce shied as he put his foot in the stirrup, picking up on the tension among the other riders. His ankle forgotten, Travis swung up into the saddle and followed his father and the others towards the distant yellow boulder.

* * *

The yearling's carcass lay behind the tall outcrop. Flecks of fresh blood spotted the rough stone. The animal's throat was gone, its stomach ripped open. Entrails, blue and grey in the rising light, spilled around it. Travis tried not to gag as the smell hit him. This was more than a hungry animal hunting for food. Whatever had done this had killed for pleasure. A heavy trace of ammonia and decay clung to the rocks, the predator's scent strong even against the dead yearling.

"There's tracks over here," Candy yelled. Travis turned Deuce towards her. Another ravine, barely wide enough for a single rider to fit through, led westward through the cliff face. A pair of tracks was plain in the sandy floor. One was curved and neat, a horse with iron shoes on its feet. The other was three-toed and alien, menacing somehow in its design. Jim McClure stared straight ahead, his eyes cold as he turned and started up the tight draw. It took every grain of resolve Travis had to turn Deuce up the little canyon and tag along behind.

The wadi twisted, the walls worn smooth by endless cycles of rain and drought, too slick to climb. Again and again it would open out only to close up once more, and Travis couldn't shake the thought that it was like riding through a snake's stomach. Ahead, something large and dark lay on the bottom of the ravine.

"Stay alert." Jim McClure took down the carbine and jacked a shell into the chamber. He dismounted and motioned for the others to do the same. On foot, they moved closer. Travis gathered up the horses' reins and walked in the rear, his chest so tight he thought he was being squeezed to death by invisible coils. They drew closer, the ammonia reek stronger with every step. Without warning, the dark shape on the ground moved, a spasmodic twitch. Travis jumped back so quickly he startled the horses. Jim McClure waved the others back and moved forward, the carbine at his shoulder.

"Dad..." Travis tried to call him back, but his throat was too dry to do more than whisper. He watched, terrified, as his father stood above the dark, writhing form. A shot rang out, the report sharp in the narrow ravine. Everyone ran forward. Travis wished he hadn't.

Lefty's horse kicked feebly as it died, the bullet far more merciful than the deep wounds that covered its body. Blood lay everywhere, a bright red pool around the animal. The saddle was still on, one of the stirrups ripped loose. Travis gasped for air, refusing to be sick, and managed to speak.

"Where's Lefty?"

"Up there." Candy pointed, her face suddenly pale. Travis followed her gaze. A twisted body lay huddled against the canyon wall. They dashed forward and ringed the bloodied rider. McClure kneeled down and pressed his hand against Lefty's throat.

"Travis, get the first-aid kit." He set the carbine down within reach. "And hurry. I don't think we have much time."

CHAPTER EIGHTEEN

Lefty's breathing was shallow, his chest barely rising as he struggled for air. He was covered in blood, though how much was his and how much from his horse, Travis couldn't tell. His good eye was squeezed shut, but his artificial eye was open, a pale blue gem staring blindly upward. Jim McClure pulled out his knife and cut away Lefty's coat and shirt. A pair of neat puncture wounds, deep enough to poke a finger inside, was punched into his ribcage. McClure grabbed a spray can from the first-aid kit and filled the holes with a sticky white foam. The foam turned pink as the blood flowed into it, but slowly the bleeding stopped as the spray hardened.

"How's his pulse?" Candy Ness joined McClure beside the injured man and picked up his hand, her fingers pressed against the inside of his wrist. "I can't even feel a heartbeat."

"Maybe you ought to give him a shot of epinephrine," said the third rider, a dark-skinned man with a puckered scar under his lip.

McClure shook his head. "I don't know what that would do to him. He's lost a ton of blood."

"Dad..." Travis stepped forward, hesitant to bring the subject up. "Lefty was drunk last night. I don't know how much he had, but it was enough that he was having trouble talking."

"Great." McClure sat back on his heels and rubbed the bridge of his nose. Travis had never seen his father look this way, as if he had reached the end of his rope and had no options left. He looked over his shoulder at Travis. "I hate to ask this, but do think you could climb out of this gulch and try to call in a med-team from Base Camp? You'd have a better chance of getting up those rocks than the rest of us."

"I..." Travis looked doubtfully around him. The walls were steep, the rock crumbling and unstable. He recalled seeing a small fissure near the dead horse that he might scale if it didn't close up near the top of the ravine. He looked down at Lefty, the old rider so pale he already looked dead. "I can try."

His father handed him his radio, the look in his eyes plain. "Be careful." Travis clipped the radio to his belt then jogged back to where Lefty's horse lay. The crack was wider than he remembered, and he pushed his arms inside it and pulled himself upward, wedging his hands and feet against the soft, crumbling stone as he climbed. A few metres up the face, the crack widened, and he managed to crawl inside it. Using his back and his legs, he scooted upward. Rocks broke loose and clattered downward, hitting and jumping as they bounced off the cliff face to the sand below. Travis ignored them and continued, his eyes locked on the rock in front of him. Near the top the fissure widened into a shallow V. Panting from exertion and relieved to be safely on top, he scrabbled away from the edge and took a moment to catch his breath before he attempted the call. His hand shook as he pulled the transceiver off his belt and held it beside his mouth.

"Camp Seven, Travis McClure, come in?"

To his relief, Alice Prevoroski's voice responded almost immediately, the signal surprisingly clear now that he was out of the network of ravines and washes. "Camp Seven. What's up, kiddo?"

"Alice," Travis said, speaking slowly, his voice even. "We need a medical team. Fast. Lefty Eicks has been attacked."

"Attacked? By who?"

"That thing that came after me." Travis let the information sink in. "They'll need climbing gear. He's down inside a narrow ravine with no way to land a flyer near him. And you better tell them to hurry. He's in bad shape."

"Roger that," Alice said. "Stand by."

Travis waited, the seconds dragging as he looked around the alien landscape that had somehow become his home. Aletha Three was, in its own way, a beautiful world, but it was a beauty laced with danger. The badlands stretched away for what seemed for ever, a twisted, confusing maze of canyons and mesas. Further to the south, a dull grey haze stretched from horizon to horizon, the rich pasture lands somewhere behind the dusky wall. A hard day's ride still lay between them and the next range, the broken, rocky desert an anvil to hammer themselves against.

The radio in his hand crackled back to life.

"Travis," Alice said. "Base is sending a medi-vac. Can you turn on your tracker for them to home in on?"

"That's affirm." Travis looked around the flat, rocky bench. Clumps of sage and rabbit brush stuck out of the thin soil, waving in the wind. "I'll try to get a fire going, too. They should be able to see the smoke from a long way out."

"Great. I'll relay the info. Keep us posted, all right?"

"I will," Travis said. "Thanks." He clipped the radio to his belt, but left it on in case another call should come, switched on the little tracker in his pocket, then set out to gather as much brushwood as he could for the fire. He heaped it near the edge of the ravine, then kindled a fire beside the pile. Acrid smoke rolled out from the dry branches. Travis let the smoke wash over him, anxious to chase the stench of the kill from his mind. Satisfied the fire would burn, he sank down beside the flames, counting the minutes until the flyer appeared in the pale yellow sky.

A sleek orange-and-white triangle hovered above the ravine, so close the guide wings nearly brushed the jagged edge as the flitter's pilot fought to maintain position. Unlike the jump-bugs, the flitter relied on a trio of rotors hidden in its smooth belly to stay aloft, the engine whine so loud it was painful to the ears. A pair of long black ropes fell from the floor hatch, drawn tight by the basket litter rising gently from below. Travis watched as the crew hoisted Lefty inside, the injured man little more than a lump bundled inside a padded cocoon. Within seconds, the med-team that had descended into the narrow gap followed him up, their climbing belts clipped to the same ropes.

The machine tore away as soon as the hatch had swung shut, dust and grit blasting around it as it skimmed the broken tabletop. The machine gathered speed, then pulled up and banked eastward. Travis shielded his eyes as he watched it vanish into the haze. He turned off his tracker, then took out his dad's radio once more.

"Alice, are you standing by?"

"Go ahead, Travis," she replied, the signal weaker

now. "What have you got?"

"The medi-vac just lifted off with Lefty aboard. You should be able to contact them by now."

"Thanks. What are you guys going to do?"

"I'm not sure yet." Travis glanced over the lip of the cliff. Twenty metres below he saw his dad and the pair of riders standing near the horses, talking and waving their arms in discussion. He stepped back from the edge. "I'm going to climb back down, so we'll probably be out of communication again. We'll try to contact you later."

"Okay. Be careful. Camp Seven out."

Travis clipped the radio to his belt, then walked carefully to the little cleft where he had ascended. The narrow crack looked far more menacing going down than it had coming up, and he took a moment to gather his nerves before starting down. Above the horizon the twin suns were so close to each other that their edges nearly touched as their mutual orbits swung tiny Alpha behind the much larger Beta, an unending cosmic reel. Within a few days only one of the stars would be visible as the eclipse began, a single sun in a blood-red sky while another of Aletha's periodic "winters" arrived, a ten-day period of cooler weather and wild storms. Hot as it was, Travis still hoped they had the cattle moved before the cold spell started.

His dad met him at the bottom and helped him to the floor of the winding ravine. It was cooler in the shadows, and Travis took a moment to rest, leaning against the rough rock wall. Nearby, the horses shuffled and snorted, their nostrils wide, nervous at the strange scents riding the wind.

"How's Lefty?" he asked. His dad shook his head slowly.

"Not good."

"So." Travis glanced at the horses. "What now? I could see the herd's dust about six klicks out. Looks like they've slowed down again."

"Good." Jim McClure said it as if it didn't matter. His eyes were narrowed, the little hollows in his cheeks drawn in. Travis knew the look all too well. "You guys should be able to catch up with them without any problem."

"Where are you going?" Travis asked, though he already knew the answer. An empty, broken feeling raced through him as his father picked up his carbine and slung it over his shoulder. "Dad, you can't go after that thing by yourself."

"Somebody has to," McClure said quietly, his voice harder than steel.

"Then I'm going with you. It's too dangerous to face it alone."

"The kid's right," Candy said. "Lefty tried, and look where it got him. I think we all should go."

Jim McClure closed his eyes a moment, weighing the odds, then slowly nodded in agreement. "All right. But no crazy chances, understand? I'm not sending anyone else out of here in a sling." He stared pointedly

179

at Travis, then wandered back to the horses and checked his cinch. "Let's saddle up."

They picked up the predator's trail, long scuff marks gouged in the sand, the animal on its toes and moving fast. After an hour's ride through the wandering chasms, the ravine emptied onto a broad alkali flat ringed by eroded foothills and steep mesas. The heat lay sullen across the emptiness. Jim McClure held up his hand and signalled a stop. Grateful for the break, Travis stepped to the ground and joined his dad.

"Can you still see the tracks?" he asked.

"No." McClure kneeled down and tried to pick up the trail. The ground had changed, the surface littered with pebbles, too dry to hold a footprint. He stood up and looked around the barren landscape. "Let's spread out. But, stay in sight of each other, okay? I don't want anyone wandering off alone."

Everyone nodded, then climbed back aboard their horses. Deuce tried to turn around as Travis swung up. Travis pulled the tired horse to the right and nudged him into a slow trot away from the others. A low dune lay nearby and he climbed to the top. Deuce whickered as the other horses drew away, the four riders spread in an uneven half-circle as they searched for tracks.

"Don't worry, fella." Travis reached up and scratched under the bridle. Deuce twisted his neck and leaned into the welcome touch, bobbing his head happily.

Thirsty, his mouth caked with dust, Travis pulled out his canteen. To his dismay, it was empty. He had been too tired to fill it last night, and now paid the price for it. "I sure hope this doesn't take much longer," he grumbled. Deuce whickered as if he agreed, then started once more along the narrow ridge.

A half-kilometre ahead, something low and grey peeked over the ridge line, then vanished behind a bone-white crag. Travis's heart jumped. As brief as the sight had been, he knew exactly what it was he had seen. Below him, riding in the shallow valley between dunes, his father looked like a toy. He turned Deuce and let him run, desperate to reach McClure before he blundered into the predator.

"Dad!" he yelled as he pulled alongside. "I just saw it."

"Where?"

"Up ahead, about five hundred metres." Travis pointed at the white bluff.

"You're sure?"

"Trust me," he said, wishing he was wrong. "I know that thing when I see it."

"Okay. Stick with me." McClure spurred his horse forward, the carbine ready across his legs as they rode up the little hill. A boulder patch lay on the other side. Hundreds of jumbled stones, some as big as houses, covered the wide flat. Travis groaned inwardly. If ever there was a place for an animal to hide, this was it. Beside him, his dad took out his radio.

"Candy," he spoke into the little unit. "Stay sharp. Travis just saw the thing ahead of us."

"Gotcha," she replied, the signal thick with static. "We're on our way."

As quietly as possible, they rode into the boulder patch. Travis swung his head from side to side, watching every shadow, hyper-aware as they moved through the jumbled stones. He had a sense of enormous ruins, of tumbled columns and fallen walls, as if a great city had once stood on the empty plain. The horses were nervous, heads high as the hot, flinty wind moaned through the rocks, a discordant song that rose and fell in pitch as if the planet were breathing. Travis felt it too, the tension nearly unbearable. Cold sweat rolled down his sides, his chest tight with knife-edged fear. Despite the harsh glare, he felt blind, his sense of direction confused by the constant twists and turns as they meandered among the boulders.

A sharp, ammonia-laced scent washed over him. Deuce stopped, his front legs planted firmly in the gravel. Travis tried to make him go, but the old horse refused. Ahead, the low, white bluff rose like a temple. A wide basin lay beyond, filled with endless, rippled sand. He swallowed, his throat raw. A familiar shape, long neck stretched level with its tail, slunk between dunes. The creature swung its narrow head and stared over its shoulder at them.

"Dad..."

"I see it." Jim McClure stepped gently to the ground,

his knuckles white around the carbine's stock. Travis eased out of the saddle and took the reins for both horses, his eyes locked on the predator. The animal flicked its long, snake-like tail, the little row of feathers on its back ruffled into a crest. It watched them as they advanced, but made no move to flee, as if it was utterly unafraid of the pathetic pair of humans. McClure edged closer and stopped in the bluff's shadow. The creature opened its mouth and hissed.

"Wait here," McClure whispered. "And keep the horses ready."

"Dad, be careful." Travis's fingers tightened around the leather strands in his fist as his father moved towards the creature. The predator whipped around, its thin, reptilian body presenting a poor target. Horrified, Travis watched the thing stalk towards them. Less than fifty paces lay between them. It crouched low, powerful legs bunched, ready to attack. McClure sank to one knee beside the low white bluff and raised the carbine to his shoulder, taking his time as he aimed.

A shadow fell across him.

"Dad! Above you!"

Travis ran forward, his own fear forgotten as a second creature leaned over the edge of the bluff. Larger than the first predator, the feathers on its back a dull green, it swung its head as Travis charged ahead and screamed in rage. Below it, Jim McClure swung the carbine's barrel skyward and fired. The creature on the bluff jumped sideways as the bullet sped past, then darted away. Heart pounding, Travis turned back towards the dunes, certain the first creature would rush them. To his amazement, the animal was no longer there, its retreat so swift it seemed to have simply vanished.

Rifle at his shoulder, McClure backed slowly towards Travis and the horses, his eyes locked on the bluff above him. Hoof beats pounded closer as Candy and the other rider galloped in.

"What happened?" Candy said, out of breath, all colour drained from her face. "We heard a shot. Did you get it?"

"No," McClure said. He was shaking, his voice uneven. "There's more than one of the things."

"That's what I was coming to tell you," she said. "There's tracks all over the place on the other side of this rock patch. Looks like maybe a dozen or more."

"They're hunting us," Travis said, the words flat in his ears. He fought to stay calm. The thought that not one, but a pack of the creatures was out there seemed unreal, a nightmare scenario that refused to go away. "What do we do now?"

"Now?" Jim McClure took his horse from Travis. "We get the hell out of here before those things come back."

CHAPTER NINETEEN

Travis relaxed as the last of the herd stormed down the rocky hillside towards a small, twisting stream, the animals mad with thirst as they crowded the muddy banks. He and the others in the hunting party had rejoined the rest of the stockmen just before noon, the cattle once more together, plodding through the badlands. The last push had seemed endless, everyone – cattle horses and humans – exhausted from the long trek. Try as he might, Travis couldn't shake the sensation of cold yellow eyes on his back, thoughts of the vicious, hungry pack never far from his mind.

A vast meadow lay before them, the grass tall and

yellow, the herd grazing as it scattered across the plain. Travis watched the cattle move away, dark shapes spreading into the twilight. Normally, this was the best part of any drive, the arrival, a time to relax and joke while the cows mothered up with their calves. But not tonight. Not until they found some way to drive off the horrors lurking in the shadows.

"Let's get those lights up," Jim McClure shouted nearby. "And keep the horse picket close to where we bed down."

"We going to keep the same watches tonight?" one of the other riders asked. McClure shook his head.

"No. Nobody goes out tonight. The herd's on its own. We'll stand guard around camp instead." He took the carbine off his shoulder and held it over his head. "We only have one rifle with us. Whoever's holding it stays on top of the crawler. And if so much as a jackrabbit moves outside the lights, shoot it."

A murmur of surprise ran around the dust-streaked riders. One of them, a tall man with a moustache so long it hung below his chin, whistled low. "Never thought I'd see Jim McClure spooked like this."

"Yeah?" Travis turned and faced him. "Trust me, if you'd seen what he did today, you'd be spooked too."

But the night was quiet, and the next morning Travis set the saddle on Deuce's back, anxious to be on the move. The riders strung out in little groups, the crawler bringing up the rear as they started the long trip back. By mid-morning the heat fell over them as if an oven door had been opened. No one spoke, the clip-clop of hoofs broken only by the wind and the steady rumble of the crawler's tracks against the unforgiving ground. Without the herd to push they made better time, and by noon had reached the dry lake bed they had camped at the night before last. Across the wide flat, Travis could just make out the other crawler's dark shape where he had crashed it into the canyon wall. A flitter sat near it, no doubt mechanics from Base Camp sent out to make field repairs.

Tempke's jump-bug lay near it, too.

"Oh, great." Travis swore under his breath. He could just imagine what the supervisor was going to say when they arrived. His dad rode out ahead of the others and met Tempke beside the disabled crawler. Travis chewed on his lower lip, screwed up his courage, and spurred Deuce towards the two men.

"We've got trouble," McClure said as he reined his horse up.

"Really? I hadn't noticed." The sarcasm in Tempke's voice made him sound petulant. "Do you have any idea the legal hornets' nest your little escapade has stirred up?"

"To hell with the lawyers." McClure stepped out of the saddle. "That thing that Travis found? It's not alone."

Travis watched Tempke's face. The man seemed nervous, but hardly surprised. His eyes narrowed to

187

slits, his thin face pale compared to the weather-beaten riders gathering around him. He stared around the ragged circle, then spoke slowly, making certain his voice carried.

"You can all consider yourselves on suspension until I get this sorted out."

"Didn't you hear the man?" Candy Ness pointed her thick arm at McClure. "There's a whole pack of those things walking around out there. What are you going to do about it?"

"What *can* I do about it? This is out of my hands."

"You could start," McClure said softly, "by getting us some more rifles."

"Oh, that's rich." Tempke's cheeks drew in, his anger rising. "I didn't want you to have that one you're packing around. Do you think the Company is going to authorize me to give the rest of your people guns?"

"If they have any sense, they will." McClure stepped towards the other man, so close their noses nearly brushed. "I don't know where these things came from, and to be honest, I don't care. But, I'm telling you straight out, we have to get rid of them."

"This is not your concern. Your job was to watch that cow herd you were ordered not to move, but did anyhow. And thanks to you, my job is now ten times harder than it needs to be."

The riders drew in, anger plain on every face. Travis felt his own fists bunch together, his blood ready to boil. All the frustration and pent-up fear of the last few days gathered inside him, a storm on the rise. He joined the others as they crowded closer. Jim McClure raised his hand and waved everyone back, his eyes still locked on Tempke.

"Whose side are you on? None of this would have happened if you hadn't let that Lebrie walk all over you."

"Don't you dare pin this on me." Tempke shook his finger at him. "I will not take the blame for what your actions have caused."

"And just what is that supposed to mean?" Candy Ness said, so mad she could barely get the words out.

"It means your little stunt has already cost one life." Tempke looked around the circle, no trace of emotion on his sharp face. Without warning, the light dimmed as Alpha slid behind Beta, the eclipse begun. A chill fell as Tempke continued. "Lefty Eicks died yesterday before they could get him to the infirmary at Base Camp."

Camp seemed deserted by the time the herders straggled in. Travis led Deuce to the corral and pulled off his saddle.

"Here you go, fella." He poured a can of oats into a low, scuffed feed pan. Deuce ate with amazing speed, oats dribbling out his mouth as he hurried to slick the plastic container clean. Travis found a brush and curried away the cinch marks and dried lather from his pony's hair. As tired as he was, he didn't feel like facing the rest of camp and the thousand questions that were sure to be waiting. It had been a long, difficult ride, and the only thing he really wanted was a cold drink and a chance to put it all out of his mind.

Finished at last, he turned Deuce inside the pen. He frowned as he noticed that Twitch and the paint gelding Adrian Lebrie had been riding were still gone. Bart Caddy's horse was missing too. Travis had an uneasy feeling that they might have gone out again looking for the predator.

"Dad?" he asked as he joined Jim McClure outside the mess tent. "Where are the Lebries?"

"Huh?" McClure scratched the stubble around his chin. He looked haggard, more tired than Travis had ever seen him. After a moment, he shrugged. "I don't know. Maybe they've gone back to their ship."

"Their horses aren't back yet."

"To be honest, Trav, I don't care. Considering what they've cost us, the longer they stay away, the better." McClure walked away. Travis watched him go, unable to shake the sensation of dread. As mad as he had been at Riane when they left, the idea of her being out there with not one, but dozens of the strange predators, chilled him. He wandered past Bachelors' Row, his shoulders slumped, the light around him a dull russet. He stopped on the outskirts of camp and stared into the distance, still hoping to see more riders come in, as if wishing it might make Riane appear.

Without warning, a pair of arms grabbed him from behind and nearly squeezed the breath out of him.

"Thank goodness, you're back!" Angie McClure spun him around and kissed him on the cheek, then crushed him in another bear hug. His dad wandered in from the direction of the corral, and she threw her arms around him next. "I just heard what happened out there. I don't know if I should kiss you or strangle you."

"I'll take the kiss, if it's all the same to you." McClure's dust-covered face twisted into a lopsided grin. Angie pulled his head down and kissed him. Travis looked away, embarrassed, as the kiss showed no sign of stopping. Nearby, someone cleared their throat.

"Sorry to break this up," Alice Prevoroski said as she stepped around the edge of the nearest trailer, "but I've been waiting for you to get back." She held a flat-screen reader out to McClure. "Thought you'd want to see the latest weather report. There's a blow on the way. A big one from the looks of it."

McClure's face darkened as he took the reader and studied it. "How long until it hits?"

"Tomorrow night at the latest. We better get the camp locked down tight. This is going to be a doozy."

"Thanks, Alice." McClure handed the reader back to her, then hurried off towards the mess tent, Travis's mom keeping pace alongside. Alice rolled up the little screen, then glanced at Travis.

"How are you holding up, kiddo? Sure is too bad about Lefty Eicks."

"Yeah." Travis's throat was suddenly so dry he could barely speak. He swallowed and forced himself to calm down as he framed his next sentence. "Alice, have you heard from Lebrie or Bart lately?"

"No, and I've been trying to raise them on the radio all day."

"Any idea where they went?"

"Well, they mentioned something about looking south, down by Scratch's Dooryard."

Travis's eyes widened, shocked at the information. The dormant volcano basin was some of the worst country to be found anywhere on Aletha, a labyrinth of jagged cliffs and broken cinder cones. It also, he realized, lay on an almost straight line between Camp Seven and the mouth of the badlands where they had discovered the pack.

"Shouldn't someone ride out and find them before the storm hits?"

"Probably, but not tonight." Alice smiled. "Don't worry, I'm sure she's okay."

She gave Travis's shoulder a friendly squeeze, then walked away. Travis stood a long time, wind ruffling the loose hair that poked out from under his battered hat until, at last, it grew too dark to see.

CHAPTER TWENTY

The sound of engines woke Travis. It was still dark in the tent, a single feeble lamp the only light. Both his parents were gone, their sleeping bags a tangled mess as if they had left in a hurry. Concerned, Travis dressed quickly, pulled on his boots and hat, and went outside.

A pool of bright light washed over the landing field, growing smaller and brighter as a cargo flitter settled to ground. An explosion of grit burst out underneath the enormous vehicle as it gunned the rotors to cushion the landing. The pilot shut down the engines, a high-pitched whir fading away as the turbines spun down. A crowd of people pushed towards the machine and formed a line, a crawler idling nearby, the cargo hatch opened. Travis jogged across the field to join them.

"Just in time, kiddo," Alice Prevoroski laughed as he stepped in line beside her. "Thought you might miss all the fun of unloading this puppy."

"I didn't know the supply drop was coming in this morning." Travis felt a little ashamed at having slept in, despite the fact that it was still an hour before dawn.

"Nobody knew about it." Alice grabbed a heavy, plastic-wrapped bundle from the man on her other side, twisted at the waist and slung it into Travis's outstretched hands. "For once the Company used a little common sense and sent it out early before the storm hit."

The bundle fell into Travis's hand, so heavy it nearly pulled his arms out of their sockets. He let the weight of it pull him around towards the next in line, dropped it in the waiting hands then twisted back for the next. Alice shoved another bundle at him. Before long, his forearms ached, the steady stream of supplies relentless. Then, just when he thought his arms would cramp and never move again, it was over. A warning horn screeched above the roar of the flitter's engines as the machine buttoned up and rose sluggishly on a cloud of grit and exhaust. Travis watched it bank east as it climbed away.

"Sure are in a hurry." He rubbed his hands, his fingers stiff from the workout.

"I don't blame them," Alice said. "They've seen the weather maps, too."

A familiar figure ambled out of the dissipating line of people. Jim McClure noticed Travis and waited for him to catch up, the lopsided grin once more on his face. "Well, we might all be fired, but at least we won't starve."

"Dad?" Travis fell in step as first light broke over the horizon, a pale red wash without warmth or cheer. "Alice said Lebrie hasn't checked in yet. Think someone should go out and find them?"

"With a sandstorm on the way? Don't think so."

"But they don't know this storm's coming." Travis tried to keep his voice casual. "They can't be very far away. Not with Bart guiding them. You know how lazy he is."

"Trav, I just don't have the time to break away." McClure sighed, his eyes showing a genuine regret. "And I can't very well ask someone else to go look for them. Not with a blow coming."

"I'll go," Travis said. His mother angled out of the retreating crowd and joined them.

"Go where?" she asked.

"He wants to find the Lebries and warn them about the storm," McClure said reluctantly.

"Absolutely not!" Angie McClure's eyebrows drew into an angry V. "You are not going out alone. Not today."

"But..." Travis's voice shot up in pitch. He took a deep breath, desperate to sound reasonable. "It's not like I'd be gone long. I'd stay in radio contact, and I promise if I don't find them, I'll turn back."

"No," his mother said again, more forcefully than before.

He turned towards his father, dreading what he had to say next. "Dad, they don't know there's more than one predator out there."

Jim McClure chewed on his lower lip as he considered what Travis had told him. The frown on his mother's face deepened as she saw the tide turn. She opened her mouth to say something, but he cut her off. "Trav, I'll give you until noon. If you haven't found them by then, you high-tail it back here. Understand? And I don't want any heroics, okay?"

"Okay." Travis turned to go, unable to meet his mother's eye. "I'll be careful." Before he had gone five steps, his dad called after him.

"Make sure you have your radio and your tracker." McClure paused. "And, Travis? Take my rifle."

Travis nodded, then hurried down to the corral. The horses were restless, the approaching storm keeping them on edge. Deuce stood near the far side of the pen beside his dad's big grey mare. Both horses were tired, their movements stiff and slow. No way could he ride old Deuce without giving him a few days' rest first. A lean bay mare with a white star raced past, her tail streaming out behind as a gust of wind rattled the metal panels. Everybody called her Sweetheart, though why, Travis wasn't sure. He had ridden the tough little mare before, and while she was no outlaw, she was no gentle old plug, either. Still, she was fast, and today speed mattered. Travis found a halter, then climbed in the corral and caught the bay. She whickered as he led her out the gate, baulking as another gust swept past.

Travis tied her to the fence then retrieved his saddle. He paused and looked southward. Somewhere out there a trio of fools needed to get to safety, and he had only six hours to find them. The wind was stronger, an electric sense of dread buried within it. No matter how he looked at it, it was going to be close.

Sweetheart wanted to run. Travis kept the reins short in his hand, constantly fighting the urge to pull up the bay mare. While he hated to deliberately slow his pace, he knew that letting the horse have a run away wouldn't do him any good either. Instead, he aimed her up a steep hillside and let her have her head, hoping the climb would tire her out.

Scratch's Dooryard wasn't far from camp as the crow flew, less than ten klicks, but the rugged terrain slowed their progress. The landscape changed as they neared the arid basin, rolling foothills replaced by low cliffs and rills, as if the ground had been folded like a worn-out piece of paper. Sweetheart grunted as she broke over the top of a little rise; pebbles scattered behind as she struggled over the loose scree. Travis pulled her to a stop so he could get his bearings. A shallow crater lay in front of him, the hill an almost perfect cone. More of the dormant vents stretched out into the distance, the ground between them nearly void of life. Even the sagebrush and tumbleweeds couldn't find purchase in the unyielding lava.

Travis took his radio out of his pocket. "Camp Seven, Travis McClure, come in?"

"Go ahead, Trav." Alice Prevoroski answered almost immediately, as if she was sitting beside the transmitter. Given the weather, Travis decided, she probably was. "What's your location?"

"I've just reached the edge of the Dooryard." He squinted back in the direction he had come, looking for landmarks. "Call it eight klicks south-west of camp."

"Roger that. Any sign of Lebrie?"

Travis shook his head, then felt like a fool as he realized she couldn't see him over the radio. He pressed the device closer to his mouth to shield it from the wind. "Nothing yet. Are you sure they said they were coming this way?"

"Almost positive." A burst of static wiped out part of Alice's reply. "Said they wanted to check out the hot springs near Mount Hobbs. You know where that is?"

"Yeah. That's affirm."

Travis stared across the lava basin and sighed. Mount Hobbs was the largest of the cinder cones. From where he sat it poked up against the skyline, a jet-black triangle, the summit punched in to form an irregular oval that spread down nearly a third of its bulk. It was at least an hour's ride across the broken country to reach the odd-looking mountain, more if he picked the wrong trail. He glanced at his wristwatch, glad to see that, for once, it was keeping steady time. It would be past noon by the time he arrived. He keyed the transceiver again.

"Alice, what's the storm doing?"

"Radar shows it's picking up speed. Call it five hours before it hits." More static crackled down the line. "Trav, your mom wants me to remind you of your promise to turn back if you don't find anything soon."

"Roger that." He sighed. "I'll give it another hour and a half, then come in."

"Stay in contact, okay?"

"I will. Travis out." He stuffed the radio back in his pocket, then turned Sweetheart downhill. The mare sank down on her hind legs as they slipped down the loose slope to the hard ground below. A dry stream bed wound nearby, and he turned up it, using the gravel-covered bed as a road.

The stream bed twisted back and forth, then abruptly ended at the base of a low, bright orange cliff. A steep ravine split the cliff face in half, wide enough to ride through. The little bay mare swung her head back and forth as Travis tried to force her up it.

"Come on, girl." He gave the horse a sharp nudge in the ribs with his heels. She hopped sideways, but started up the narrow draw. Travis couldn't help feel trapped, thoughts of other ravines and snapping jaws spinning in his imagination. Relieved to reach the top, they broke out on a wide shelf covered with knee-high dunes. Mount Hobbs towered above him, less than a kilometre away. The jagged crater gouged in its flank stared down at him like a great blind eye. As hot as the wind was, he felt cold inside, dwarfed by the mountain.

Without warning, Sweetheart spun around and whickered.

Travis pulled the reins back a little faster than he wanted, and the mare backed up, her head high, ears laid back. He let the reins slacken again, and tried to see what was making her so nervous. The hair on the back of his neck stiffened as he spotted a dust cloud tearing across the sandy basin. Something was on the move. Too far to make out details, he grabbed the compact pair of binoculars off his belt and tried to focus on the runners. The image danced and jiggled as Sweetheart shifted around, refusing to stand still. Annoyed, Travis jumped to the ground and tried again.

The ground blurred as he scanned across it. Suddenly, a pair of horses seemed to leap across the lenses. Travis focused the binoculars on the animals as they raced towards the next cinder cone. One was Bart Caddy's, the other the paint Adrian Lebrie had been riding. Both were saddled.

Neither had a rider on its back.

"Oh no." Travis scanned the ground behind them, but couldn't find any trace of the two men, nor of Riane and Twitch. His hand shook as he pulled out his radio.

"Camp Seven, come in?" No one replied, and he tried again. "Camp Seven, this is Travis McClure. Come in. I've spotted two of the horses, but no riders." He waited a moment for Alice to reply, then gave up. The terrain was blocking his signal, the radio useless until he reached higher ground. He stuffed it and the binoculars back in his pocket, then swung up on Sweetheart's back. She tried to wheel around and chase after the fleeing pair of horses, but Travis turned her once more towards Mount Hobbs.

Wind poured over his face as he let the mare run, his own panic building. The carbine banged against his shoulder blades, a steady *thwack, thwack, thwack* in time with Sweetheart's hoofs. Thoughts of what might have become of Lebrie and Riane lay hard on his mind. He forced himself to calm down and think. The best-case scenario was that Bart had failed to tie up the horses and they had simply run away.

He didn't want to think about the worst-case scenario.

A dark stain came into view as he neared the base of the mountain, deeper black against the dark stone. It looked like a cave. Travis swerved towards it. As he approached, he spotted a third animal standing near the mouth of the cleft. For one hopeful moment he thought it might be Twitch, but just as quickly realized it was a mule. The tethered animal brayed and pulled back on the rope that tied it to a picket line strung between two boulders as he and Sweetheart pulled closer. Travis jumped to the ground and, leading the sweat-covered mare, hurried towards the mule.

Two sets of broken reins dangled from the picket line, swinging in the wind. Travis breathed a little easier. At least, he decided, he had been partially correct. Bart hadn't bothered to change the bridles for halters, and the horses had obviously jerked back hard enough to break the thin leather strands. Behind him, from the mouth of the narrow cave, someone shouted.

"Did you find them?"

Travis looked up. Adrian Lebrie stood at the edge of the fissure, Bart just behind him. The exo-biologist hurried down the little slope towards him.

"Did you see them? The horses I mean?"

"Yeah," Travis nodded, too relieved for the moment to say anything else. Lebrie looked around and scowled.

"Where are they?"

"Halfway to camp," Travis said.

"Why didn't you catch them?" Lebrie demanded. Travis ignored the outburst as he looked around the area, his concern once more building.

"Where's Riane?"

"She's safe," Bart said, as if that explained everything. Travis pressed the issue.

"Safe where?"

Lebrie and Bart glanced at each other, as if they were reluctant to say more. Travis stepped towards them, Sweetheart's reins gripped tight in his fist. Finally, Bart shrugged. "We found an abandoned starship a few klicks from here."

"A starship?" Travis said, his doubt plain. "What would a starship be doing out here?"

"How should I know?" Bart said.

"It's an old-style freighter," Lebrie interrupted. "It looks as if it's been here quite some time. Riane stayed there to see if she could access the computers, while we tracked the neo-raptor."

"The what?"

"The near-apter," Bart repeated, mangling the word. "That's what we're calling that thing you found."

"You saw the predator?" Travis felt his stomach tighten, a painful grip. "Where?"

"Actually, we found its tracks," Lebrie said. "They led us here. We think the creature has used this cave as a den."

"But..." Travis's pulse pounded in his ears. He forced himself to speak slowly. "Why did you leave her there?"

"Because it's safer there than it is out here," Bart said, his old swagger in full glory. "I told you. We tracked the thing this way."

"You idiot," Travis said, his voice as cold as he felt inside. "There isn't just one predator. There are dozens of them. And you damn fools left her alone for them to find."

A hard gust blew around the western edge of the mountain, strong enough it seemed to shake the ground. Travis looked up. Streams of clouds shot past the summit of the pointed cinder cone and gave the illusion that the mountain was swaying. The view made him dizzy. Angry, and more frightened than he wanted to admit, he snugged the cinch up tight around Sweetheart's chest, then swung aboard.

"Where do you think you're going?" Bart glared at him, stung by the accusations. Travis ignored him and turned the mare until he faced Lebrie. He had to shout to be heard as another wave of hot, gritty wind swept by.

"Where's this freighter you found?"

Lebrie's face had turned pale, the implications of what Travis said all too plain. He pointed southward. "It's on the far side of this mountain. There's a dormant geyser basin on the south-west flank. The ship is inside a large crater beside it. I'll show you the way."

"No." Travis shook his head. "There's a sandstorm headed this way. A big one. The best thing you can do now is hole up inside that cave and wait it out. I'll find Riane."

Bart sneered, and tried to say something, but a sharp gust blew his hat off his head and sent it rolling across the ground and under the mule. He chased after it, careful to avoid the nervous animal's feet. Lebrie stepped closer and looked up at Travis.

"I had no idea we were leaving her in harm's way." He took a small radio, far more compact than the one Travis carried, from his pocket and pressed it into his palm. "We're using different frequencies than your Company. With luck, you can contact her once you've cleared the side of this hill. Please, hurry?"

"I will." Travis tried to look confident. "Don't worry. She'll be all right."

He whirled Sweetheart around and started round the side of the mountain. The wind struck harder, and he leaned against it as the mare broke into a lope.

CHAPTER TWENTY-ONE

Nothing mattered but speed. Travis let his horse gallop along the base of Mount Hobbs. The sand was deep and Sweetheart stumbled, rose and charged on. Finally he reined her in and let the tired horse walk, her legs unsteady. He could feel her gasping for breath, her ribs moving in and out under his legs as they crossed yet another dune, using the low hill to block the rising wind. Wispy curls of grit snaked along the ground, at times so thick he couldn't see the path, while Beta burned at the zenith, a dull red spot in a haze-filled sky. The mountain lay behind him now, its dark bulk no longer a shield against the coming storm.

Again and again, the mare tried to turn around, but Travis forced her ahead, hoping to see the geyser field with each dune they topped.

"Come on, Sweetheart." Travis spat to the side, his mouth full of fine sand. "Just a little further."

A blast of heat hit him as they broke over the top of the next rise, the hot wind choked with dust. Travis stared in dismay at the western horizon. The jagged line of peaks was gone, hidden by a surging wall of sand at least a kilometre in height. Relentless, the sandstorm rolled towards him, no more than ten minutes away. A flash of lightning arced in front of it, the thunder lost in the hurricane roar.

Something beeped in his pocket. Frantic to answer the call, Travis dug Lebrie's radio out and hit the transmit button. "Riane? Is that you? Come in?"

The beep sounded again, still in his pocket. Disappointed, he brought out his own radio and turned up the volume. "Travis here, go ahead."

"Travis..." Static choked the message. He pressed the receiver close to his ear and tried to hear the rest. To his dismay his mother's voice, not Alice Prevoroski's whispered out the cheap speaker. "Can you hear me?"

"Roger that," he replied. "Your signal is faint, but I can read you. Go ahead."

"Storm is stronger...come back in...Travis, please respond."

"Mom?" He swung the stubby antenna around, but it

didn't seem to improve the signal. The storm was too close, the static electricity kicked up by the swirling sand disrupting any transmission. "I can barely hear you."

"Travis? Thank goodness." For a moment, the static cleared. "Get to shelter. You can't outrun the storm. Understand? Get to shelter."

He looked around him. Beyond a few low, wind-polished boulders, the landscape was bare. The closest shelter was the cave Lebrie and Bart had found. If he turned now, he could still reach it before the storm arrived. Squinting against the wind, he shifted in the saddle and stared out at the rolling dunes. A low butte lay ahead, directly in the path of the onrushing sand. That had to be the geyser field, he decided. The radio crackled again, and he pressed it to his ear.

"Travis? Can you hear me? Get to shelter now."

He shut his eyes, fighting with the choice he had to make. Behind him lay shelter. Ahead, lay Riane. If he could find her.

"Travis, come in?"

"Sorry, Mom," he said out loud without pressing transmit. He shut the radio off and stuffed it back in his pocket, then turned his horse towards the geyser field.

Sand gave way once more to barren lava as Travis climbed onto a wide, irregular escarpment dotted with tiny cones. Some of the extinct geysers were as white as a bleached skull, while others were stained garish shades of orange and red and copper blue. Deep pits which once housed hot springs lay like traps across the wide, rocky bench. Though it had been centuries since they last erupted, the reek of sulphur still clung to the porous stone, a reminder of the fires that raged not so far beneath Aletha's crust. As much as he wanted to run, Travis held Sweetheart to a walk, the terrain too treacherous to gallop over.

A grey wave crested over the field and pelted him with fine sand, the gust front nearly on top of him. He needed to find the crater Lebrie had told him about before all visibility was lost. Harsh grit scraped against his cheeks and ran down the back of his shirt. He wrapped his blue bandana around his mouth and nose. Sweetheart pawed the ground, a broken, angry rhythm. She whickered, the cry so shrill it hurt Travis's ears.

"Easy, girl."

The mare whickered again, then spun around, her rump to the storm. Travis turned her towards the low bluff directly ahead, her ears flat against the back of her head. Her legs were stiff as springs, her back arced, a dangerous signal that she had reached the limit of her patience. On a better day, Travis would have pulled the nervous mare around in tight circles, spinning her first in one direction and then the other until she was tired of the game. But today, with the sandstorm only minutes away, he had no choice but to ignore her little tantrums and push on.

The bench sloped upward in front of him towards a low mound made of dark, walnut-sized pebbles. "This has got to be the crater," Travis muttered. Somehow, the sound of a voice, even if it was his own, made him feel better. He turned Sweetheart towards the low rise and flicked the reins. She started up the crater wall, then spun back around. Tired of her endless baulking, Travis jerked her head back to face the hill as he dug his heels behind her shoulders. She tossed her head and tried to run. Anger replaced caution, and he kicked her again.

Too late, he felt the jump coming. The mare planted her feet and lunged to the left so fast Travis had no time to ready himself. Off balance, he leaned out over her right shoulder, scrabbling with his other leg to pull himself back into the saddle. Sweetheart bucked once, her muscles as explosive as an overcharged fuel-cell. One moment Travis was clinging to the saddle, the next he was pitched violently to the unyielding ground.

He landed shoulder first beside the mare's front feet. Travis rolled to his side, instinct outweighing pain, and narrowly avoided her hoofs as Sweetheart jumped past him, spun around and raced back in the direction she had come. Travis tried to stand up, but the pain in his shoulder had spread through his entire body and he toppled forward again. His goggles were gone, lost in the fall, and coarse bits of lava gouged his skin. His father's carbine slipped off his back and clattered beside his face. Furious with himself and with the fleeing horse, Travis managed to sit up long enough to catch his breath.

Beta, visible only moments before, suddenly vanished, swallowed by the swirling brown cloud as the sandstorm arrived. Travis picked up the carbine and staggered to the top of the crater wall just as the storm swept over the basin. He looked down and caught a single glimpse of an enormous machine less than a hundred paces ahead. The freighter rested drunkenly on the crater floor, the hull scoured raw and partially buried beneath the dune that curved behind it. The cargo hatch was open, a gaping black hole set amidship on the lowest deck. A slim figure stood inside the broad opening, fighting to pull a rangy bay mare inside.

"Riane!" She looked up, startled to hear her name. Travis started down the hill towards her. Fifty metres from the abandoned ship, he stopped dead, as if his feet were planted in the rusted stone around him.

Travis stared in horror as another figure slunk around the freighter's nose, its whipcord tail stuck out weathervane straight. A strip of bright green feathers fluttered madly along its narrow spine as, unseen by Riane, the creature bunched low and prepared to pounce.

"No!"

Instinctively, Travis threw the rifle to his shoulder and fired. The stock shoved against his shoulder as if someone had punched him, a trace of sweet-hot gunpowder smoke brushed away by the screaming wind. The predator spun towards him and screamed, rows of dagger-sharp teeth gleaming in the pale half-light. Travis jacked another round into the chamber and took better aim, the sights dancing in front of him as he tried to steady his arms. Gently, he squeezed the trigger. The creature leaped sideways and started to bite at its own flank as it spun in tight, fast circles. Suddenly it stopped, neck low above the ground, and stared at Travis. He fired again, but missed.

Before Travis could aim once more, a surging, boiling wall of sand broke over the crater rim and threw Travis to the ground as easily as a dog might shake a rag doll. Around him, the light faded until nothing remained but a dull, swirling grey fog that stung his eyes and threatened to scour the flesh off his bones. Rifle at the ready, Travis clambered to his feet, leaned into the wind and stumbled down the low hill, the next fifty paces the longest of his life.

CHAPTER TWENTY-TWO

Blinded by the storm, Travis staggered on, his shoulder to the wind, one direction the same as another. Despite the bandana tied around his face, the dust found its way into his mouth and nostrils until he thought he would suffocate. His eyes burned, every bit of exposed skin scrubbed raw.

An unseen stone caught his left foot and he sprawled to the ground. On hands and knees he crawled forward, ignoring the pain. A faint metallic clatter rang nearby, sand battering the freighter's hull. He rose to his feet and pressed towards the sound. He could only hope it was the right direction.

Something large and soft, and immensely strong struck him on his left side.

Travis yelled as he was knocked once more to the ground. A large foot struck a hand's breadth from his face. To his relief, the leg was covered in coarse brown hair, not scales. He rolled quickly aside before Twitch could step on him, and using the carbine as a crutch, climbed to his feet.

"Riane," he shouted. "You have to get Twitch inside."

"What do you think I'm trying to do?" A sharp, frantic shout somewhere in front of him. Travis shouldered the carbine, then leaned against Twitch's hind leg. The mare shied away, but he pressed hard against her to keep her from kicking as he slipped his right arm behind her rump and heaved. Twitch took a faltering step, then stopped. Travis pushed again, so hard he thought he might rip his arm out of the socket.

Finally, the frightened mare took another step, then lunged ahead. Travis clung to her as she charged through the open cargo hatch into the abandoned freighter. He tripped over the threshold and landed on the sand-littered deck. Behind him the doorway seemed to glow, a wide, perfect rectangle, sand still pouring through the opening.

"Help me close this," Riane shouted, gasping for breath.

"How?"

"There's a hand-wheel on the other side of the door. Turn it clockwise."

Travis stumbled upright and scrambled past the wide

hatchway. Fumbling in the dim light, his hands brushed over a large steel ring inset in the inner hull. He grabbed the wheel with both hands and tried to turn it, but the door was jammed. The wheel refused to budge more than a half-turn in either direction.

"Hurry!" Riane shouted from the other side of the hatch.

"I'm trying! It's stuck."

"Then try harder."

Angry at her rude commands, Travis threw all his weight against the wheel. Without warning, it broke free. The force more than he had expected, Travis's hands slipped off the steel ring and smashed against the hull. He swore loudly, but grabbed the wheel again and spun it as fast as he could. Slowly, the heavy, steel hatch slid across the doorway. What little light remained inside the unlit hold faded as the two halves inched towards each other. Once again the wheel stopped as the left side of the hatch hit the limit of its travel. Sweating, blood pouring off his scraped knuckles, Travis darted past the narrowing opening to help Riane close her side of the hatch.

"Travis, behind you!"

Startled, he jumped away from the door. A nightmare head on a serpent's neck shot through the narrow gap and snapped at his legs. Acting on instinct, he swung the carbine off his shoulder and pointed the muzzle point blank at the predator's face. A flush of hot rage swelled inside him as he pulled the trigger.

Nothing happened.

"Travis! The hatch!"

Frightened beyond anything he had known, he brought the carbine up to his shoulder and swung it like a club at the predator's hissing face. Wood struck bone, the strike so hard his hands ached. The creature hissed, its breath foul as it pulled back through the narrow slit. Travis rushed towards Riane and grabbed the other wheel. The hatch ground against the rails, but moved. Together, they closed the hatch until only a finger's width of light showed through. He gave the ring a final tug, and then even that was gone.

Darkness reigned inside the freighter. It was hot, the air so thick it seemed like water. Travis pulled the bandana away from his mouth and tried to catch his breath. Sand pounded against the hull until it seemed the curved walls might collapse beneath the constant barrage. Twitch shuffled somewhere behind them, snorting in the musty, ammonia-laced air. A faint light sifted down from the far side of the enormous cargo hold, an open stairwell plain against the other wall. Riane's face rested near his, so close he could smell the fear on her breath.

He understood exactly how she felt.

Exhausted, his legs suddenly unsteady, Travis leaned against the hull and slid down to the deck. Thoughts of the predator prowling outside leaped into his mind, and he groped around the metal deck until he found the carbine.

"Why didn't you shoot that thing?" Riane's voice trembled as she sank down beside him.

"I tried to." He jacked the action open. A spent cartridge tumbled out and struck the floor with a sharp ping. Travis pressed his fingers inside the action to see if it was jammed, but found nothing. "It's out of ammo."

He reached inside his jacket for the box of cartridges his dad had given him before he left, but his pocket was empty. He frowned, and tried the other pocket. It was as empty as the first. He shut his eyes and tried not to be sick as he recalled striking the ground after Sweetheart bucked him off. In his haste, he hadn't noticed the little box fall out. Hating to admit what had happened, Travis turned to face Riane, little more than a dim figure an arm's length away.

"I think I lost the rest of the bullets."

"Wonderful," Riane said. "Got any more good news for me?"

Twitch moved somewhere behind them. Travis jumped at the sound, then took a long slow breath. He needed to sort things out. "Riane, is there another way inside this ship?"

"I don't think so."

"Are you sure?"

"Yes." Her voice faltered. "I'm almost sure. Maybe we should make for the upper deck? If anything did get in, we could at least hold it off from climbing the staircase." She pointed towards the narrow set of open stairs. A dim, rust-hued light spilled down from above, the only illumination inside the cavernous cargo hold. Carbine in hand, Travis struggled to his feet and followed her across the metal deck. Their footsteps echoed in the darkness, muffled by the howling storm outside. Twitch tried to follow them, but stopped at the stairs.

"Hold this." Travis passed the carbine to Riane, then eased closer to the frightened mare. Clumsy in the darkness, he loosened her saddle and let it fall to the deck, then slipped the bridle off her head. She made a plaintive, whuffling sound as Travis rejoined Riane on the steps and started to climb towards the upper decks. He looked over his shoulder at the horse and wished he could somehow bring her upstairs with them. The idea of leaving anything alone in the dark, sweltering hold tore at him. "I'm sorry, girl, but you'll have to stay down here."

"She'll be all right, won't she?" Riane asked, her face backlit by the dim light. Travis felt a newfound respect for her as he noted the genuine concern in her dark eyes.

"Yeah. As long as that thing out there doesn't find another way in, she'll be fine." He patted the horse once more, then began to climb. Again, he paused. Something was missing inside the abandoned hull, and suddenly he realized what it was. "Riane? Have you seen any mice in here?"

"No." She shook her head slightly for emphasis. "No mice. No rats. No rodents of any kind. It's the smell in here."

Travis frowned as he sniffed the air. A faint trace of ammonia and oily rot drifted on the breeze circulating through the empty hold. He stiffened. "The predator has been inside here, hasn't it?"

"I think it was born in here," she said quietly. "Wait until you see what's upstairs." Riane turned and climbed through the hatch. Travis followed her. The stairs opened into a narrow corridor, the walls padded for zero-gee. A long skylight lay above, the outer shields drawn back, but the glass was so pitted that only a dull, swirling haze could be seen through it. The decrepit freighter was tilted slightly on its belly, the deck askew, and it left Travis dizzy as he moved along the empty passage. Hatchways opened off either side, the chambers beyond dark and menacing. He felt relieved as they reached yet another staircase and climbed into the cockpit. Like the skylight, the narrow, forward windows were unshielded, but nothing could be seen through them but the sandstorm.

"How long has this ship been here?" Travis asked as he looked around the small chamber. Thick dust covered everything, the panels, the screens, the five scuffed and ratty flight couches. The ceiling was so low he had to duck his head to avoid bumping it. Dark gaps littered the panels where portions of the equipment had been removed, nothing but dangling power cables left behind. He slipped into the co-pilot's station and sat down. Something crunched under his feet. Dozens of data sticks lay broken, the shards scattered everywhere around the deck. "What tore this place up?"

"Not what. Who." Riane eased into the pilot's chair. The vinyl creaked as she reached beneath the padded seat and retrieved a thick stack of paper bound in a hard-backed folder. She passed it to Travis. "Somebody went to a lot of trouble to erase all the records from this flight, but they forgot this when they left."

Travis took the folder from her. It was heavier than he had expected, the pages inside yellowed with age. He leafed through them, the rustle of paper unfamiliar in his fingers. It had been a long time since he had felt real paper. The light was fading, and he strained to read the reams of technical data. Most of it was utter gibberish.

"I can see why they left it." He shook his head and passed the folder back to Riane. "You'd have to be pretty desperate for reading material to take this along." He smiled, but she missed the joke, her face deadly serious. She opened the file again, shuffled through the pages, then pointed at what looked like a requisition form. A sloppy, hand-scrawled set of initials covered the lower corner of the form.

"There are dozens of requisitions like this inside, all signed for with the same initials."

Travis leaned across the low panel between the seats and squinted at the barely legible writing. As far as he could tell, the signature simply read "AT". Riane flipped a few pages, and pointed out more of the initials.

"See? The same person signed for all the equipment aboard."

"Well," Travis said, trying to understand what she was getting at, "it would make sense, wouldn't it? Probably the pilot or purchasing agent, I'd guess."

"Uh-uh. None of the forms are flight related. Everything is about the incubators."

"Incubators?" The cold, heavy lump returned to Travis's chest. Riane nodded slowly, her eyes never leaving his.

"The deck below us is filled with cold storage units and incubators. Expensive ones, too. Most universities would kill for equipment this good."

Around them, the hull vibrated in time with the wind, a discordant, undulating note that rose and fell as if a choir of banshees was singing. Despite the heat inside the tightly sealed cockpit, Travis felt chilled. This was the ship that had brought the predators to Aletha Three. He cleared his throat and wished he had a drink of water to wash away the taste of sand. Riane closed the folder and placed it once more beneath the seat.

"So, you understand," she said softly, "this is how that creature out there arrived. It was grown from an egg after the ship landed, then released."

"There isn't just one of them," Travis said, his chest tight. "We saw tracks of at least a dozen after Lefty got killed."

"Someone was killed?" She stared open-mouthed as the colour drained from her face.

"Yeah." Travis nodded slowly. "One of the herders. We were trying to rescue him when we discovered there's a whole pack of these things."

"I'm not surprised." Her exotic, off-world accent, normally so faint, was stronger. "This is an animal bred for survival. Advanced Terraforming was very thorough about that."

Travis looked up, surprised, not certain he had heard her correctly. In the dim cockpit, her hair was perfectly black, the shadows accentuating her delicate features. She tried to smile, but it faded quickly. She sighed. "Yes, the Company was behind this. What else could AT stand for?"

"I..." Travis stammered. His head was swimming, the implications too stark to deal with. "That doesn't make sense. Why would the Company sabotage their own project?" He paused, a sudden thought bright in the haze. "Riane? When you landed, you thought Allen Tempke was going to meet you. Why?"

She cocked her head to the side, a puzzled expression on her face. "We were invited to Aletha by Mr. Tempke. That was why we were so surprised when he seemed not to know we were coming. He had been very adamant when he contacted my father prior to our departure. He said the Company wanted independent oversight of what you were doing. But, when we arrived, it seemed like he had totally forgotten. Unless he was just pretending not to know who we were. But why?" Her eyes widened. "*O, mon dieu!* What if 'AT' stands for Allen Tempke? Travis, what if Tempke is responsible for all this?" She waved her arm around the ruined cockpit.

"I...don't know." Travis sank back into the battered seat and said nothing. He didn't have to, the impact was all too clear. For some reason – why, Travis couldn't understand – it looked as though the man left in charge of their operation had deliberately sabotaged the project. And, not only put everyone on Aletha at risk by doing it, but had already got one man killed. Travis tried to make sense of the seemingly impossible facts, but couldn't. Nothing seemed real any more. Nothing beyond the storm and the darkness gathering inside the cockpit.

It was long after nightfall that Travis finally drifted to sleep, lulled by the constant vibrations and the howling wind, and the softness of the flight couch. He dreamed he was still aboard the starship that had brought him to Aletha. In his dream he was eleven again, a boy setting out on a grand adventure. None of his friends had even left Earth, and certainly none had travelled through hyperspace. As sad as he was at leaving, the thought of what lay ahead was too seductive to ignore. He wandered through long, empty corridors, driven by thirst, the dream's landscape a hazy version of reality. Lost inside the dream, he blundered into the ship's shadowy cockpit, the panels lit with bright, dancing displays. The pilot's and co-pilot's seats swung around as he ducked under the low hatch. But, instead of the flight crew, it was his mother and father staring at him, their faces ghostly white, the flesh around their throats slashed open.

"No!" Travis bolted upright. The silver emergency blanket Riane had found for him inside one of the cockpit lockers fluttered to the deck. He took a moment to catch his breath, his pulse as loud in his ears as the sandstorm raging outside. The storm was, if anything, worse, the rattle of tiny pellets against the windscreen steady as rain. He felt, more than saw, Riane watching him from the pilot's couch.

"Are you all right?"

"Yeah, I'm fine." Travis's throat hurt, his mouth dry. "Is there any more water?"

"Yes." She fished around in the dark and came up with a two-litre water bottle, already more than half empty. Travis took it and drank gratefully. He was so thirsty he could have finished the water in a single pull. He closed the cap and passed it back to her before temptation could overwhelm him. "Riane? How much water do you have?"

"Six litres," she said. "Counting this one. Is that a problem?"

"Might be." He thought about Twitch, the horse left alone in the cavernous hold two decks below the cockpit. The horse would be as thirsty as he was. "We'll have to give at least one of those bottles to your horse.

That doesn't leave much for you and me."

"How long do these storms last?"

"Hard to say. Sometimes, they can go on for three or four days without letting up."

"Three or four days?" Riane swore under her breath, too low for Travis to tell what she said. "What a lovely little planet you have here. What possessed you people to come to a place like this?"

"Same reason most people do crazy things. Money." Travis tried to make it sound like a joke, but his words fell flat in the dark, cramped cockpit. The dream looped in his mind, his father's face haunting him. Old memories came back, memories of the hard times before they left, of the desperate arguments his parents had every night, the tears on his grandmother's face the day they boarded the transport for Aletha. "We were going to lose our ranchif Dad didn't find some way to make the payments to the bank."

"Oh." Riane's voice sounded impossibly small. "It must mean a lot to you. Your ranch."

"I guess. I mean, it's not a big place or anything, but it's home, right? My dad's family has owned it for, like, three or four generations. Never much money in it. Barely enough to get by most years. It got really tough when my grandpa got sick. The doctors kept promising they could save him, but it took more and more money and, pretty soon, there wasn't any money left." Travis couldn't keep the bitterness out of his voice. "He died anyhow, but the doctors still wanted their money. Big surprise, huh? Then, when the inheritance taxes came due, the bank dropped us. So, we leased the place to a neighbour and came here. Guess Dad didn't have many options left."

"I didn't know. I'm sorry."

"Not your fault," Travis said.

"It is if our audit closes the project permanently. If…" She paused, as if it was painful to ask the next question. "If you go back now, will you still lose your ranch?"

"Probably. Dad's been counting on the bonus the Company promised him at the end of his contract. Without it, this has all been for nothing."

The hull shook as another blast of gritty wind rolled across the caldera. Chilled, Travis groped around the deck beside the co-pilot's seat until he found the thin blanket and pulled it back around him. Across from him in the pilot's couch, Riane snuggled deeper into her own blanket, the silvery foil crinkling as she drew it around her shoulders.

"What will you do if you lose your ranch?"

"I really don't know," Travis said. "Sometimes, I wish we'd just let it happen so we could get on with our lives." He laughed sourly. "You know something? You're the first person I've ever admitted that to."

"I'm honoured," Riane said. She was teasing, but there was genuine warmth in her tone as well. Travis felt better about her, but that only made what he wanted to ask her more difficult. He took a deep breath, then launched into the subject he had been avoiding since she showed him the requisition forms with Tempke's initials. He was still struggling to come to terms with the idea that the man who represented the Company might be trying to sabotage the project. But there was something else on his mind too.

"Can I ask you something?"

"Of course," Riane said. "What is it?"

"Do you think your father knows what Tempke is doing?" Travis expected Riane to be angry. Instead, when she finally answered, she sounded thoughtful instead.

"I don't think so. My father is not someone who can keep a secret. He is too passionate, too..." She sighed. "Too hot-headed, yes? He has something of a temper."

"Well," Travis said, "at least he and my dad have that much in common."

She laughed softly, but fell serious again. "If my father knew anything about this, I would have known, too. The question is, why would someone like Tempke sabotage his own project?"

"Yeah," Travis admitted, "it doesn't make sense. I mean, if the Company wanted to shut down, they would have just shut us down. As cheap as that outfit is, they would never go to this kind of expense just for an excuse to give up." A new thought occurred to him. "Maybe Tempke is working for someone else, someone who stands to gain if the Company pulls out?"

"Yes," Riane said, "that could explain it. I just wish we knew who it might be."

For a long while, neither spoke, and Travis thought Riane might have fallen asleep again. The wind's howl slackened off a bit. She turned on her couch and faced him.

"When the storm ends, what do we do? What if that thing is still waiting for us outside?"

"Don't worry." Travis tried to sound more confident than he felt. He glanced at the carbine propped against the control panel beside him. Even if he had ammunition, the idea of facing the predator terrified him. Without bullets, it seemed impossible. He smiled, though he doubted she could see it. "We'll think of something."

CHAPTER TWENTY-THREE

Riane got up and hunched over the control panel, feeding data into it with rapid keystrokes. Now and then her actions would be met with a ping or a flash of numbers across one of the screens, but little else. She swore softly with each failure. Travis didn't recognize the words, but he had a pretty good idea what they meant.

"Worthless junk," she muttered. "There is power from the reactor, but nothing will work."

"Are you sure you should be playing with that stuff?" he asked. "I mean, you won't blow up the ship or something, will you?"

She turned and glared at him. "Some of us learned to ride horses when we were babies, some of us learned how to fly starships. Don't worry, I won't blow us up."

"Sorry. Didn't know you were so touchy about it." He rolled over and tried to go back to sleep, but couldn't. Instead, he lay quietly until it was light enough to at least find his way down into the hold without breaking his neck. Even with Beta fully up, the red glow that penetrated the swirling sand outside did little as it poured through the skylights and tiny windows that periodically dotted the inner hull. Water bottle in hand, he felt his way back down the open staircase into the dim hold.

For a long, uncomfortable moment he couldn't see Twitch, and his mind jumped to the worst conclusion. Then the bay mare snorted behind him. She hurried closer and bumped him with her muzzle.

"Hello, girl. Glad to see you, too." Relieved, Travis pushed her aside, then searched around in the gloom until he finally found a rounded plastic lid from a disabled incubator and filled it with water. Moving carefully, desperate not to spill a single precious drop, he shuffled back towards Twitch, stumbling on a discarded power-cell in his path, and placed the makeshift water dish before her.

A piercing blue light cut down from above. Travis threw his forearm up to protect his eyes from the harsh glare. "Why didn't you tell me you had a thumblight?" he demanded.

"You never asked." Riane flicked off the tiny light and held a foil-wrapped packet towards him. Travis took it, surprised that it held liquid instead of food. "I found a couple of juice boxes in the cockpit."

"Do you suppose they're still good?"

"I hope so. I already drank mine." She laughed softly, the sound welcome against the unending wind outside. Travis found the thin plastic straw attached to the packet, peeled it off and jabbed it through the stout foil. The liquid inside was sweet, with a slight lemon flavour that lingered on his tongue after he had sucked up the last lukewarm drop.

"Thanks," he said. "You don't suppose there might be a couple of cases of those laying around somewhere?"

"I doubt it. I searched the ship pretty carefully when I first arrived." She shrugged. "We can look again, if you want, but I doubt it will do much good."

"What else have we got to do?" Travis offered his hand and helped her off the steps. Riane smoothed her tunic over her hips, then lit the tiny thumblight again. He fell in step behind her, letting her pick the way with the miniaturized flashlight. Together, they examined the cargo hold, but as suspected, found nothing useful. Riane paused near the heavy airlock and made certain it was still secure. Then, she turned towards the staircase.

"Wait a minute." Travis pointed towards the far end of the deep, cylindrical hold. "There's a door back that way. Where does it go?"

"The power room, I think."

"Didn't you check it out?"

"No." A note of fear crept into her voice. "I thought it best to leave that door sealed."

"Why? I mean, of all the places we might find something we can use, surely it would be the engineering section."

"Travis... This ship, it is an old-style fusion burner, yes?" Riane pointed her light towards the aft wall. Travis could just make out the heavily shielded hatch nestled in it. A dust-grimed placard picked up the light and tossed it back. Three black triangles against a yellow circle seemed to glow, the warning unmistakable. "If there is a radiation leak in there, we could contaminate the entire ship if we open that hatch."

He stared longingly at the hatch. "I'd still like to look around." Finally, he started back towards the staircase. Twitch shuffled past, still trying to lick the last trace of water from the pan. They waited until the mare was out of the way, then returned to the cockpit, the heat inside the old starship almost more than Travis could take.

The day dragged on, an unending symphony of heat and thirst and howling wind. Travis tried to doze, but couldn't, the stale air inside the abandoned ship stifling. His tongue was thick, as if he'd been eating handfuls of spiderweb, so dry he could think of little else but a long, cold drink of water. Bored, he checked his watch, but it had stopped working again.

"What time is it?" he asked. Riane hadn't spoken in a long time, but he was sure she was awake.

"It's twenty-six forty-five," she said, her voice rough. Travis sighed. At least three more hours before Beta set and the air might cool off. He pushed his matted hair off his forehead, then sat up and ran his hand along the control panel until he found the pair of radios where he had left them. Out of habit, he checked the frequency, then pressed the little communicator to his lips.

"Camp Seven, Travis McClure, come in?"

"Why do you keep trying?" Riane asked, the words barely more than a whisper. "They can't hear us."

"We don't know that for sure. At least, if they pick up the signal they'll know we're alive." He set his own radio back on the panel, then grabbed the one Lebrie had given him. "Travis McClure to Adrian Lebrie. I'm with Riane in the freighter. We're both all right for now." He set the little device beside the other one, then sat a long time staring out of the narrow windows at the sand swirling outside. His eyes drifted down to a thumb-sized adhesive patch glued to the top of the control panel, the circle in the centre of it a dark grey.

"What's that thing?"

"A radiation patch. They tell you if the levels are getting too high." Riane frowned. "Why?"

"Think there are any more of them up here?"

"Maybe. Why?" she asked again.

"I'd really like to look around the power room. We could use one of these patches to see if there's a leak from the reactor, right?"

"Maybe." She propped herself on an elbow so she could face him. "But if you open that hatch and it is contaminated inside, it would already be too late by the time the patch went dark."

"I know. But, we could stick it on the hatch and check back in the morning. Wouldn't that tell us what we wanted to know?"

Her frown deepened, but at last she bobbed her head. "Yes, it would work, *if* the hatch shielding isn't too thick."

"Okay, so it's a risk. But it's still worth a try. Look, if we had ammo for my dad's gun, I could just climb up on top of this ship and pick off those things the second they popped up. But we don't have that option any more."

"So, we wait until my father arrives. He knows where we are."

"Riane..." Travis hesitated. He didn't want to bring up the subject, but had to. "As soon as this storm breaks, your dad is going to hurry over here. But there's a pack of those things waiting out there. He could ride straight into them and never know it until it was too late. Our best chance is to make a run for it the minute the storm ends, while the creatures are still denned up. If we're lucky, we can slip back to your dad and then home before they come out again. But we need something to even up the odds in case things go wrong. We need to find something to use as a weapon."

She closed her eyes. Travis wasn't sure, but he thought she was fighting back tears. Finally, without a word she reached into an overhead bin and pulled out a small patch wrapped in silver foil. She handed it to him.

"But," she said, her eyes stern, "neither of us goes inside until morning. Deal?"

"Deal." Travis took the radiation patch and crawled off the flight couch. Riane called to him as he started down the narrow stairs.

"Take this." She tossed him the thumblight. "You might need it."

He caught the little light out of the air, then hurried down to the hold. The heat below was intense, the hull holding the high temperatures like a kiln. Twitch still stood near the empty pan, her head low, her breath laboured. Without water, the horse wouldn't last much longer. Travis patted her on the shoulder, then hurried to the aft of the compartment. The predator's reek was stronger here, and twice he stepped on bits of bone and eggshell. This freighter had obviously been home to more than just the first generation of the creatures. He reached the sealed hatch and ripped open the little packet with his teeth. The radiation warning glowed above him in the thumblight's sapphire glare. He almost expected sparks to shoot out when he slapped the adhesive back against the heavy steel door, but nothing happened. Finished, he hurried back to the cockpit to wait out the night.

They drank the last of the water at daybreak, then, still thirsty, wandered down to the hold together. Unlike the night before, the temperature inside the freighter had not fallen, the driving wind outside hot even in the darkness. Travis was covered in sweat by the time he reached the hold. Twitch barely noticed as they passed. Travis tried not to think about her as they worked their way aft. Riane swung her light towards the patch. A faint grey smudge ringed the circle's edge.

"Well?" he asked.

She leaned closer until her nose nearly brushed the sealed hatch. "We'll be okay if we don't stay in there very long. But if that door has heavier shielding than most ships, this patch won't be accurate. If that's the case, we won't know it until after we've absorbed a lethal dose."

Travis nodded. "I'll be quick."

"No," she said quietly. "We do this together." She reached past Travis and slapped the door switch. To both their surprise, the sound of electric motors whirred to life as the door slid back.

Red emergency lights flashed on as they stepped inside the maze of machinery and conduits that filled the chamber. Riane brushed past Travis towards a pallet of barrels beneath a chain hoist. He hurried to catch up.

"What's in there?" he asked.

"I don't know." Riane kneeled down beside one of the plastic containers. "It's not for the engines, I can tell you that much. The warning label say they're full of organic synthetics, but I've never seen anything like it."

Travis sniffed the air. The scent was definitely stronger now, the predator's reek so acrid he nearly gagged. A sticky brown residue covered the top of one of the barrels as if someone had spilled some of the contents while pumping it out of the small, round bung.

Riane had already wandered off into the tangled collection of pumps and colour-coded pipes that serviced the fusion core. Her boots clicked against the deck as she wandered in and out of the machinery. She frowned as she studied a tangle of wires running out of the main power unit and leading off towards various other units. Many of them looked to have been hastily spliced together, as if whoever had done the wiring was in a great hurry to finish. "These engines have been tampered with," she called out. "Looks like they're rigged for self-destruction."

"You're kidding, right?"

"I wish I was." Riane looked very uncomfortable. "I could be wrong, but I think we're sitting inside a giant bomb."

Travis started towards her, but stopped when he noticed a crate tucked against one of the heavy steel buttresses that crossed the inner hull. He pushed the lid back and stared at the contents. A double row of finned tubes lay nestled in packing material, the noses tipped pencil-sharp. He lifted one of the metre-long missiles out of the crate and held it at arm's length. The metal tube was heavier than it looked. A green light flashed on above the arming switch as he turned it over. He had seen geologists use missiles like this for seismic tests around the foothills, and knew just how dangerous they could be. He smiled to himself, then called over his shoulder.

"I think I found something we can use against those things."

Riane didn't answer. Worried, he placed the missile back in the crate, but before he stood up, he heard her call his name.

"Travis?" Riane's voice echoed out from the far end of the chamber, muffled by the network of tubing. "You better see this."

He rushed through the jungle of conduits until he spotted her beside a dust-covered control panel. Something lay at her feet. Travis ran the last few paces, then stopped cold. A mummified body was sprawled face down on the deck, shrivelled in the heat until little remained but bones wrapped in dried skin and bits of hair. The blue coveralls it wore were still intact, save for a small hole between the shoulder blades from which a dark brown stain spread. Though he couldn't be certain, the hole looked like a bullet wound to Travis. He forced himself to breathe, the shock more than he expected. Riane turned towards him, her eyes wide.

"I think this man was murdered."

"I think you're right." Travis started to say more, but stopped. One glance at Riane convinced him she was thinking the same thing he was. Not only was Allen Tempke a saboteur. Now, he was also the prime suspect in a murder.

"Let's get out of here," Travis muttered. Riane nodded, and together they hurried back out into the main hold, stopping long enough to grab a pair of the heavy, shoulder-fired missiles. He didn't relax until the hatch slid shut once more behind them. "What happened out here?"

Riane started to say something, but stopped. She held up her hand for him to be quiet as she listened, her head cocked to one side. "Do you hear that?"

"Hear what?"

"The storm," she said. "I think it's stopping."

Travis listened. The howl had almost died away, the sand pinging against the hull quiet for the first time in two days. He stared at the main hatch and shifted the heavy missiles on his shoulder. "We better hurry. If we're going to go, now is the time."

CHAPTER TWENTY-FOUR

The light inside the cargo bay brightened as the sandstorm faded. Travis saddled Twitch while Riane climbed back to the cockpit to gather their gear. He stroked the mare's neck and hoped she would be stronger once they left the oven-like hold. As it was, the horse could barely walk, let alone carry them should they have to make a run for it. Footsteps clanged down the narrow stairs. Riane jumped the last three steps to the deck, her bag slung across her back. She held his dad's carbine out to him, but Travis shook his head.

"You'll have to carry that." He picked up the pair of

missiles he had found in the power room and hoisted them over his shoulder. "I'll need both hands free just in case."

They moved to the main hatch. Twitch lagged behind, her steps slow and uneven. Riane moved to one side of the broad hatch and grabbed the steel ring. "So, how do we do this?"

Travis snugged his hat down, then glanced at the exhausted horse, hating what he had to say. "You and me will open the doors. We'll send Twitch out first."

"If one of those things is waiting out there, she won't have a chance."

"I know." He felt like a traitor. "But it's better they attack her than you or me." Travis leaned the pair of missiles against the hull, then wrapped his hands around the heavy wheel. "Okay. Let's do this."

He leaned against the stubborn mechanism, using his weight to turn the wheel. A thin crack of light appeared in the hatch as the two sides began to retract. Travis gave a sharp jerk on the ring, and the hatch split open. Fresh air poured inside, the flinty taste of sand and pulverized rock as welcome as rain compared to the stale odours inside the derelict freighter. He spun harder and the gap widened enough to walk through.

"Okay, step back."

Travis barely had the words out his mouth when Twitch lumbered past him, nearly knocking him to the deck in her haste to get outside. He snatched up one of the missiles and flicked the arming switch. His thumb rested above the tiny trigger as he crept to the gap and kneeled down.

The seconds dragged on, the only sound Twitch's slow footsteps outside. Travis tried to swallow, but his throat was too dry. His legs felt heavy, as if they were glued to the deck. Silently, he counted to three, then darted outside.

After two days inside the dim hold, even Beta's feeble glow seemed bright. Travis squinted, swing his head back and forth, looking at every shadow. Sand had piled up around the freighter, the landing gear nearly buried in the coarse red grit. Riane joined him outside.

"Do you see anything?"

"No." Travis ducked back inside for the other missile and threw both of the projectiles over his shoulder, then hurried to catch Twitch before she wandered too far. Together, they moved across the crater floor towards the dark bulk of Mount Hobbs. Riane wrapped the reins around her hand while Travis stepped out in front. Ankle-high dunes slowed their progress, the sand soft and uneven. The missiles dragged him off balance, and he had to stop frequently to shift them on his shoulders. At this rate it would take hours to reach the little cave where Lebrie and Bart Caddy had sheltered. Travis staggered to the top of the crater rim, every step an effort, and looked around.

The wind had scoured most of the vegetation away; even the twisted bits of sagebrush had been stripped bare. Fresh dunes stretched toward the badlands like ripples on a frozen pond. Mount Hobbs towered on their left. Frothy pink cloud twisted in the sky above it, more remnants of the storm's passage. Nothing moved across the landscape except them. A wave of relief washed over him as they started down the other side. Then Travis stopped, the hair on the back of his neck rising as he caught a familiar scent.

"Travis..." Riane whispered, her voice thick with fear. "Look behind you."

He turned slowly and stared back at the caldera's rim. A narrow grey head on a snake's neck swung back and forth, silhouetted against the pale sky. The predator's tongue flicked in and out as it searched for their scent. Suddenly, it stopped, its yellow, slitted eyes staring straight at him.

"Get on the horse," he said.

"But..."

"Don't argue with me." He sank to one knee, his eyes never leaving the predator perched twenty metres away on the crater lip. "Please. Just for once don't argue. Get on that horse and go."

"What are you going to do?"

Travis flicked the arming switch again. The green light flashed to red as he slid the safety latch away from the trigger then set the missile on his shoulder, the tip trained on the predator. As if it sensed what was about to happen, the creature hissed, then dropped back down the other side, hidden from sight. Every nerve in his body said run, but he fought down the panic as he scanned the horizon. "Riane, get on that horse...now."

Without warning, the sand above them erupted. The creature leaped over the rim and charged. Travis waited until its green-grey body filled the crude sight window, then squeezed the trigger.

The stubby missile whooshed off his shoulder, a white vapour trail curling behind it. Travis held his breath as he watched the projectile speed towards the advancing animal. At the last moment, the creature twisted aside. The missile thumped into the deep sand behind it and buried itself. Instinctively, Travis crouched lower. He had watched the geologists detonate dozens of the little warheads, and despite their compact size, knew how potent they could be. His heart sank as nothing happened. Instead of a flash and burst of shattered rock, an oily mist spread around the impact. The predator screamed in rage and jumped, its powerful hind feet splayed wide, the deadly, sickle-shaped claws ready to slash. Terrified, Travis fumbled for the second shot.

Too late, he realized he didn't have time to arm the missile before the creature would be on him. He pulled the second projectile to his chest and spun around, desperately searching for cover. An ancient geyser rose out of the sand forty metres to his right, a steep, curved cliff behind it, with a small ledge near the summit. Travis ran towards the cliff, hampered by the missile. A twisted bit of sagebrush poked through the sand and snagged his foot, and he slammed to the ground. He could almost feel the deadly talons sink through the unprotected flesh in the small of his back.

"Travis!" Riane shouted at him from the top of the next dune. "Look behind you!"

He rolled to his feet and stared back at the predator. Instead of attacking him, the animal was spinning madly around the spot where the first missile struck, snapping and striking at the air around it. The bright feathers along its spine stood high, fluttering as the animal leaped and twisted, sand churning beneath its feet. Above it, a second creature arrived and screamed, the wail so loud Travis winced. It pounced high and struck the first creature in the ribs, and together they rolled down the incline, kicking and gouging each other.

Hoof beats struck the hard ground nearby. Travis twisted around and saw Riane kicking her heels madly into Twitch's flank, trying to force her down the slope towards him. The horse shied as another of the creatures arrived, its whip-thin tail slashing the air.

"Riane, no! Get away!" He could barely get the words out. Missile in hand, he dashed once more towards the dormant geyser, desperate to reach the ledge before the fighting creatures noticed him again. His lungs burned, his muscles already spent as he stumbled more than ran the last ten metres and slammed painfully into the cliff.

Gasping for air, he struggled to climb. The stone, far from being solid, crumbled as he fought for purchase and he slipped back to the ground less than a metre from the geyser's throat. The dry fissure twisted deep into the lava beneath his feet. One misstep would send him tumbling into the bottomless chasm. To the west, yet another of the creatures had arrived, but instead of joining the melee near the first strike, it charged arrow-straight towards the cliff. Travis tucked the second missile to his side and tried once more to scale the low pitch.

The creature closed on him, then suddenly stopped. It twisted its long neck back and forth as if it couldn't decide whether to attack Travis or the rest of the pack. Travis wasted no time and climbed faster, still making slow progress. Rocks broke free under his hands and spun downward, bouncing and clattering into the throat. His left foot slipped and he nearly fell backwards, but he found another toehold. Frantic now, he reached above his head with his free hand. His fingers slipped over the ledge. With what strength remained in his exhausted muscles, he pulled himself onto the narrow shelf.

Below him, a scene from hell unfolded. Three more of the predators had arrived, juveniles by their size, screaming and spitting at each other as they converged on the free-for-all along the caldera rim. The nearest of the creatures turned once more towards where he clung and advanced, neck stiff, the blue and green feathers on its back raised like a crest. Travis flicked the arming switch on and slid the safety back on the remaining missile. The monster grew in his sight, a writhing blur of scales and leathery skin. He held his breath and tracked the creature closer. He was only going to get one shot.

Without warning, the ledge beneath him crumbled. Rocks pounded down the low face as Travis began to fall. Unable to do anything else he tossed the missile away and scrabbled to find handholds in the soft rock. He slid halfway down the face before he caught another ledge, barely wide enough to stand on. Five metres below, the little projectile hit the ground, rolled towards the geyser's throat, then stopped.

"Stay where you are!" Riane shouted. Once more on foot, she darted out from the edge of the cliff and ran headlong towards the chasm.

"No! Get back!" Travis yelled. She ignored him. The creature raised its neck and screamed. Riane scooped up the fallen missile and pointed it at the thing's chest, then, unexpectedly, swung the nose away towards the barren dunes behind it. Before Travis could stop her, she squeezed the trigger.

The projectile tore away, twisting along its flight path as it flashed past the creature on the other side of the pit and struck harmlessly in the sand a hundred metres away. Instead of climbing up towards him, Riane huddled at the base of the cliff, her gaze locked on the creature.

"What are you doing?" Travis shouted down at her. "Get up here!"

"Wait." She raised her hand and gestured for him to be quiet. Travis felt sick as the animal inched along the edge of the geyser, stalking Riane. It paused, twisted its head to the side, then turned around. An oily, ammonia-laced scent washed over them, carried on the breeze from where the second missile had detonated. To his amazement, the creature charged towards the shallow pit the strike had gouged out. Several of the others broke away from the first battle and hurried to meet the newcomer.

"Come on." Riane waved him down. "It won't hold them long."

Travis slid the rest of the way down the cliff, the rock rough against his body. Riane grabbed his hand and dragged him back the way she had come. Twitch stood around the far side of the little cliff, the reins wrapped around a boulder at her feet. Her nostrils flared as they arrived.

"She's too weak to ride any further," Riane gasped. Travis nodded, grabbed the reins and untied the mare. The screams of the creatures battling less than a hundred metres away on the other side of the little cliff filled the air. Together, they ran as fast as they could, and didn't pause until they reached the edge of Mount Hobbs.

"What..." Travis leaned forward, hands on his knees, and tried to catch his breath. A deep pain twisted in his side from the headlong run. "What happened?"

Riane tried to answer, but began to cough. She

doubled over and sank to her knees as she fought to regain control of her lungs. Finally, she raised her head. "It's their scent. That's what was in the missiles. Somebody was using them to bait the creatures in."

Suddenly, Travis understood. He recalled hearing how trappers back home had used scent as a lure. The memory of the freighter's hold flashed in his mind. "That's what was in those barrels, wasn't it? But why would it make them attack each other like that?"

"Scent was the most powerful sense among tyrannosaurids and other predatory dinosaurs." Riane nodded to herself as she spoke. "Certainly, they would have used it to attract mates. And many modern reptiles will fight to the death if they catch the scent of a rival male. Why should this predator be any different?"

"All right. I can buy that," Travis said. "But why would anyone want to gather them all together in the first place?"

"I wish I knew," she said. Travis helped her to her feet, then took a look around to get his bearings. The ground sloped gently away down a long, barren slope stripped clean by the sandstorm. To the east, a dust cloud moved towards them, and for one sickening moment Travis thought another pack had picked up their scent. He put his hand over his eyes and squinted at the cloud, then grinned. Two riders on horses, one a tall bay, the other a squat, black and white paint, raced towards them. Behind followed another bay and a sturdy grey mule. He pointed at the riders.

"There's your dad."

"I see him." Riane waved her hands over her head to catch the riders' attention. The little group veered towards them, and within minutes had reached the top of the low rise. Adrian Lebrie nearly fell off the paint gelding in his haste to reach his daughter. He threw his arms around her and practically smothered her in a long hug. "*O, mon dieu!*" he said as he finally released her. Travis laughed quietly. He had heard Riane use the same expression at least a hundred times over the last two days. The exo-biologist wiped the dust-streaked sweat off his high forehead. "We feared the worst."

"We're all right." Riane's smile faded. "But we can't stay here. Too many of those creatures are back there."

"What creatures?" Bart Caddy said, his face suddenly pale. "Are you talking about that near-rapter thing?"

"Yes, of course," Riane said, dismissing him as if he was a child asking stupid questions. She stepped beside her father and pointed at the extinct geyser field still in view. "Wait until I show you what I've learned about their behaviour."

Travis laughed inwardly at the way she conveniently ignored any contribution he had made in the discovery, but said nothing. Sweetheart stood nervously beside the mule, a makeshift lead rope coiled in Bart's hand. Travis took the rope from him, then gently approached the rangy mare, careful not to startle her. His hands slid down her neck and under her belly as he searched for injuries. "You okay, girl?"

"She came wandering in not long after you left us the other day. That's when we thought you might be in trouble." Bart actually sounded apologetic. "We wanted to come after you, but the storm hit."

"Did you radio the camp yet?" Travis asked.

"Been trying all day." Bart shrugged. "Either we got sand in ours and they're busted, or the wind took the camp's antenna out again."

"Yeah. Mine doesn't work either." Travis gave Sweetheart a closer look. The mare seemed none the worse for her adventure. She shifted under his weight as he swung up, but made no attempt to toss him out of the saddle. He started to breathe easier, until he remembered the pack of predators fighting each other less than two kilometres away. He moved up beside Riane.

"I think we better go."

She nodded, but her father seemed not to notice. His gaze was locked on the little collection of dry fumaroles to the south. Dust still churned where the animals fought one another, driven mad by the scent-laced missiles. Riane took him by the sleeve and pulled him around. "Father, we are not safe here."

"But this is the chance of a lifetime. We may never get another opportunity to study them like this."

"It doesn't matter," Riane said, more forcefully. She lead Twitch a little closer, then untied the carbine from the saddle horn where they had lashed it after leaving the derelict freighter. She handed it up to Travis, then climbed aboard the tired mare. "We have no protection. The gun is empty."

"It's what?" Bart's voice rose in pitch, his eyes wide. He led the paint gelding towards Lebrie. "I think she's right, Doc. It's best we get a move on."

Reluctantly, Lebrie took the reins and climbed aboard, still clumsy in the saddle. He twisted around for one last look, the resentment plain on his face, then fell in step with the others as they rode away.

CHAPTER TWENTY-FIVE

They stopped at the tiny cave on Mount Hobbs's flank to retrieve Lebrie's gear and water the horses before starting out once more. Twitch drank every last drop left in the pan and would have drunk more had there been any, but seemed to recover her strength as they turned north across the rolling hills. Travis kept to the back, constantly looking over his shoulder every time the wind shifted or a rabbit crossed their path. Ahead of him, Lebrie sat on the paint gelding, lost in thought. Travis noted with resentment that Riane and Bart rode side by side, talking and laughing as if they were out for a picnic.

"Gee, thanks for saving my life, Trav," he muttered. Sweetheart flicked a neatly pointed ear at the sound of his voice, but no one else seemed to notice he even existed. He thought about racing ahead and tapping Bart on the shoulder just to hear him shriek, but knew he wouldn't. As much as he hated to admit it, if Lebrie and Bart hadn't arrived when they did with fresh horses and water, he doubted they could have stayed ahead of the pack.

He was getting awfully tired of people saving his life.

A thick brown haze surrounded Camp Seven as they topped the final ridge south of the ragtag encampment, the dust cloud heavier than usual. Suddenly, a low, thumping growl, overlaid with a high-pitched whine shook the air. Startled, he craned his neck back as a heavy transport thundered overhead. The machine banked towards the landing field, hovered a moment, then settled to ground.

"What's going on up there?" Bart asked, confused.

"I don't know," Travis answered. "But I'm about to find out."

He dug his heels into Sweetheart's ribs. The mare needed no more urging, and broke into an easy lope across the alkali flat. Travis let her run. The closer he drew to camp, the tighter the lump in his chest became. Everywhere through the dust he saw men and women scurrying back and forth as they carted heavy bundles inside a long line of crawlers idling along the edge of the compound. As he pulled up outside the meteorology trailer, Alice Prevoroski saw him and waved.

"Look what the wind's blown in." She set down the box she was carrying and hurried towards Travis. "Good to see you, kiddo. You don't know how worried everyone's been about you."

"Yeah, well..." He let his voice trail off as he stepped to the ground. His legs were stiff from the long ride. "I kind of got sidetracked. Are we moving south?"

"No." Alice shook her head. The little spikes in her hair flopped back and forth. "We're pulling up stakes and returning to Base Camp."

"Why?" The lump tightened a bit more inside him. "What's going on?"

"Travis." Alice hesitated, her smile forced. "The Company's recalled everyone. They're shutting down the project permanently."

"They can't do that," Travis blurted. "Not yet. Where's my dad?"

"Out looking for you." Alice flexed her thin eyebrows, a discreet warning. "He wasn't too happy about your being gone during the storm." She reached out and gave his shoulder a squeeze. "I'll see if I can raise him on the radio and let him know you're back."

"Thanks," Travis said, his mind elsewhere. He led Sweetheart through the tumult towards the corral. The tack trailer was already hitched to a crawler, and he had to rummage through the crates and tightly packed gear to find enough grain to feed her. He poured the rolled oats in a pan and let her eat while he unsaddled her, then turned her loose in the pen. A familiar whicker caught his ear as the gate swung open. Deuce trotted out of the herd and nuzzled Travis under the arm, cadging an extra bite of grain.

"Hey, take it easy!" Travis laughed as the old horse nearly knocked him off his feet in his eagerness. "Glad to see you, too."

He went back outside and returned with a pan of oats for Deuce, then stood beside him as he licked it clean. Travis sighed as he stroked the horse's neck. Outside, the activity had picked up, everyone hurrying to finish before darkness fell. Even the sight of Bart leading Riane off towards the mess tent, his arm slipped neatly around her waist, couldn't distract Travis from the hard reality that the project was dead. He gave Deuce a final pet, then left the corral and turned towards his own tent.

Bachelors' Row was already gone, nothing left but the imprints of the tents in the sand. He saw his mom standing over a low mound of sleeping bags and gear. She looked exhausted, her hair tied up with a scarf, dark streaks running down her forehead. She saw Travis and threw her arms around him.

"Oh, thank goodness." She squeezed harder, her arms wrapped tight.

"Mom, I can't breathe."

"Sorry." Angie McClure laughed, the worry lines slipping away. She took Travis's hat off his head and pulled him closer again, her face buried in his hair.

Suddenly, she pushed him away, the smile replaced by an angry glare. "What possessed you to pull a stunt like that? You promised you'd be back before the storm hit."

"I know." He felt ashamed now that the ordeal was over. He had barely given a thought to how worried his parents might be during the long days behind him. "I'm sorry. I really am. But it's a good thing I went. Riane could have been killed if I hadn't." He didn't add that she had saved his life as well. He put his hat back on and tugged it down, then set his gear and the carbine on top of the pile. "Mom, wait till you hear what we found out there. Someone sabotaged the project, and we think we know who."

Angie McClure sighed. Travis had never seen so much hurt and fear in her deep green eyes before. "It really doesn't matter now. They're shutting us down permanently."

"They can't just shut everything down. Can they?"

"I don't think they had any choice. A Federated cruiser broke out of N-space yesterday to enforce the injunction. Word is there's a garrison of troops aboard. One way or the other, I'm afraid it's over." She tried to smile but couldn't. Her gaze drifted outward to where a small party of riders approached, their shadows long against the hard, uncaring ground. She nodded at them. "That'll be your dad, coming in. Better go tell him what happened."

"Yeah." Travis took a deep breath, dreading the meeting ahead as he trudged back towards the corral.

Jim McClure reined in his horse and let the other riders go on, waiting until he and Travis were alone. He stepped off the big grey and let the reins fall to the ground. Travis flinched as he walked towards him, unsure what to expect. He knew his dad's temper all too well, but McClure simply stopped in front of his son and took off his sunglasses.

"Well?"

"Dad, I..." Travis's words failed. He swallowed and tried again. "I know it was stupid, what I did. And I shouldn't have done it, but, I couldn't just leave them out there to die, could I?"

"Might have been better for all of us if they had." Jim McClure put his glasses back on and stared off into the distance, his jaw clenched. When he spoke again, his voice was low, filled with cold, aching resentment, a man betrayed. "You heard they're shutting us down?"

"Dad, we have to stop them. We can't let them close the project down."

"Funny," McClure said. "I'd have thought you'd be thrilled by the news, considering how much you hate this place. Thought you and your girlfriend would have been dancing for joy."

Travis stared down at his feet. "That's unfair."

"Oh? Well it's true, isn't it? If it wasn't for Adrian Lebrie and the Free Planet people who hold his leash, none of this would have happened." A gust of wind shook the metal panels as one of the transports lifted off. McClure stared at Travis, his eyes unreadable behind the dark glasses. "Guess I know which side of the fence you stand on."

"Dad..."

"You risked your life to save the man who's shutting us down." McClure turned his back and started away, his steps long and even. "Hope you're happy with the choices you made."

Travis watched his father walk away. He was shaking, his legs unsteady, his fists bunched tight at his side. A single fat tear rolled down his face. He swiped it away. The things his father had said stung deeper than he could have believed a few days ago. Another transport circled the landing field, then set down in a cloud of dust. Not far behind it, a single-seat jump-bug descended nearly vertically and touched down beside it. Allen Tempke crawled out of the cockpit door and jogged towards his office, the trailer already hitched behind a crawler. Travis's shame turned to anger as he watched the man strut around, tossing orders at every person he passed. His resolve returned, he spun on his heel and started after his father.

He found him standing beside the rolled-up tent, talking to his mom. Travis stepped closer, stopped and cleared his throat to get his attention.

"Dad, everything you said might have been true once. I did hate this place. Maybe I still do. But before you accuse me, you ought to know everything I've done, I did for you." The words poured out, and he couldn't have stopped them if he'd wanted to. "Do you really think I don't want to save the ranch? It's the only home I've ever known, unless you count this hellhole. But I was even willing to put up with Aletha, because I knew we had to. And if I've done anything wrong, it was because I had to do it. I was doing my job, just like you would have if you were in my shoes. So don't blame me for sticking to something, because that's the way you raised me."

He stood, ready at any moment to feel the back of his father's hand across his cheek. Instead, Jim McClure's shoulders slumped, the lines on his face so deep they looked like rivers etched in his weather-beaten skin. He took off his dark glasses and Travis saw tears rim his eyes. He took his son in his arms and pulled him close.

"Trav, I didn't know you felt that way. I'm sorry."

"So am I." Travis's own eyes blurred with salty tears, and he didn't try to hold them back.

Angie McClure joined them, and they stood together, arms wrapped around one another for what seemed an eternity, before the sound of yet another transport spooling up for take-off broke the moment. Embarrassed by his unexpected display of emotion, Travis wiped his face with his sleeve and looked back towards what remained of camp. "Dad, there's something you need to know. I don't know if we can prove it yet, but I think I know who brought the predators to this planet. It was Tempke."

"What?" McClure's eyebrows pinched together. "Why would Tempke sabotage his own project?"

"I don't know, but we found the ship that brought the things here. It's abandoned out in Scratch's Dooryard, and there was a notebook on board full of invoices with Tempke's initials on them. And there's all sorts of incubating equipment and scent-lure in the hold."

"Are you sure?"

"Pretty sure," Travis said. "Riane told me Tempke was the one who contacted the Free Planet Society, not the other way around. Why would he have done that if he didn't want Lebrie to find those things?" Travis paused, recalling suddenly how eager Tempke had been for him to pick up the creature's trail after his own encounter with the predator. He stiffened, the implications suddenly all too real. Tempke wanted the creatures to be found so the project would be shut down. "There's something else you should know. At least one of the crewmen on the freighter was murdered. We found his body in the engine room. Looks like he was shot in the back. There might be others, but we didn't have time to look for them."

"That worthless..." Jim McClure's voice trailed off as his gaze drifted towards Tempke's office. "I wonder if Alice could access his off-planet records?"

"I don't know," Travis's mom said, cold determination in her voice. "But I know how we can find out if he's been at that freighter." She glanced at the jump-bug. "Watch my back a minute, okay? I'm going to go take the inertial guidance logs out of his transponder. I doubt he's found a way to erase those yet."

"Be careful," Jim McClure said to her. He turned to Travis and clapped him on the shoulder. "You stay here and keep an eye out for trouble. I'll go talk to Alice about the commo records."

"Okay." Travis settled down on the pile of gear to wait, and tried not to look too suspicious as he stared around the rapidly dwindling camp. From the pace things were going, nothing would be left to pack by the time night settled in. He twisted at the waist and looked towards the corral. A small group of people was marching towards it, Bart Caddy in the lead. The heavy lump returned deep inside Travis's stomach. He saw one of the geologists who had helped them drive the cattle south a few days earlier, and ran towards him.

"What are they doing at the horse pen?" Travis asked, panting from the run.

"Turning the horses loose, I think." The man scratched the stubble under his chin. "Tempke said we can't take them with us."

Travis shut his eyes, the thought of Deuce being torn to shreds by the predators more than he could handle. His mother and Tempke's jump-bug forgotten, he rushed towards the pen, nothing in his mind but the need to stop Bart Caddy before he opened the gate.

CHAPTER TWENTY-SIX

Dust swirled up from inside the pen, churned by the horses, as Bart reached for the latch. He didn't see Travis until he slammed against him and knocked him from his feet. They struck the ground and rolled apart. The others at the pen stepped aside as Travis jumped to his feet. Bart stared up at him from the manure-speckled sand.

"What was that about?"

"You're not turning those horses loose." Travis kept his eyes on Caddy as he moved in a loose circle towards the gate and blocked the latch with his body.

"Look, Trav..." Bart Caddy crawled to his feet and

winced as he rubbed the spot under his armpit where Travis had hit him. "I don't like the idea either, but what are we going to do? Tempke said turn the horses out."

"I'm not moving."

"Don't be a jackass." Bart stepped towards him. "What did you expect the Company to do? We're lucky they'll pay to boost us off this place before they shut it down. Now, move over before I knock you on your butt."

New thunder rattled the pen as yet another transport, sleeker than the others, its black hull studded with weapon ports, settled to ground. Travis pulled closer against the gate as Bart advanced. His resolve started to slip. What Bart said was true, the Company would never pay to move the horses off-planet. Not now, not with the terraforming project abandoned. And, he thought sourly, at least they hadn't ordered the animals to be put down. Behind him, Travis felt something soft and warm against the base of his neck and twisted around. Deuce stood at the rail, begging another bite of grain. Travis turned back around.

"I'm not moving," he repeated.

"You spoiled little brat." Bart's hand closed over Travis's shoulder as he yanked him away from the latch. "Get the hell out of my way."

Almost as if someone else was in charge of his reflexes, Travis felt his right fist swing upward in a lightning fast arc. Bart's own inertia worked against him as he pulled Travis away from the fence, the movement adding force to the blow. The flesh around Bart's jaw sank in as the uppercut struck. The larger, older Caddy staggered backwards, a stunned expression on his face as he landed on his backside. A trickle of blood seeped out of his lower lip.

"You little..." Bart's hand went to his mouth. His eyes squeezed to slits as he saw the blood on his fingers. Faster than Travis could believe, Bart leaped to his feet and threw his body against him. Sharp pain exploded under his ribs as Bart's fist slammed into his stomach. Travis felt his feet leave the ground, and before he could recover, a second punch landed above his left eye. Flashes of white flame danced past his vision as he toppled to the ground beside the fence. He tried to crawl to his feet, but a kick from Bart's scuffed boot sent him rolling away from the gate.

"Stay down unless you want some more of this." Bart stood over him, the blood from his lip pouring out faster. "Understand me?"

"Go to hell." Travis struggled to his feet, blinded by anger, his only thought to pay back some of the pain and humiliation Bart had just given him. Head down like a bull, he charged. Bart sidestepped the clumsy attack, stretched out his leg and sent Travis sprawling once more in the dust.

"I warned you." Bart edged closer. "I told you to stay down. This time, I'm going to put your smart-ass lights out."

"Not unless you go through me first." Jim McClure burst out of the growing crowd gathered around the fight. He struck Bart in the face, then stepped back as Caddy staggered against the gate. Unable to stand, he crashed to the ground and curled up, knees drawn against his chest. McClure faced the crowd. "What's wrong with you people? You'd stand there and let a grown man beat up a kid?"

"Hey," said one of the bystanders, a technician in oil-stained coveralls and a welding-burned cap. "Your kid was the one who started it. Bart was just trying to do what he was told."

"Yeah?" McClure's scowl deepened until his eyes seemed like two points set in stone. "Well guess what? No one is turning these horses loose. Not until we get a few things straightened out around here."

He helped Travis to his feet. "You okay?" McClure asked quietly.

Travis nodded. The pain in his stomach had faded to a dull glow, but he felt sick, his legs wobbly. He took up position on his father's left side, the two of them all that stood between the crowd and the horse pen.

"Look, Jim..." The technician with the dirty coveralls stepped forward. "It's over. Don't get yourself fired over something as stupid as this."

"Fired?" McClure started to laugh. "Is that all you people think about? After everything that's happened, you're still worried the Company's going to fire you?"

"That's right," the technician said, his face flushed

with anger. "Maybe you've got it made when you go home to Earth, but the rest of us don't."

Travis snorted at the irony of it, that the people he had spent the last five years working side by side with would turn on them as if they had no stake in the outcome. He cleared his throat and spat, ignoring the fire in his side where Bart's boot had landed.

"Don't any of you get it?" Travis looked around the ring of faces. "This is all a set-up. Tempke has been using us. I don't know why, but he's the one who brought the predators to Aletha. And he's the one who made sure an injunction got slapped against us."

"Kid, seems like every time there's trouble, you're mixed up in it." The technician pointed at him and shook his finger. "I don't know where you come up with these stories, but we're getting sick of them."

"Shut up, Bob." Candy Ness stepped out of the ring. "I want to hear what the kid has to say." She turned towards Travis. "What makes you think Tempke's behind this?"

"Well..." He tried to explain, but the sea of angry questioning eyes seemed to steal the words from his throat. Beside him, Jim McClure nodded for him to continue.

"Go ahead and tell them what you told me."

Travis squared his shoulders. "Those creatures, the predators that killed Lefty and have been going after the stock? They were genetically engineered and brought here aboard an unmarked star-freighter.

It's still down at Scratch's Dooryard where it was abandoned. And, it's got a bunch of hand-missiles loaded with the creature's scent in the hold. Somebody has been making sure those things would be out there to cause us a problem." A low murmur ran around the circle. "Whoever brought the things here wanted them to be found. They wanted the project shut down."

"But what's Tempke's part?" Candy asked, loud enough for her voice to carry. By now, most of the camp had turned out, a mob on the verge of a riot.

"I'll tell you." A thin figure with spiked black hair pushed towards the horse pen, elbowing her way through the crowd. Alice Prevoroski waved a flat-screen over her head like a flag. Everyone drew in as she handed McClure the little reader. Quietly, she said, "Tempke was smart enough to purge his call records, but he didn't bother with his tax returns. I hacked the computer at Base Camp and got a look at his financial statement. He's bought heavy into New Earth."

Travis's eyes widened. New Earth Enterprises were the second-largest terraformers in the business, and the Company's only serious competition. Alice smiled at Travis and winked.

"You done good, kiddo. Tempke's the man, all right." She turned back to the crowd and raised her voice. "Allen Tempke has been buying stock in New Earth for the last six or seven years. And not just a little bit, either. He's into them several million dollars. My guess is he's working both sides of the fence. Advanced Terraformers hired him as a foreman, but New Earth is paying him off to make sure the project fails. Then, when the Company pulls out, guess who moves back in and finishes the job?"

"Lies. Every word of it."

As one, the gathered people spun around. Allen Tempke stood on the edge of the circle, a tight squad of uniformed men in full battle-gear behind him. More Federated troops poured out of the black-hulled transport as he spoke. He moved towards a nearby crawler, a small pack clenched in his left hand, and climbed up on the tread so everyone could see him.

"These people," Tempke pointed at Alice and the McClures, "are trying to excuse their own incompetence at my expense. Jim McClure was the one who got Lefty killed, not me. He's the one who moved the herd south against orders. Now, he's trying to stop all of you from being evacuated before it's too late. You want to listen to him, fine. But trust me, when the last ship breaks orbit, there won't be any more. Unless you want to spend the rest of your life stranded here, I'd suggest you load up in those transports now."

"Don't try to lie your way out of this," Travis shouted, so mad his voice jumped in pitch. He struggled to stay calm. "This is all your doing, and we know it."

"Really? Where's your proof?" Tempke smiled, but his eyes were cold. Travis glared at the older man.

"There's a requisition book aboard that freighter with your initials all over it. I'll bet it has your fingerprints in it, too."

"Really?" Tempke snorted with pure disgust. "So where is this mythical starship, huh? How do we know that it even exists? The only thing we know for certain is that you have a little tendency to tell big stories."

"You're lying!" Travis shouted. "I'll take anyone out to the ship this minute and prove it."

"Forget it." Tempke waved his hand dismissively. "Face it. You've got nothing."

"We already know the freighter is real," Jim McClure said. "And that's enough to ask for a full investigation from Base Camp. And until we get an answer from them, no one leaves this camp."

"You already have your answer." Tempke leaped off the tread and faced one of the troopers with him. "Sergeant Garcia, would you escort these people out of here?"

"Yes, sir." Garcia barked over his shoulder and pointed at the ground near his left foot. "Form left, here!"

The troops swung into a tight semicircle, then stepped forward in a single, unbreakable line. Tempke smirked as the crowd began to spread out, the herders and technicians uncertain what to do. Travis saw their chance slipping away, and as loud as he could, shouted at Tempke, "Why don't you tell us what happened to the freighter's crew? Who's the dead man in the power room?"

Everyone, troops and herders alike stopped. They stared first at Travis, then turned towards Tempke. The foreman clenched his jaws, the tendons along his throat so tight it looked as if they might snap. "Don't try to turn this around with another one of your wild stories. We've heard enough of those already, Mr. McClure."

"Why don't you answer his question?"

Travis spun around, amazed to see it was Bart Caddy who had shouted. Despite the dirt and blood on his face, he stood straight and pointed at Tempke. "I know I'd like to hear a little more about it."

"Why ask me?" Tempke sounded confident, but his face had lost all colour. "I've never shot anyone."

"I never mentioned that he was shot," Travis said.

"Yeah, that's right," Candy Ness said. "So how come you know about it?" More people started shouting questions at Tempke, everyone speaking at once. Tempke's lips moved, but no words came out. He backed up a few steps until he stood behind Garcia and his troops, then waved his arm at the mob inching toward him.

"Damn it! Disperse that crowd, Garcia."

The soldiers shifted the stubby rifles in their arms and held them waist high, the muzzles trained on the people gathered around the horse corral. Tempke's face fell further as, instead of breaking, the crowd pulled in tighter around the gate. Some of them crossed their arms over their chests while others shook their fists at the troopers. Jim McClure stepped out until he was only a few paces from the man named Garcia.

"Is this how it's going to be?" McClure said. "Are you and your men prepared to kill us over a pen full of horses?"

Garcia stared at him, his expression unreadable. No one spoke, the only sound the rising wind. Travis pushed his way through the crowd and stood beside his father. Alice Prevoroski and some of the others moved forward too. After what seemed for ever, Garcia lowered his weapon. Tempke, panic building on his face, shoved the nearest trooper forward.

"What's wrong with you? You have your orders. Fire!"

"Mr. Tempke." Garcia pushed his heavy helmet back from his forehead. "My orders were to make sure this evacuation proceeded in an orderly fashion. They don't say anything about shooting unarmed civilians." He put his rifle on safety, stepped towards Travis and his dad, then took his place in line with them. A wry grin split his face as he spoke quietly to McClure. "Grew up on a ranch myself. Never could stand guys like that one." He pointed at Tempke. "Corporal, would you escort Mr. Tempke to his trailer until we can get someone from Advanced Terraforming here to take over?"

A woman in battle armour, a few strands of blonde hair peeking out from beneath her padded helmet, stepped towards Tempke, but he twisted away. Something bright flashed in his hand. "Look out," she shouted. "He's got a cap-knife!"

Tempke swung the blade around him then darted inside the crawler and slammed the cab door shut. People and soldiers alike scattered as the machine roared to life. The treads kicked dirt high into the air as it swung towards the landing field. Running at full speed, the bulky machine bounced over the rock-littered terrain, and before anything could be done, rammed the black-hulled transport head on. The horrible crunch of metal on metal and shattered plastic ripped around camp. A loud hiss came from the vehicle as an icy-white cloud spurted out from beneath it.

"He's ruptured the fuel cells!" someone shouted. "Get down!"

Travis hit the dirt only seconds before the two machines, the crawler and the troop transport, burst into flame. Pieces of hot steel whirred overhead as the hydrogen tanks aboard the aerial personnel carrier exploded. Against the backdrop of flames he saw two figures moving towards the other transport. From the looks of them they appeared to be fighting, but before he could see more a wall of acrid smoke rolled over the camp. Travis climbed to his feet, and began to cough as the smoke poured down his throat. Blinded by it, he stumbled upwind, desperate to reach fresh air. Other engines revved up, and through the roiling haze he caught a glimpse of the last transport rising above the flames. The machine struggled awkwardly into the air and banked away. Eyes burning, Travis followed his father and the others upwind, out of the toxic fumes.

Across the field, a lithe figure ran towards them, waving her arms frantically to get their attention. Travis wiped his eyes and squinted at her, certain it was Riane.

"Help," she yelled. "Tempke has my father."

CHAPTER TWENTY-SEVEN

"It happened too fast." Tears streamed down Riane's face, her words broken by hiccups as she tried to explain the situation. She was covered in dirt and soot from the fire, an angry red scrape high on her left cheek where something had struck her following the explosion. She ran her fingers through her hair and pushed it off her forehead, her jerky motions betraying her fear. Travis wanted to say something to make her feel better, but couldn't find the words. For all her cool exterior, he realized, inside she was just as frightened and vulnerable as he was. Alice Prevoroski handed her a water bottle and made her drink. Riane nodded gratefully, then continued.

"We were in Tempke's office, trying to place an off-planet call before the camp moved and we lost the sat-link. We heard people arguing, and stepped outside just as the crawler hit the transport. My father thought it was an accident and went to investigate. I stayed in the office, but then heard him shout something. I ran outside, but before I could get there, Tempke had already taken my father as a hostage."

"Tempke had a cap-knife." Sergeant Garcia screwed up his face in disgust as if just mentioning the weapon left a foul taste in his mouth. Capacitor knives were notorious for the pain they inflicted, the electric stun-prods as deadly as the razor-sharp blade itself. "Lucky he didn't use it."

Riane took another drink. "I ran towards them, but the explosion knocked me to the ground. By the time I got up again, Tempke had already forced my father aboard the last flyer." She coughed, the convulsions so deep her entire body shook. After the spasm passed, she looked up at Jim McClure. "Please, you have to help him."

"We'll do all we can."

Another person arrived. Travis glanced over his shoulder, relieved to see his mom hurry forward, a first-aid kit in hand. She kneeled down by Riane and gently began to work on the cuts and burns across the girl's face and hands. "Hang tight, okay? This might sting a little." She twisted at the waist until she faced Travis's dad. "Travis was right about Tempke. The auto-log in his jumper shows he's been down to Scratch's Dooryard at least a dozen times over the last year or so." She bent back to the first-aid kit.

Riane flinched as antiseptic spray hissed over the welt on her cheek. Uncertain what to do, Travis took her hand. She squeezed down so hard on his fingers he thought they might break, but relaxed as the pain cleared. She smiled at him, her eyes full of worry. Embarrassed, he looked away towards the ruined troop-transport. The machines continued to burn, gaping holes in both hulls where the metal had already been consumed, the smoke thick and black as it snaked along the ash-stained ground. Behind him, he heard Garcia talking to his father.

"Where do you think he would go?"

"Well…" McClure paused as he considered Tempke's options. "He has to get off-planet one way or another, but unless he has an accomplice somewhere close, he won't make it. The flyer he stole only has a range of about two hundred klicks. My guess is he'll make for the starship Lebrie and his daughter came here in. It has some damage, but it's still the only flyable ship in the area. That's why he took Lebrie as a hostage, to make sure he can get the ship prepped for a fast launch."

"Makes sense." Garcia rubbed his eyes. "How far away is Lebrie's starship?"

"Not far. Less than ten klicks from here," McClure

said. "If we hurry, we can get there before he has it prepped for launch."

Garcia stared doubtfully around the camp, most of the tents already loaded aboard the line of crawlers. "You got anything faster than cargo haulers to get us there?"

"No." McClure shrugged. "Fastest bet is on horseback. Can your people ride?"

"A few of them." Garcia waved at several of his troops and beckoned them closer, then turned back to Travis's dad. "You willing to show us the way?"

"Yep." Jim McClure bent down and gave Travis's mom a kiss, then started towards the corral. Travis stood up, ready to follow him, but he held up his hand, palm flat. "You stay here. Both of you." McClure looked pointedly at Riane. The harsh lines on his face softened. "You did good, Trav. Real good." He smiled, then hurried towards the horses. Travis sank down to the ground beside Riane.

"Don't worry," he said, hoping he sounded more confident than he felt. "They'll get there in time."

Riane nodded, but her eyes already said she didn't believe a word of it.

A column of dust rose into the afternoon sky, kicked up by the pair of crawlers running at high speed across the arid plains towards Adrian Lebrie's starship. Dozens of technicians and Federal troopers rode the bulky machines, anxious to reach the starship before it launched. A smaller dust cloud drifted ahead of the first where Jim McClure led the assembled troops and herders on horseback towards the broad mesa the ship had landed on. Most of the herders left in camp had volunteered to go, the desire to catch Tempke stronger than their dislike of Lebrie.

Travis stood on the edge of the landing field and watched the columns twist in the wind and wished he was with them. He snugged down his hat as a gust fanned the stubborn flames still licking at the burned-out transport. Disappointed at being left behind, he turned and wandered back to where his mother sat with Riane, still fussing over the injuries she had taken in the explosion. Something tugged at his memory, something Riane had said while they were searching the power room of the derelict freighter beside Mount Hobbs. Already, the event seemed like ancient history to him, the details fuzzy.

Suddenly, he remembered what it was.

His chest tightened, the lump once more heavy in the pit of his stomach. He tried to act bored as he settled cross-legged on the ground beside Riane, then smiled at his mother, desperate to get a few minutes alone. "Is the mess tent all packed up, Mom?"

Angie McClure nodded. "'Fraid so. If you're hungry, I could probably rustle up some field rations for you."

"No thank you." Riane actually shuddered. Travis suppressed a laugh as he recalled how much she hated the bland, dehydrated meals. Struggling to keep a straight face, he leaned closer.

"You really should eat something." Travis caught her eye and hoped she understood what he was getting at. For a moment she stared back at him, her thin eyebrows bunched into a tight V. Travis waited until his mother wasn't looking, then poked Riane with his elbow to get her attention. Comprehension finally dawned on Riane's face.

"Oh. Maybe I am a little bit hungry," she said.

"I'll see what I can find." Angie McClure stood up and brushed the dirt off her backside, then sauntered off towards what little remained of camp. Travis wasted no time, and as soon as his mom was out of earshot, he scooted closer to Riane.

"I didn't want to say anything around my mom," he said. "She's worried enough as it is. But, do you remember what you told me in the freighter's engine room? That it was rigged to explode?"

"Yes, I remember." Suddenly, her eyes widened as she stiffened. "*O, mon dieu!* Tempke. He's the person who did it. He intends to cover his tracks by destroying the evidence. He's not going to our starship at all."

"How big an explosion would it be?" Travis asked.

"I...I don't know. It all depends on how much fuel is left in the tanks. If there is enough it could incinerate everything inside the crater." A waxy sheen of sweat broke out on her forehead. "My father is still with him. Can you call your father and tell him to turn around?"

"I can try, but odds are the storm took out the relay tower again. We always lose commo after a sandstorm." Travis fumbled in his pocket for the little radio and flipped it on. A hiss came out the speaker, but no reply to any of his attempts. He paused, wishing he had a better solution than the one in his mind. "You told me the other day you can fly a starship. Can you?"

"Yes."

Travis took a deep breath, then nodded towards the only vehicle remaining on the landing field, Tempke's little single-seat jump-bug. "Can you fly that thing?"

"I..." Riane's voice faltered. After a moment, she nodded, her old confidence returned. "Yes. I can fly that machine."

"Good. But, if we're going to go, it better be now." Before he could say anything else, Riane jumped to her feet and started towards the sleek little craft. Travis had to jog to catch her. "Hey, slow down."

Riane turned and faced him. "Unless you haven't noticed, that is a single-seat craft."

"Well, yeah." Travis stood on tiptoe and glanced through the tinted side window, just able to see inside the cramped cockpit. "There's a cargo space behind the seat. I'm sure I can squeeze into it."

Riane sighed. "I've never flown anything like this before. I might very well crash on take-off. I can't ask you to go along."

"Who's asking? I just volunteered." Before she could stop him, he popped open the hatch and wormed inside the ridiculously small cargo area until he was able to sit with his knees drawn up to his chin. Riane eased into the cockpit and peeked over the back of the seat.

"Are you sure you want to do this?"

"No," he said. "So let's get going before I change my mind."

A lurch told Travis they had left the ground, the engine roar so strong it rattled his teeth. He felt as if he was falling first backwards, then forwards as Riane fought to control the unfamiliar craft. Travis grabbed the edge of the seat and tried to look over it at the control panel, but before he could pull himself up, Riane pushed the throttle ahead. The acceleration was more violent than Travis had expected, and he tumbled back to the floor of the cargo compartment and struck his head. G-forces pinned him as they rose, his face crushed against the dirty floor. The world seemed to tilt around him as the machine banked. His stomach rose into his throat, the light around him fading to brown as the blood was driven from his brain.

Just when he thought he was going to pass out, the roar cut out, leaving them briefly in free fall at the top of the arc. Travis's stomach lurched as he rose off the floor only to crash down again as Riane once again pushed the throttle ahead.

"Ow!" He smacked the side of the cargo hold, but managed to get his arms around the back of the chair.

Finally able to see out of the windshield, Travis stared in horror at the ground, the familiar terrain rendered tiny by their altitude. Instinctively, his arms tightened around the chair as the jump-bug nosed over and started down, nearly vertical.

"Would you let go of the seat!" Riane shouted. "You are making it hard for me to concentrate."

"I thought you said you could fly?"

"I can! But this is different from flying in space." She pulled back a bit too sharply on the joystick, and the machine arced up once more, red sky now filling the view ahead. More gently, she brought the nimble little machine level. Sweat poured down her face, her hair damp with it. Finally in control of the craft, she eased into a slow bank westward. "Where is the derelict?"

Travis forced himself to look out the window, his stomach in an uproar. Nothing seemed right, the usual landmarks little more than bumps and ridges against an endless expanse of red sand. As they turned a slow circle, the light suddenly changed, silver burning the reds to yellow, a second shadow slipping out alongside everything on the ground far below. Travis didn't have to look up to realize Alpha had swung out of eclipse, both suns once more visible. An irregular patch of orange ground beside a dark, cone-shaped mountain swung past beneath them. Travis could just make out the volcanic crater the freighter sat in.

"It's straight below us," he shouted over the engine roar and pointed out the window. Riane nodded, her fingers clenched around the joystick as she put the machine into a slow, descending spiral. Mount Hobbs grew at an alarming rate as they dropped, and it took all of his nerve not to bother Riane as she searched for a landing spot. Instead, he watched the control panel. Most of the instruments were pure gibberish to him, their purpose unknown, but one indicator he knew all too well. Unable to remain quiet, he reached over Riane's shoulder and tapped the digital gauge, the green bands already slipping into red. "Look at the fuel. We're getting low."

"You think I don't know that?" Riane pulled the throttle back slightly. "Would you please shut up and let me fly?"

More frightened than angry at her rebuff, he sank to the floor and wrapped his arms around his knees. Unable to do anything else, he shut his eyes and waited for the end. Pictures flashed through his mind – his father yelling at him for being so stupid, his mother crying over a lonely grave dug in the hard red soil. Before his mind could concoct any further nightmares, he felt a hard bump against his back. The machine bounced up, tilted on the point of toppling over, then thumped down again. The cockpit noise faded to a low whir, the thrusters finally silent. Amazed to be alive, Travis opened his eyes.

"See." Riane smiled, though her voice shook with spent fear. "I told you I would get us there." She released the latch and the cabin door swung open.

Riane stepped out, and Travis followed, tumbling without ceremony to the hard-packed sand. Legs stiff from the wild ride, he managed to stand and get a good look around him.

An all too familiar scene waited, the caldera walls brighter than he remembered in the double sunlight. The freighter still sat askew, partially buried, the main airlock gaping open. Beside the abandoned starship sat the stolen transport. Travis took a grim satisfaction in knowing he had been right. Tempke had returned to cover his tracks.

"Do you see him anywhere?" Riane asked, her hand above her eyes to shield the glare.

Without warning, something flashed inside the freighter's door. Travis grabbed Riane and shoved her to the ground as a missile streaked past just in front of them.

A second, and then a third missile hissed past, thin white vapour trails curling in their wake. The projectiles struck the crater wall half a kilometre across the caldera and popped harmlessly against the rocks. The predator's scent drifted towards them as the canisters released their payload.

"Stay down," Travis said. "He's shooting at us."

"I don't think so." Riane pointed as yet another missile struck the rim, an oily cloud pouring out as it detonated. "I think he's calling your old friends home."

Travis turned away from the freighter and stared in shock at the caldera rim. Dozens of writhing, angry shapes leaped over the crater top and hurried towards the strikes, driven mad by the scent the projectiles had released. His feet felt as if they were nailed to the ground, unable to move as he watched the packs converge less than half a kilometre away. The animals screamed at each other as they fought, a wild melee of snapping jaws and churned dust. A voice behind him made him spin towards the freighter once more. Tempke stood in the doorway, Adrian Lebrie clutched in front of him, the cap-blade pressed against the base of his neck.

"Travis? Is that you?" Tempke shouted. "You shouldn't have come out here."

Riane stepped forward, her entire attention focused on the pair of men framed inside the airlock door. "Let my father go. I don't care what you do after that."

"Really?" Tempke actually laughed. "I didn't know you were in any position to bargain. Come down here and we can talk about it."

"Riane..." Travis whispered, but she continued to advance towards the ship. Unable to think of anything else to do, he lagged behind her. The creatures' screams rose in pitch as more of the predators arrived inside the shallow crater. Ten paces from the derelict starship, Tempke jerked Lebrie's head back and pressed the blade tighter, the stun-prods along the hilt leaving little indents on the exo-biologist's unprotected throat.

"That's far enough." Tempke pushed Lebrie ahead until they stood with only a few metres between them.

"Best thing the two of you could do now is turn around and leave."

"He's right, *chérie*." Lebrie gasped. The knife against his neck made his accent more pronounced. "Go back."

"No. Not without you." Riane took a step forward, but Tempke pulled her father's head back further, the warning plain.

"I said stay back."

Travis heard the nervous fear in the foreman's voice. The veins along the side of his face pulsed madly, his skin so white it seemed to glow in the harsh sunlight. Sensing an advantage, Travis spread his hands in front of him, palms up. "Where you can go? No one is going to let you off the planet if you kill him."

"I'll worry about that later," Tempke said. "Right now, all I want is for you two to turn around and leave."

A loud hiss, like steam dumped down a pipe, echoed out of the freighter's hold. Travis tried to look past Tempke to see what had caused it, but couldn't. The battered hull began to shake so hard dust drifted out of the partially open hatch. "Riane," he said quietly. "He's set the ship to blow. Maybe we should get out of here."

"Not without my father."

"Fine." Tempke's too-quick movements betrayed his panic. "You want him? Here, take him." Serpent-quick, Tempke pulled the cap-knife away from Lebrie's throat, then plunged it deep into his shoulder. The odour of burned skin and ozone drifted out as the capacitor discharged. Adrian Lebrie twitched spasmodically as the voltage coursed through his nerves. Riane leaped forward as her father toppled to the ground, a dark stain spreading down his tunic. Tempke, the blade still in hand, stepped back, then spun around and ran towards the transport. Travis, his own fear forgotten, charged after him.

"Travis!" Riane called after him. "Help me. His heart has stopped!"

He hated to go back. He wanted more than anything else to tackle the fleeing Tempke and drive his face into the harsh sand. But he couldn't. Shaking with rage and fear, he turned around and ran back to where Riane knelt, her hands on her father's chest. Tears rolled down her cheeks. She grabbed Travis's left hand and pulled him down, then placed his palm against the gash in Lebrie's shoulder.

"Press down hard."

"Okay." Travis pushed his hand against the wound. Blood, hot and sticky, seeped between his fingers, and he pressed harder to stop the flow. He had helped his own dad take care of too many injured animals for the sight of blood to bother him. He had also seen too many animals die not to know how close to death Lebrie lay. "You better hurry."

"I am, I am." Riane put both her hands on Lebrie's sternum and pushed down three fast strokes. Air hissed out of his nose, but he made no other response. She pressed again, so hard the blood gushed against Travis's fingers as she compressed her father's heart. With a jerk, Lebrie's eyes shot open and he gasped. Travis pressed harder against the wound so the man couldn't rise. Colour returned to his face, the blue in his lips fading back to a healthier red as the injured scientist began to breathe normally. Relieved, Travis took Riane's hand and placed it over the gash, then stumbled to his feet. Behind him, above the growing rumble inside the freighter and the predators' screams across the caldera, he heard the transport's engines come to life.

"Where are you going?" Riane shouted. He ignored her as he ran headlong towards the starship's airlock and into the darkened hold. A wave of heat washed over him, ripe with the stench of overheated coolant. He had no idea how long it would be until the fuel in the tanks ignited, but knew it wouldn't be long. He stumbled in the darkness to the power room. One missile remained inside the crate, and he snatched it up, then rushed back outside. The missile banged against his legs and hampered his movement, and he reached the airlock just as Tempke lifted off. Dust swirled beneath the triangular flyer as the heavy machine rose, swaying on the cushion of air. Travis dropped to one knee then hefted the missile to his shoulder.

The safety snapped back with a satisfying click, and from the corner of his eye Travis watched the red light turn green. Armed, he pointed the stubby projectile at the belly of the departing craft and pulled the trigger.

The missile shrieked away. For a heart-stopping instant, Travis thought he had missed, but at the last moment the missile arced up and struck the machine beneath the starboard rotor. The transport swerved madly, then dipped down. To his credit, Tempke was a better pilot than Travis could have imagined as he righted the crippled flyer and continued away. Dark smoke began to pour out of the shattered rotor housing, an inky trail drifting on the wind as the transport vanished out of sight over the caldera's rim. Travis watched it go, elated that his shot had run true. The elation vanished as his anger seeped away and the cold, unalterable fact that he had just tried to kill a man sank in. He shut his eyes as a dull, heavy thud echoed out from somewhere beyond the caldera rim. Though he couldn't be certain, he thought it was the transport striking the ground. Another, closer sound – a squeal of rage – caught his attention, and his eyes snapped open in time to see two of the predators fighting near one of the other missile strikes. The animals fell on each other, biting, and gouging with their back feet, blood flying around them as they rolled across the rock-strewn ground. He stared as more and more of the creatures arrived. It would be only a matter of minutes before the scent dissipated and they turned their attention towards the freighter.

"Travis?"

Riane's voice pulled him back to the moment. Behind him, deep within the dying ship, metal popped as the pressure rose. He jogged away from the freighter and sank down beside Riane and her father.

"How is he?" Travis asked. Riane shook her head slowly.

"His heart is steady, but he's lost a lot of blood." Riane's voice shook so badly Travis had to strain to hear her. She had ripped open her father's tunic and made a crude bandage of the torn cloth. Already, it was soaked with bright red blood. "He needs a doctor."

"Come on." Travis put his arms under Lebrie's shoulders and heaved himself upright. Clumsily, he began to drag the wounded man towards the jump-bug. Riane caught up with him, grabbed her father's legs, and together they carried him to the little machine. "Put his feet in first," Travis said as they eased him into the cargo compartment.

"What if there isn't enough fuel to get me to camp?" Riane asked as she tried to cradle the unconscious Lebrie to the floor.

"You have to chance it. We don't have much time before that ship explodes." Travis stared at the hulking starship. Heat waves rippled beneath its rusted thrust cones. The predator's scent drifted around them, mingling with the smoke and burned oil from where the missile had struck the fleeing transport. Travis glanced across the crater and shuddered. The far side of the pit seemed to writhe with fighting animals, a carpet of fangs and claws slashing each other to bits. A few of the bolder ones caught the scent from the missile, and turned towards the freighter. Riane grabbed Travis by the shoulder and pulled him around to face her.

"There isn't room aboard for you."

"I know."

"But..." Riane stammered, comprehension dawning. "I can't leave you here."

"You have to. Get your dad to camp." Travis tried not to sound as terrified as he felt. "Send someone back for me. I'll try to get to the cave where your dad waited out the storm."

"What about the freighter? What are you going to do when it self-destructs?"

"What am I going to do?" Travis managed a weak grin. "I'm going to run like hell."

Lungs burning, legs shaking, hot air down his throat. Travis reached the crater rim and started up. His boots slipped in the loose stones and he slid back to the floor. A muted roar made him glance over his shoulder, certain the freighter's tanks had finally burst. With relief he watched the jump-bug struggle into the air. The machine hugged the ground as it became a speck, then vanished from sight. Travis's relief was short-lived. From the corner of his eye he caught movement. A pair of the creatures rounded the freighter, their longs necks stretched out as they searched for his scent. As one, they turned towards him and broke into an easy lope.

"No," Travis muttered under his breath as he scrabbled up the steep rim. Rocks rolled down behind him, every footstep an invitation to trip. Closer now, one of the predators screamed, and he climbed faster, pulling with his hands. "No, no, no."

The geyser field leaped into view as Travis broke over the lip and fell down the other side, stones gouging his shins and elbows. He reached the bottom of the slope and rolled to a stop. Blood and grit covered his left elbow, the skin scraped away. Travis ignored the pain and stood up, then ran, limping slightly as he sprinted towards a nearby boulder. Behind him, a scream of pure animal triumph echoed, and he stopped long enough to see one of the predators standing on the crater rim. The beast swung its narrow face towards him and screamed again as its partner joined it at the summit. Mad with fear, his only thought to escape, Travis rushed towards the shoulder-high rock thirty paces ahead.

Just as he reached the boulder the air shook. Travis felt himself lifted off the ground as easy as a tumbleweed on the wind. Face first, he struck the ground beside the boulder, and crawled on his hands and knees behind it.

The explosion inside the crater sent rocks high into the blood-red sky, dark specks arcing towards the glowering bulk of Mount Hobbs. Stones clattered around him, and he curled as tightly as he could against the rock, arms above his head a poor shield from the downfall. A cloud of sand raced past, oven hot as it spread across the dormant geyser field. The rain of pebbles slowed, and Travis peeked out from under his arm. Without warning, something soft and wet thumped down in front of him. A pair of gaping jaws studded with dagger-sharp teeth snapped a hand's breadth from his right foot.

"No!"

Travis screamed as he leaped sideways. Then, relieved beyond words, he began to laugh as he realized the creature was dead, killed by the explosion when the freighter self-destructed. The smell of ammonia and charred flesh was replaced by the stench of unburned fuel drifting in the wake of the blast. Still dreading what he might see, Travis crawled on hands and knees back to the rim and peered over the crest. Below him lay a charred patch of ground littered with pieces of the now destroyed freighter, many of them smoking, sending up an acrid cloud. Around it, their bodies broken and burned, lay dozens of the predators, tossed aside by the blast. None of them moved.

Travis sat for a long time, laughing until tears rolled down his face. His body ached, pummelled by the roll down the crater rim and the violent explosion, but he didn't care. It was over. Travis wiped the tears and blood off his face, stood up, and started walking towards Mount Hobbs, anxious to reach the little cave on its northern flank before darkfall.

Ahead, nearly lost against the jumbled pile of black lava, a column of smoke drifted, driven sideways by the relentless wind. Travis shut his eyes, his guilt returned as he spotted the transport piled up against the side of the unforgiving mountain. Resigned at what he would find inside it, he started uphill towards the wreckage.

The machine wasn't as badly broken as he expected. Winded and tired from the long climb, Travis surveyed the scene. Tempke had somehow managed to keep the craft upright when he crashed. Silver streaks covered the dark basalt where metal had gouged against rock as the craft skidded to a halt, bits of glass and plastic and torn aluminium scattered about. Dreading what he would find, Travis crept towards the hatch.

A chemical stink lingered around the machine, burned plastic and spilled hydrogen. He started to gag, and quickly wrapped his bandana around his mouth and nose. Eyes burning, he reached the narrow hatch. The metal door swung back on one hinge and banged against the shattered hull.

"Come on, Travis," he told himself. "You've got to look." The hair on the back of his neck rose as he stepped up to the hatch, then slipped inside.

It was brighter inside the cockpit than he had expected, the windshield torn away. The pilot's seat faced away from him and blocked his view. Travis took a deep breath, then spun the chair around, fully expecting to see Tempke's body slumped in the harness. He felt as if he had been granted a reprieve when he found the padded chair empty. Blood spattered the control panel, but Tempke had obviously survived. The power controls were in the off position.

"Thank you," Travis said aloud. He sank into the empty seat and rested a moment, his guilt gone. He hadn't killed Allen Tempke. Better still, the man couldn't get far on foot across the desert before someone would find him and see that he faced the charges he deserved. Travis searched the cockpit, still expecting to find Tempke lurking somewhere, cap-knife at the ready. Instead, he found an emergency kit under the chair filled with dehydrated rations and other field gear. A water bottle was nestled with them, and he drank from it greedily.

Anxious to leave, Travis squirmed back outside and squinted in the afternoon sunlight. His eyes burned as he scanned the horizon, and he frowned as he spotted a small figure silhouetted against the skyline. From the way Tempke dragged his leg, Travis decided, he was injured. He ducked back inside for the first-aid kit, then as an afterthought, searched the ruined cockpit for a weapon just in case Tempke became unreasonable. A flair pistol was nestled at the bottom of the canvas kitbag, three small flares strapped to the grip.

"Better than nothing." Travis stuffed the ungainly pistol in his belt, then went back outside. Tempke had moved higher, though not far, his progress slow. Travis smiled to himself. It would be easy to catch up to him. His smile faded as he spotted a second figure further down the mountain. Low and lean, nearly as dark as the stone beneath it, the creature climbed towards Tempke, slowly closing the gap between them.

At least one of the predators had survived the explosion.

Nothing grew on the side of Mount Hobbs. No grass, no weeds, nothing but cinder and dark, pitted boulders left behind by the ancient eruption. Travis climbed, zigzagging up the slope. Part of him desperately wanted to turn around and leave Tempke to his fate, the thought of facing one of the predators again, especially to rescue someone as worthless as Allen Tempke, was almost too much to contemplate. But, as much as he hated the man, he knew he couldn't do it. Not after the guilt he had felt after he had hit the fleeing transport with the missile. Like it or not, he had to at least try and save the man. He stopped a moment to catch his breath, but with sunset less than an hour away, couldn't afford to lose so much as a second. Desperate to be finished before nightfall, he pushed on.

The mountain narrowed as he neared the summit, the cone broken by the deep, egg-shaped pit on its north face where once an explosion had blasted away millions of tons of the mountain. Travis stepped carefully towards the lip of the crater. His stomach reeled as he looked over the edge, the sides nearly vertical. Far below, jagged spires lay bathed in shadow. He picked up a rock, tossed it over the side and watched it fall. Long seconds passed until he finally heard it strike one of the outcrops and shatter into dust.

"Watch that last step," he muttered as he backed away from the edge. "It's a doozy."

He kept to the side of the crater, using it as a guide as he worked his way up the mountain. Wind pushed against him, so strong it threatened to drive him off the summit. Travis wrinkled his nose as a familiar scent washed past, a trace of ammonia and oily, rotting flesh. He stiffened, certain the predator was nearby, but to his relief he saw only Tempke stagger into view forty metres above. The man was at the end of his endurance, his left leg sticking out at an odd, disjointed angle. The predator's scent grew stronger, and Travis realized it came from the injured man, no doubt from handling the scent-filled missiles before he escaped in the transport. With a start, Travis remembered that he, too, had handled one of the scent-loaded missiles. How much of the lure did he splash on himself? He had to hurry. Using hands and feet to climb, Travis rushed up the mountain, anxious to catch Tempke before the predator arrived.

A low growl made Travis stop and turn to his left. The predator was nearly upon them, its long neck stretched out as it climbed across the tumbled boulders towards Tempke. Its tongue flicked in front of its face as it tasted the air, the feathers along its spine laid flat by the howling wind. Shaking with fear, Travis cupped his hands around his mouth and shouted.

"Mr. Tempke, stop!"

Tempke straightened, startled by the sound of another voice. He looked down towards Travis and frowned, as if he couldn't quite grasp the idea that someone had found him. His face was pale, dried blood crusted in his hair where his head had smashed into the transport's control panel when he crash-landed.

"Travis?"

"Mr. Tempke, listen to me." Travis's lungs burned from exertion, making it hard to shout above the wind. He spotted a pair of broken lava columns near the crater's edge, the space between them wide enough to take shelter inside, and pointed frantically at them. "Get under those boulders. Hurry!"

"What?" Tempke shook his head, confused. Travis started towards him but stopped as he caught a flash in Tempke's right hand. The injured man pointed the tip of the cap-knife at him. "That's far enough."

"Listen to me." Travis took another step towards Tempke, then stopped and called again, punctuating each syllable. "You're in danger. One of those predators is directly below you."

"Nice try. They're dead. I made sure of that." A crooked smile lifted Tempke's lip. Despite the pain, he shook his head and laughed. "Nothing could have survived that explosion. Do you really think I wasn't ready for something like this? Trust me, a lot of planning went into this operation, and I'm not about to give up on it now." Tempke turned and climbed a few steps higher, his path taking him within spitting distance of the crater's edge. He grimaced as his foot slipped, and then he sank to the ground, holding his injured leg with one hand, the knife in the other.

"You've got to believe me," Travis shouted. "It's the scent! They can smell it on you."

"Of course they can smell it," Tempke said. "That's what it was designed for, to lure them back if I needed to kill them all. And that's exactly what I've done. You can drop the scare tactics."

"I'm not kidding," Travis shouted, but Tempke cut him off.

"You're a sharp kid, Travis. We both know you deserve better than wasting your life on a rock like Aletha Three." Tempke managed to stand again, but didn't try to climb higher. "This place is finished. But, you don't have to be. I have a lot of friends who can get me off-planet, but I need help to call them. On top of this mountain there's a rock cairn. Inside there's an emergency transmitter. You bring me that transmitter, and you can name your price. Understand?"

"Mr. Tempke, please." Travis climbed a little closer. Out the corner of his eye he could see the crater, and it left him dizzy. Once again, he thought seriously about turning around and leaving Tempke to his fate. "Get to cover, now! There is one of those things left, and it's coming straight at you."

"Travis." Tempke sighed. "I really thought you were smarter than that. Come on, kid, quit playing the fool.

Go get that radio, and you're rich. Don't waste your life like your old man."

Travis gritted his teeth at the insult, but before he could reply rocks rattled nearby. The blood rushed from his face as the predator swung into view ten metres above Tempke, nostrils flared as it tracked the man's scent-soaked clothing. Afraid to draw attention to himself, Travis slowly drew the flare pistol from his belt, snapped it open and pushed the first of the three tiny flares into the breech. Tempke saw the pistol and drew back. Travis raised the gun as the creature lowered its narrow head towards the unsuspecting Tempke.

"Don't move," Travis said.

"You're not going to shoot me," Tempke said, still refusing to listen. "Not with that. We don't have to be enemies."

"Shut up." Travis clutched the pistol with both hands and took sight. Suddenly, his fear was gone, nothing in his mind but making the shot. "Stay where you are and don't move."

He squeezed the trigger. The flare tore out, a trail of sparks behind it. Tempke flinched as it tore past his face, and stumbled. Finally seeing the creature, he screamed as the flare struck the animal in the chest. The predator hissed and snapped at the air, but otherwise seemed unhurt as the little flare dropped to the ground in front of it. Suddenly, the flare ignited, so bright Travis looked away to keep from being blinded. The predator screamed in rage and leaped away, so near the crater's edge its tail whipped out into the emptiness.

Hands shaking, Travis struggled to reload. The flare pistol was a distraction, but little more. If he ran now, while the creature was startled, he could make it to the boulders and shelter beneath them. But that meant leaving Tempke to certain death. He snapped the pistol closed and took aim once more.

"Tempke," he said quietly. "Get down here. Now!"

The first flare burned out, leaving nothing but a charred spot on the rocks at the creature's feet. Faster than Travis thought possible, the enraged animal jumped downhill, straight at Tempke. To his credit, the man stood his ground and met the attack, driving the cap-knife deep into the predator's shoulder as it struck him. The creature reared back and screamed, and for a moment staggered as the capacitor discharged. Just as quickly, it righted itself and knocked Tempke to his back with its tail. The man landed on the edge of the cliff, the knife still clutched in his fist. The predator snapped at the weapon. Tempke cried out and tried to pull away as its jaws closed around his wrist. Blood erupted out of the torn flesh where his hand had been. The knife spun away in a long slow arc and dropped over the cliff.

"No!" Travis rushed forward, ignoring the danger and fired the second flare. It dropped near the creature and ignited, a fountain of crimson sparks blazing in the wind. The predator hissed and stepped backward.

For one hopeful moment, its left leg strayed over the edge, but it quickly righted itself and jumped once more towards Tempke as the man tried to rise. Before Travis could fire the third flare, the creature struck the wounded man again. Tempke, his balance lost, rolled towards the crater's edge, then as if he had never been, fell over the side. His terrified screams stopped abruptly as he hit the jagged rocks far below.

"Damn you!" Travis shook, not with fear, but with rage. The animal finally noticed him, lowered its head and turned towards him. Blood stained its muzzle, its teeth bared as it took a step closer. Travis raised the pistol once more and stood his ground.

"I'm really getting sick of you."

The predator crouched, ready to leap. Travis's finger tightened around the trigger. He held his breath, then pointed the pistol at the ground. The flare struck in front of the creature's face and exploded. Startled by the burst, the animal leaped sideways, its momentum carrying it over the ledge. It twisted as it began to fall, and fought to grab the crumbling edge of the cliff with its powerful toes. Seeing his chance, Travis snatched up a rock and hurled it at the thing's chest. The stone struck the creature in the ribs and drove it over the side. It snapped at him even as it fell. A low thump rose up as the animal joined Tempke somewhere in the shadows on the crater's floor.

Travis sank down and wrapped his arms around his knees, too spent to move. The pistol fell away from his hand and clattered against the jumbled carpet of stone. Travis didn't bother to pick it up. He began to shake, unable to control his reactions now that the terror was finally over. Far in the distance, Travis could just make out a line of riders racing across the rolling plains towards him. The sky faded to silver as Beta sank, leaving only tiny, pitiless Alpha to burn above the horizon. Still trembling, Travis staggered to his feet and started down to meet them.

CHAPTER TWENTY-EIGHT

Like an ungainly phoenix, by morning Camp Seven had risen again on the edge of the badlands, not far from the little river where they had crossed the herd a week before. Travis wandered through the rows of crates and equipment waiting to be unpacked. It had been less than twelve hours since his final encounter with the predator, but he had been so busy he had scarcely had time to absorb what had happened. He wished he could forget the entire chain of events, but knew he never would. Even now, he could close his eyes and see the terror on Allen Tempke's face as he tumbled over the cliff on the side of Mount Hobbs.

"Travis?"

Startled, he turned around and found his mom behind him. She smiled sadly, then nodded towards the newly erected landing field on the edge of camp.

"Honey, Sergeant Garcia would like to talk to you."

"Okay." He started towards the little group of Federated soldiers, then stopped cold. Several of the uniformed troopers were carrying something on a stretcher towards a waiting shuttle. Despite the fact that it was covered head to toe in a thick plastic bag, Travis knew without a doubt it was Tempke's body. Angie McClure put her hand on his shoulder and gave him a reassuring squeeze.

"It's all right, honey. There was nothing else you could have done. You know that, don't you?"

"Yeah. I guess so." Dreading the meeting, Travis trudged towards the waiting soldiers. Garcia's lips were drawn in a thin, tight line as he listened gravely while Travis told him what had happened on the mountain. One of the other soldiers kept an omni-corder trained on him, recording the account. When he finished, Garcia held out his hand and waited for Travis to shake it.

"I just want you to know," Garcia said gravely, "I will have to mention your part in what happened to Tempke in my report." His face softened slightly. "But, I doubt you'll ever hear anything back. As far as I'm concerned, you acted appropriately."

"I understand," Travis said, feeling somewhat better.

"You're an amazing young man, Mr. McClure. I'm not sure I could have done what you did up there." Garcia smiled. "If you ever consider a career in the service, I'd be proud to have you in my unit."

"Thanks," Travis said, embarrassed at the unexpected praise. "But if it's all the same, I think I'll stick to driving cattle."

Garcia and his men climbed aboard the shuttle and sealed the hatch. Travis watched as the craft broke ground and banked away from camp before it ignited its main engines and blazed skyward. Soon, even its thunder was lost on the wind.

A slim figure walked out of camp towards him. Riane smiled, but her dark eyes betrayed how uncomfortable she was. Since his return, this was the first time she and Travis had been alone together, and he sensed she had been waiting for a chance to talk to him.

"How are you?" she asked.

"I'm fine." Travis smiled for her benefit. "I promise."

"I feel so bad about leaving you behind. If I had any idea what was going to happen..."

"You did what you had to do. I'd have done the same thing if the tables were turned." Travis pushed his battered hat a little further up on his forehead. "How's your dad?"

"He'll be all right. The doctors want him to spend a couple of weeks at Base Camp to make sure the knife wound is healed, but I doubt he will stay that long. He wants to recover as much tissue and bone as he can from the creature you killed. He's convinced he can find enough genetic markers to trace it back to the lab that created it in the first place and put them out of business." Riane shrugged. "Between you and me, I think he's a little obsessed with the whole idea, but then, you know how stubborn he can be."

"Yeah." Travis stared across the compound and caught sight of his own father directing the construction of the horse corral. He grinned. "I've met the type before."

Another transport arrived, kicking up a cloud of dust as it settled to ground. Travis watched as a handful of people sauntered towards it to begin offloading the cargo it carried. Without turning, he said, "Why do you think he did it?"

"Who?" Riane asked. "Tempke?"

"Yeah." He nodded. "Was it just for money?"

"Money can be pretty powerful," Riane said quietly. "Especially to someone like Tempke. From what my dad said, he must have been planning this for years. No telling how much New Earth Enterprises paid him to sabotage the project here. But, once Advanced Terraforming pulled out, you can bet they would have been on this planet in a matter of weeks. Think about it. A whole planet for the taking, and all because Allen Tempke was willing to sell out."

"But still, to actually kill people. And all of it for nothing." He shook his head sadly.

"Travis..." Riane's smile faded. She stood a moment, uncharacteristically silent, kicking at the ground with her foot. Finally, she looked up at him and held his gaze. "I know we caused you and your family a lot of trouble, but we really thought we were doing the right thing."

He nodded. It would have been easy to lash out at her, but after what they had shared, he couldn't imagine hurting her. "I guess doing the right thing depends on which side of the line you stand on."

"I suppose." Her smile returned. "So, with the injunction thrown out, I suppose you will be staying on Aletha?"

"Looks that way. Whether I want to or not."

"I'm glad. It would get awfully boring around here without someone to argue with." She looked around the camp. "We'll be here a while too. Maybe we can get together sometime and do something." She paused, a puzzled frown on her face. "What exactly do you do around here when you're not working?"

"Well..." Travis laughed. "To be honest, there isn't much to do."

"Okay. Well then, maybe we can do nothing together." To his surprise, she leaned forward and gave him a quick kiss on the cheek, then sauntered away. She waved over her shoulder. "*Au revoir*."

"Yeah. See you around." Feeling three metres tall, Travis strolled back towards Bachelors' Row, in no hurry to get back to work. Jim McClure noticed him and walked out to meet him.

"Hey, Trav."

"Hi, Dad." Travis waited for him to continue.

"Look, I haven't had a chance to tell you how proud I am of what you did." McClure cocked an eyebrow and stared down his nose. "Or how badly you scared your mom and me."

"Sorry about that."

Somewhere in the middle of the camp an air-hammer rattled as the crew drove tent pegs into the unyielding ground. The horses, still tied to their picket line, shied at the noise. Both Travis and his dad started towards them but stopped when they realized the animals were all right. McClure laughed at their mutual reaction.

"Gets to be a habit, doesn't it?" He sighed. "Maybe it shouldn't be. Look, I know I dragged you and your mom away from everything that mattered to you. At the time, I thought I was doing it for all of us, but, looking back, I guess I was doing it for me. I wanted to hold onto the ranch so bad I let my priorities get turned around."

"Dad, it's okay..."

"No, it's not okay," McClure continued. "What I'm getting at is this. Maybe it's time we went home. Back to Earth."

"Are you serious?"

"Yes," Jim McClure said, his grey eyes heavy as stone. "What do you say? Are you ready to turn back?"

Travis looked out towards the low mesas on the

other side of the narrow river, out where little bands of cattle grazed on the scrubby grass. Somewhere high above, a hawk screamed in the pale yellow sky, twin shadows racing along the ground as it flew past. Like it or not, he realized, he couldn't go home. He was already there. Travis took a deep breath and turned back to his father.

"Yeah, maybe we should head back." He grinned, feeling happier than he had in ages. "In another season or two."

JUSTIN STANCHFIELD is a real-life cowboy, part-time snowplough driver, private pilot and occasional musician. He first began writing as a member of a local theatre group, where he was awarded the job of tacking new endings onto old plays. He then moved on to fiction and has had various short stories published in magazines and online. *Space Cowboy* is his first novel and is a combination of his favourite genres – westerns and science fiction.

Justin lives in southwest Montana on a family-owned cattle ranch with his wife, two children and a menagerie including two cats, three dogs, a pair of llamas and a quartet of hermit crabs.

If you have enjoyed

SPACE COWBOY

you'll love these other
thrilling adventures...

GRAHAM MARKS

KAÏ-RO

Stretch Wilson's world is a hard place. All he has, since his father was taken as slave labour, is his dog, Bone – until the fateful day when he discovers something extraordinary deep in the heart of Bloom's Mount, a gigantic pile of ancient rubbish and waste. Something that will change his life for ever.

Battle is inevitable as the sun rises on a world where once again Setekh, God of Chaos, and Horus, God of the Sky, walk the land. And now Stretch is the only person who can stop the evil that lives in Kaï-ro from taking control, for eternity.

"A brilliantly imagined epic adventure."

Publishing News

9780746078884
£6.99

RODMAN PHILBRICK

the last book in the universe

The one good thing in Spaz's life is his little sister, Bean. But Bean is dying. Spaz is determined to save her, but in a world devastated by an earthquake, and dominated by vicious gangs and brain-melting mindprobes, nothing is easy.

Plunging into dangerous territory, Spaz must trust in the wisdom of an old man and the stubbornness of a perfect princess to survive, as together they try to change the world...

"Gritty, moving and provocative, this is a vivid and futuristic adventure." *tBkmag*

9780746090794

£5.99

TIM WYNNE-JONES

Burl can't take any more bruises from his bullying father, so one day he runs away with just a penknife and a fishing lure in his pocket. Despite his survival skills, Burl knows he won't last long in the frozen Candian wilderness, so he is filled with hope when he stumbles across Ghost Lake, and a secret that could save him.

But his father is after him and Burl is dragged back into his dangerous games...

"Gripping – gut-churningly exciting in fact."   *Time Out*

**Winner of the Canada Council
Governor General's Literary Award**

9780746068410
£5.99